Praise for
WHAT WALKS THESE HALLS

'There is a creeping dread in *What Walks These Halls* by Amy Clarkin that builds with each page, absolutely loving it, very sharp YA for your shelves.'
Lucas Maxwell, former UK Librarian of the Year

'Deliciously creepy debut YA title. An eerie abandoned mansion, a malevolent spirit, family secrets, paranormal investigators, secrets revealed … gorgeous, gothic & utterly gripping. If you liked *Wednesday*, you'll love it!'
The Bookaneer

'A great start to a new series that is as much about friendship, love, and found family as it is about the paranormal.'
Children's Books Ireland in the *Irish Examiner*

'A thriller story about a band of young investigators who are determined to discover the truth about a haunted house in their neighbourhood. Clarkin has created a wonderfully diverse group of characters with rooted backstories that makes them altogether relatable and each one of them unique. She has a real talent for building tension from one chapter to the next, making it next to impossible to put this book down. With the door left open for a potential sequel, this could be the beginning of series ideal for thrill-seekers. Recommended for ages 12 and up.'
Irish Examiner

'*What Walks these Halls* will warm your heart while chilling you to the bone. A thoroughly gripping story, of ghosts, legacy and chosen family. I adored it.'

Deirdre Sullivan, author

'This debut has all the ingredients that fans of the genre will love – an eerie, abandoned mansion, a truly malevolent spirit, family secrets and a team of young paranormal investigators. But it also has a wonderfully diverse group of relatable characters with credible backstories ... Skilfully told from multiple points of view ... There is a real creeping sense of building menace, and one genuinely fears for the outcome for these engaging protagonists. The character dynamics are so enjoyably portrayed that I am sure readers would be delighted if this exciting debut developed into a series.'

Joy Court, Lovereading4kids

'OMG Wayfarers! I LOVED this book! If you know me, you know that I love a good scary story/thriller, especially when it's done well. And Amy honestly knocked it out of the park with this debut. I was transported into the story through Amy's storytelling and loved every second. It felt as if I was there alongside the characters trying to get to the bottom of the mystery of Hyacinth House ... I also thoroughly enjoyed all the representation within the storyline. I would highly recommend this book to anyone interested in reading ghost stories, especially if they want ones based in Irish lore. I'll absolutely be looking out for future releases from Amy Clarkin. This novel has proved her talent for storytelling and building a multi-layered plot line to keep readers interested ... fantastic.'

WayfaringBiblio

'Deliciously dark.'
@Serendipity_Viv

'A spooky book with amazing ghosts and funny characters … will keep you on the edge of your seat.'
BotsBookShelf

'The novel's small cast of main characters becomes ever more closely knit, not only through their mutual connections to the house, but their various burgeoning relationships, which simmer so intensely that they threaten to overpower the paranormal plotline … a chiller with cinematic echoes of the Hammer House of Horror and has all the spooky ingredients required for torchlit reading by those whose imaginations thrive on things that go bump in the night.'
The Echo

Praise for

WHO WATCHES THIS PLACE

'Comes to a tremendous climax in scenes that cleverly tie the ghostly elements with the emotional turmoil of the characters. Romance, ghost story, family saga – it's all of this and more and comes thoroughly recommended.'
Books for Keeps

'A YA horror with some genuinely terrifying moments. Also features an amazing found-family friendship group.'
ScorpioBookDreams

'A story with plenty of supernatural elements, including a chilling haunted portrait, but ultimately it's an ode to friendship, a cosy hug of a book that celebrates found family and relationships of all kinds ... Clarkin has built a world in which friendship can literally save the day. This is the kind of book that will make so many readers feel seen and comforted and hopeful.'

The Irish Times, Claire Hennessy

'Perfect for those who love spooky with an emphasis on paranormal investigation and will leave you either wanting to spend the night in a haunted building or never setting foot in one.'

PrythianBworm

'The plot, the pace, the setting, the emotional baggage grumbling in the background, the evocative twists and turns; all create a tale that will leave you glued to the page and on the edge of your seat. This book will haunt your dreams (or rather nightmares) for a long time. Absolutely brilliant!

Fallen Star Stories

'Readers with an interest in the paranormal will love this gripping thriller about Irish teen ghost hunters ... this book is much more than a ghost story; it also deals with loss, love and found family. Highly original and deliciously chilling.'

Irish Independent

'Spine-chilling ... with a fantastically paced plot, a growing sense of creeping dread and building panic, the story deals with not only ghosts, but also chronic illness, sexuality, mental health and acceptance.'

Children's Books Ireland's Annual Reading Guide 2024

WHERE THE SHADOWS HIDE

Amy Clarkin

THE O'BRIEN PRESS
DUBLIN

Amy Clarkin is a writer from Dublin, Ireland. Her non-fiction writing is often on the theme of chronic illness and identity, and has been featured in *Sonder Literary Magazine*, *Rogue* and *Dear Damsels*. Her debut novel, *What Walks These Halls,* was shortlisted for the An Post Irish Book Awards Teen & Young Adult Book of the Year 2023 and Great Reads Awards 2023 (School Libraries Group of Library Association of Ireland), and nominated for the Yoto Carnegies 2023. Her second novel, *Who Watches This Place,* was published in 2024.

She can generally be found by the sea, drinking coffee, talking about her dog or asking people what their favourite ghost story is.

 amyclarkinwrites

For Rebekah
BFH and proof that platonic soulmates exist

First published 2025 by The O'Brien Press Ltd,
12 Terenure Road East, Rathgar, Dublin 6, D06 HD27, Ireland.
Tel: +353 1 4923333; e-mail: books@obrien.ie; Website: obrien.ie
The O'Brien Press is a member of Publishing Ireland.

ISBN: 978-1-78849-531-8

Text © Amy Clarkin 2025
The moral rights of the author have been asserted.
Editing, design and layout © The O'Brien Press 2025
Cover and text design by Emma Byrne

All rights reserved. No part of this publication may be reproduced or utilised in any form or by any means, electronic or mechanical, including for text and data mining, training artificial intelligence systems, photocopying, recording or in any information storage and retrieval system, without permission in writing from the publisher.

2 4 6 7 5 3 1
26 28 27 25

Printed and bound by Nørhaven Paperback A/S, Denmark.

To the best of our knowledge, this book complies in full with the requirements of the General Product Safety Regulation (GPSR). For further information and help with any safety queries, please contact us at productsafety@obrien.ie.

The O'Brien Press received financial assistance
from the Arts Council to publish this title.

Previously in
WHAT WALKS THESE HALLS
and
WHO WATCHES THIS PLACE

When Archer O'Sullivan started up his parents' business again, Paranormal Surveyance Ireland, or PSI, his sister Raven, wanted nothing to do with it. She was there in Hyacinth House in County Wicklow five years ago, the night their father died during a séance. She couldn't remember what happened, but she was sure she was to blame.

Éabha McLoughlin grew up seeing and hearing things no one else could. But when she started college, she finally had the freedom to find out why. The daring Archer and his resourceful team seemed like a good place to start.

Real estate agent Cordelia Cassidy Cuevas was tasked with selling Hyacinth House. When she called on PSI, hoping they could give the property a clean bill of psychic health, Archer and his friends, Fionn and Davis, couldn't resist the chance to investigate.

The team waded through secrets – both the property's and their own – to discover the mysteries of Hyacinth House, their past, and the terrifying spirit that had haunted the house for years. Their confrontation with The Lady left its marks on PSI and revealed more than just the truth about the house.

A few months after the events at Hyacinth House, the team were asked to investigate The Merrion Hub, a private members' club in Dublin city. Tensions were running high: Éabha and Raven were clashing over Raven's new clairvoyancy gift, Fionn was feeling isolated by the team and Davis was frustrated by a journalist who was convinced PSI were frauds – and was determined to prove it.

All their conflict got pushed aside when Éabha disappeared during a survey. With the team running out of time to save her, they had to pull together or risk losing her forever. But their showdown with Adrian Fitzgibbon, the ghost in the portrait, changed their lives forever.

PROLOGUE

ELIZABETH CARMICHAEL STUMBLED DOWN the long corridor towards her cabin, resenting how much her fitted, satin Alexander McQueen dress restricted her gait and trying to convince herself the swaying was because she was on a boat and not because of the half-drunk bottle of champagne still dangling carelessly from one hand. The other hand held her Valentino Rockstud pumps, her bare feet welcoming the feel of soft, luscious carpet after an evening in heels, even as the rest of her seethed with rage. She would have stayed dancing longer, drinking in the admiring glances she'd gotten in her olive-green dress, but one of the staff had informed her it was against the ship's safety policy for someone to be barefoot on the dance floor.

She had told him that with what she was paying for a superior cabin with a sea view it should entitle her to wear whatever she wanted, but instead he'd had the *audacity* to tell her if she didn't put her shoes on, he would have to ask her to leave. And when she'd refused, he'd actually signalled to the security guard lingering unobtrusively by the wall. *Security*. As though she were some kind of *criminal*. She'd seen heads start to turn and, with as much dignity as she could muster, left before she could be ushered out. She'd noted his name, though, and the captain would be getting a strongly worded complaint about his unprofessionalism in the morning. When she'd told him that, she could have sworn he was holding back a smirk. As though it was *funny*. That was the problem with these people: give them any sort of power and they'd cling to it, trying to make themselves feel that they were in any way important. Trying to forget that they would always be there to wait on people like her.

The lights flickered overhead and she staggered, putting a hand out against the wall to brace herself.

Terrible staff, faulty electrics. She wouldn't be returning to *this* ship, that was for sure.

The lights flickered again, for longer this time, and when they flashed on she could see a figure standing at the end of the corridor.

He – she was pretty certain it was a man – wasn't moving, and she couldn't make out his face from this distance. Even through the champagne fog engulfing her, something made her pause. A sense that something was off. She stopped in the middle of the corridor.

He was completely still, staring at her. Or she thought he was. She couldn't make out his face because of a cap pulled low over his eyes.

A *cap*. On a five-star cruise liner. He must be one of the staff and had wandered up from below deck into the guest quarters out of uniform.

Maybe she'd have two employees to complain about tomorrow.

It was cold now, as though the AC had started blasting despite it being well past two in the morning, and her arms broke out in gooseflesh. What was wrong with this ship? She wrapped her rose-pink Dior stole more tightly around her. Why was he just *staring* at her?

'Hello,' she said, annoyed that it came out as more of a question than a statement. The lights flickered again and when they came back on, he was three metres further along the corridor. She stifled a shriek, dropping the champagne bottle to clap a hand over her mouth. The cold liquid splashed over her feet but her entire body felt like it had been plunged into ice.

The lights went out again.

He was just a couple of metres away when they came back on.

She didn't waste time trying to make out his features this time. She turned to flee, running barefoot up the corridor, her shoes flailing in her hands as she ran, praying the lights stayed on long enough for her to reach the end of the corridor, to where the ship opened out into a large foyer that should still have a member of crew stationed there.

They did not.

The entire corridor was plunged into darkness, a single scream cutting through the stillness, summoning the crew member on watch from the foyer.

As he stepped into the corridor, the lights came on.

It was empty, save for an abandoned pair of Valentinos and, further down, a spilled bottle of champagne.

With a shaking hand, he reached for the radio.

'There's been another one.'

CHAPTER ONE

ÉABHA MCLOUGHLIN WAS TIRED.

Actually, 'tired' was too gentle a word for what she felt. Tired didn't feel enough to capture the bone-deep exhaustion that permeated her whole body, how even the smallest movement felt like wading through wet cement, how her brain felt like it was stuffed with cotton wool and filled with buzzing and her vision was covered in gauze. How, whenever someone spoke to her, she would blink for an extra couple of seconds as her brain scrambled to process their words, understand them and dredge up a response.

Today had been a bad day. She had slept until eleven am, returned to her bed for a 'nap' from three to eight, and it still felt as though she was barely functioning when Archer and Davis collected her for the investigation. The only thing worse than the physical weight dragging her deep into an ocean of tiredness was feeling Archer O'Sullivan watching her, feeling his concern and apprehension washing over her until they were drowning her more than the tiredness. She could barely breathe with the weight of it.

Things were hard enough. She didn't need his doubt shackling her too.

She took a swig of the noxious but effective energy drink she'd cracked open a little while ago, studiously avoiding Archer's gaze as she looked around the room. They were in a terraced house in north Dublin that overlooked a graveyard, and the owners were convinced it was haunted.

'Ready to do the vibe check?' Raven O'Sullivan asked as Éabha took a second long swig of the drink, leaning against the wall beside her. Raven's silvery-blond hair was in her usual plait and she pulled her flannel shirt tightly around her. Éabha surveyed the rest of the team casually. Archer, Davis and Fionn were on the other side of the room, Fionn holding about six cables in his hands, Davis gesturing emphatically about something – a small smile fought its way through her fatigue as she saw him wave his arms dramatically, a tiny spark of curiosity managing to burn its way through the fog. Raven followed her line of sight.

'He's either discovered empirical proof of the afterlife or he's trying to convince Archer to add Coco Pops to the shopping list,' she said.

Éabha laughed softly. Davis fought just as passionately about small, mundane things as he did about the big ones. She always enjoyed seeing how the outrage he could muster over a teaspoon being left in the sink instead of the dishwasher could rival someone finding their wallet had been stolen. It could be exasperating at times, but it was something so Davis she couldn't help being fond of him for it.

'Possibly both,' Éabha said, taking another gulp of her drink.

Raven wrinkled her nose. 'Ugh, I can smell the chemicals from here.'

'Says the girl who runs on, like, eight cups of black coffee a day.'

'They're not manufactured in a lab, though,' Raven glanced at her out of the side of her eye, her arms crossed. 'You good?'

'I'm managing.'

Éabha stiffened as Raven studied her a second, and braced herself for the questioning, the doubt. Instead, Raven nodded.

'Good, I'd hate to see the carnage it would unleash if I had to take the lead on the clairvoyant shenanigans,' she said lightly, pushing off the wall and clapping her hands together. 'Right lads, we getting this started or what?'

A rush of affection for the petite, often abrasive girl rushed through Éabha as she watched her stomp over to the boys in her heavy boots. She and Raven hadn't exactly had the easiest start, but ever since the events of early spring they'd formed not just a truce, but a tentative friendship.

'We were waiting for you two to stop chatting,' Davis teased. Raven rolled her eyes at him.

'Oh, as if you wouldn't have kept ranting for another fifteen minutes if I hadn't stopped you.'

'I was just sorting out seven different types of equipment, but don't mind me,' Fionn said, handing first Raven, then Éabha a voice recorder. Éabha mustered up a smile for him as he did, and his blue eyes looked seriously at her from behind his wire-rimmed glasses.

'You feeling OK, Éabhs?' Archer asked, sliding an arm around her waist.

Éabha had to stop herself from pulling away. It didn't feel like the easy, affectionate gesture it used to be; it was more like he thought he needed to hold her up. She hadn't even taken off her tourmaline bracelet, a chunky black crystal that helped her to block out energies, but she could still feel the faint edges of his concern.

'I'm fine,' she said. 'I wouldn't be here if I wasn't.'

The words came out more clipped than she'd intended, and she saw Davis and Raven glance at each other as she stepped out from

Archer's arm as gently as she could manage, squeezing his hand to try to soften her words.

'So I have the cameras set up,' Fionn interjected, beginning a breakdown of where everything was in the house. Éabha tuned out, using the moments to breathe and try to calm her emotions. It wasn't fair to get annoyed with Archer; he was just looking out for her.

By asking her if she was OK every five minutes and giving her sceptical looks when she told him she was.

Very helpful.

Fionn finished speaking and Raven turned to Éabha, tying a long chain with a purple pendant on it around her neck as she did. It was amethyst, a crystal Éabha's aunt, Lizzie, had gifted her. Éabha and Raven were PSI's – Paranormal Surveyance Ireland's – two clairvoyants. Their gifts were similar in a lot of ways, but while Éabha's problem was keeping energy out, Raven's was lowering her walls enough to let it in. Amethyst helped enhance Raven's psychic abilities while Éabha had a range of tourmaline jewellery – her staple piece a black bracelet – that shielded her from other people's emotions. The two girls were opposite ends of the spectrum, but they worked well together. Or were learning to, anyway; Raven being willing to sacrifice herself and stay trapped in a portrait so that Éabha could be freed had been a pretty unique bonding experience.

'Next time the grand gesture is on you,' Raven had deadpanned afterwards. There was an uncharacteristic softness in her eyes as she'd spoken, a softness Éabha saw more and more as they spent time together. The events at the Merrion Hub had unlocked something in Raven, dropped part of the wall that she kept around her. She was still sardonic, still spiky, but more and more, she was becoming a version of herself that, Davis had confided, was closer to the Raven he'd known before the death of her father, Pádraig. Archer said it too, his eyes bright with hope, that he felt like the sister he'd called his best friend for most of his life was coming back.

Éabha hoped she'd stay.

For now, she could lose herself in the comfortable familiarity of a PSI survey. They'd already planned the areas to focus on in the preparation sessions, and Fionn was going around double-checking that all the equipment was set up correctly. It was the area everyone deferred to him on – what worked the best and where. For today it was thermal imaging and EMF meters, alongside voice recorders held by each of the team.

It still blew Éabha's mind slightly how at ease she was with all of this now. Less than a year ago, she'd thought the clairvoyancy stuff was all in her head, and if you'd said the words 'EMF' to her, she never in a million years would have guessed it meant 'electromagnetic field', or that it was a reliable method for PSI to detect ghosts. Now she was a member of the Paranormal Surveyance Ireland team and studying clairvoyancy with her previously estranged Aunt Lizzie.

'We good?' Davis asked, straightening up from where he'd been putting his phone – turned off, as all of theirs were – back into his bag. They couldn't risk a phone going off, or any kind of signal affecting their equipment, so they only communicated by walkie-talkie during a survey.

They were downstairs in the living room. It was one of the two rooms that the couple who'd moved into the house reported the activity in: the living room and their bedroom, both of which overlooked the graveyard behind the house. Both rooms were decorated in thick, navy-blue wallpaper, so blue it was almost black. Alice, a thirty-five-year-old marketing manager, had grimaced as she'd shown them the rooms. 'We haven't had the budget to redecorate yet,' she'd said. 'It's a bit dour for our tastes. We'd prefer something brighter, but honestly, we're just happy to have anywhere at all.' She and her partner had done their best to hide the air of dilapidation that permeated the house – a bookcase lined the majority of one of the walls in the living room; beside it, in the corner, there was a tall étagère laden with spider plants while a large, vibrant print hung on the wall over the couch, obscuring most of the wallpaper. It was the same throughout the house: photos and artwork and carefully placed furniture covering as much of the inherited décor as possible, just rogue flashes of the wallpaper appearing in the gaps between them.

No offence to the people who had lived there before, but Éabha didn't blame Alice or her partner, Neil, for wanting to change it. It made everything feel … heavier, in a way.

'Shields down?' she asked Raven, who nodded, closing her eyes as her face furrowed in concentration. Éabha followed suit, slowly guiding Raven through the breathing exercises Lizzie had taught them to help them be in a state of calm as they delved into their energy. As Éabha guided Raven to begin to reach out, she felt comforted. This was familiar. This was routine. This wasn't draining her too badly.

Yet.

She cast her senses out, brushing over Fionn, over Davis and Archer, trying to ignore the emotions coming from them.

She couldn't sense anything out of the ordinary. No presence beyond the five of them in the room, the four familiar energies she knew like the back of her hand. Opening her eyes, she looked at Raven.

'Nothing out of the ordinary on my end,' Raven said.

'Mine either,' Éabha confirmed. She sighed, steeling herself. Time for the next level.

Psychometry, the ability to pick things up by touching objects, had always been Éabha's strongest gift. So now she walked around the room, resting her hand on the different objects there, letting the feelings wash over her. When she got to the couch, which was at the back of the room, up against the wall, she felt herself stumble slightly.

Instinctively, she threw out her other hand, not to catch herself, but palm up to stop the others from speaking to her or trying to touch her.

She needed to dig deeper. Figure out whether this was her, or something she was picking up on.

Blurring fog. Confusion. Tiredness. A shortness in her breath that made every inhalation feel like a battle. She said it all out loud automatically as she felt it, both for her own voice recorder and the one she knew Davis was holding to capture their reports. It was their protocol, because the deeper she went into the layers of an object, the harder it was for her to remember afterwards what she'd picked up. That had always been the way, even before *him*, so she didn't resent it. The sensations felt familiar, as though she could recognise the feelings, but they weren't from her. They were from whoever had sat on this couch. It felt like Alice and Neil, the same energies she'd picked up on when she'd shook their hands. She reported it all, coming back into herself and letting the rest of the team finish up as she took a bag of sugar-covered jellies out of her pocket and ate a few. Sugar and caffeine were not ideal coping mechanisms, but at times like this, they were her best options. She could feel Archer watching her carefully and avoided making eye contact with him. She just needed to do her job, and it was hard when she could literally sense Archer hovering protectively around her.

They decided they had finished with the living room and moved upstairs, her ballet flats feeling like cement blocks on her feet as she climbed the stairs behind Fionn. The bedroom felt the same. The heaviness. No sense of other energies, but a weighty feeling, a shallowness in her breathing that made her feel like she was struggling for each inhalation.

She left the bed until last, resting her hand on a pillow. Alice had reported waking in the night gasping for breath and seeing a figure standing over her in the dark, the same one she kept seeing out of the corner of her eye while they watched TV in the living room or got ready for bed up here. She said it looked like it was reaching for her.

Éabha felt it immediately, her hand jumping to her throat as she took long, ragged gasps, choking out what she could feel. It was a relief to take her hand away, to take the bracelet Fionn offered her and slide it back onto her arm, dimming the sensations and memories that had flooded through her.

'There's something going on,' Éabha said frowning. 'But I don't sense the energies of anything besides Alice and Neil.'

'Me either,' Raven confirmed, folding her arms and tapping a heavy boot against the ground. 'We're missing something.' She said it like she was personally offended by that fact.

'Let's think through the timeline,' Archer said. 'They started having these experiences a few weeks after they moved in. Then the bathroom flooded and the plumber said it was a leaky pipe, but they felt it was malicious, that they'd already felt on edge before then, like they were being watched.'

'What damage was done again?' Fionn asked. 'I know it leaked down into the living room, but they said they caught it before it completely destroyed anything, right?'

'The bathroom's on the other side of this wall, isn't it?' Davis asked. He was standing beside the large, full-length mirror placed between the wardrobe and the adjacent wall and was pointing towards it.

'Yep,' Fionn confirmed.

Davis placed a hand on either side of the edge of the mirror and pivoted, lifting it out of the way with a grunt.

'That's heavier than I expected,' he said. He placed it carefully against the wardrobe before running a hand along the now-exposed wallpaper. He pulled his hand away. 'That's coming away from the wall,' he said, frowning.

'Feeling anxious and unwell, seeing things out of the corner of their eyes, shortness of breath … a heavy sensation …' Archer said out loud. He looked at Davis, and Davis gave a triumphant grin.

'Mould.'

They had to wait for Neil and Alice to come home before they could confirm it. Even clients this eager for answers might object to them ripping the wallpaper off the walls, whether or not they hated the wallpaper to begin with. So when the couple returned, they explained their findings and hypothesis, and with their consent peeled away the wallpaper in the bedroom and on the living-room wall, where the couch was, to expose thick expanses of dark mould.

'The wallpaper shade is so dark you wouldn't see it as easily,' Davis explained. 'And because it was mostly covered by furniture and artwork, there were only small gaps where you could see it at all. It's completely understandable that you missed it. The pipe was probably already leaking and the mould starting to grow when you moved in, which was why things felt off before the bathroom incident. Then once the bathroom flooded, it would have developed even more widely.'

'Mould can cause a lot of the symptoms you're experiencing,' Archer explained gently. 'It can be—'

'Really toxic,' Alice filled in. She let out a shaky laugh. 'You probably saved our lives.'

'Or at least saved us some major health complications,' Neil added.

'I'm so embarrassed. I was convinced it was a ghost,' Alice said, putting her head in her hands.

'You are absolutely not the first person we've met who had an ordinary reason for something they thought was paranormal,' Archer said reassuringly. His handsome face had a gentle smile, and his blond hair was shining under the lights of the kitchen. Éabha was always impressed by how his confidence ensured that people took him seriously; sometimes people did a double take when a nineteen-year-old walked into a meeting. The rest of the team were aged between nineteen and twenty-two, but a few moments with them, and especially Archer, showed they knew what they were talking about. Not only that, but it was always clear that all Archer wanted to do was comfort people, to alleviate any embarrassment or worry. He was an exceptionally kind person. It was one of the things she loved most about him.

'The majority of our cases are like this,' Raven added.

Éabha nodded fervently, pulling her gaze away from Archer to focus back on the couple. Davis and Fionn were already carrying the equipment out to the car, Davis brimming with his usual mix of delight at successfully solving a mystery and disappointment that it was, once again, an ordinary reason. PSI only ever seemed to find completely ordinary or extremely life-threatening surveys, and Davis was desperate for them to find one somewhere in the middle.

'A real ghost, just not a homicidal one,' was his general way of phrasing it.

Éabha said goodbye to the couple, waving to avoid shaking their hands. She felt shaky, fragile, like the barriers keeping her energy in and theirs out was brittle. Touch would be too much right now. She left Archer and Raven finishing up with them and went outside to Davis's car, where he and Fionn were just slamming the boot closed.

'You good?' Davis asked, scanning her, a faint expression of concern on his face.

She nodded.

'I am ... I just ... need to be ... not standing.'

What was the word for that?

Neither Davis nor Fionn remarked on her word choice. Instead, Davis simply opened the car door and ushered her in. Éabha collapsed against the back seat, Davis gently closing the door behind her as Fionn got in on the other side. Davis and Archer, as the tallest of the group, always sat up front.

'Raven looked wiped after that one,' Fionn said. 'It must have been pretty intense.'

'Yeah, it was a bit,' Éabha managed to say, summoning up a smile. She could have cried at his kindness. Raven, when she poked her head in the window to say goodbye before getting into her own car to drive to either her flat or her girlfriend, Cordelia's, looked mildly tired but by no means 'wiped'.

Archer and Davis got into the car, already beginning a dissection of the survey. She looked out the window as Davis drove, to avoid seeing how often Archer glanced in the rearview mirror to check on her. Experience had taught her it would be a lot.

It took her three-quarters of the drive back to Kilcarrig before she remembered the word was 'sitting'.

CHAPTER TWO

THE FAMILIAR CHAOS OF THE PSI FAMILY takeaway night washed over Fionn as he walked into the O'Sullivans' living room. Raven and Cordelia were sitting on the couch, Raven's leg carelessly slung over Cordelia's as they bent their heads together to look at something on Raven's phone. Probably a cat reel on Instagram. Davis and Éabha sat in the two armchairs by the fire, Davis talking enthusiastically about something while Éabha listened thoughtfully, a small smile on her face. Her legs were curled up underneath her and she had her hands tucked into the sleeves of her jumper. She was pale, and the concealer under her eyes didn't fully hide the tiredness there.

Éabha had always been good at putting up a front, but even she couldn't hide the effect the Merrion Hub investigation had had on her. Her aunt, Lizzie, who was deeply skilled with all things clairvoyant, was trying to help her heal from it, but this was outside of even Lizzie's remit. Whatever Adrian – the homicidal ghost who'd painted his soul into a self-portrait and preyed on the living, stealing young women into the portrait to take their energy – had drained from Éabha was taking its time coming back, to the point where, months later, Fionn was starting to wonder if it ever would.

Davis had been quietly deep diving into physical illnesses that mimicked this, to see if there was any correlation or cure. Now that the seemingly endless onslaught of essays, presentations and exams that had accompanied his final semester of university had finally ceased, he had plenty of time to research. He brushed it off as 'needing a project to keep him distracted from panicking about his results', but he obviously just wanted to help his friend in the way he knew best – via science. So far he'd narrowed in on ME: myalgic encephalomyelitis, a neurological condition that triggered a range of symptoms, including brain fog and extreme fatigue, two of the things affecting Éabha the most.

'It's been recognised since the nineteen-eighties but no one has taken it seriously,' Davis had said to Fionn when they were alone in the office, pulling his tightly coiled black hair into a low bun at the base of his neck, his sign that he meant business. 'Long Covid research is helping a bit but there's no medicine or treatment.'

'Well, that's … not helpful,' Fionn had said. What an understatement! He hated this: seeing how much it was affecting Éabha and knowing there was no way he could help.

He did, at least, know not to hover. Archer was dealing with it by trying to help Éabha with her every need – even the ones she hadn't asked him to help with. Éabha visibly tensed every time Archer rushed to do something for her, and despite both Davis and Fionn gently suggesting to Archer that he tone down the assistance, he hadn't quite managed to follow through.

'You warm enough, Éabhs?' Archer asked, coming into the room behind Fionn. Éabha nodded. 'I got you this blanket,' Archer continued, holding out a thick, fluffy blanket, ignoring the fact that she had just indicated she was fine.

'I'm fine at the moment, thanks,' Éabha said, giving him what looked to Fionn like a slightly strained smile as she took the blanket and placed it folded up on the arm of her chair.

'I can get you a warm drink?'

'I'm fine.' There was just the slightest sharp undertone in her voice now, a level that was basically default for Raven but, coming from Éabha, it sounded like a snap.

Raven cleared her throat.

'What have we got planned for dinner, Little Brother? I'm starving.'

'I'd love Thai,' Davis said immediately.

'I'd be down for that,' Cordelia chimed in.

The moment of tension passed as Fionn and Davis started enthusiastically debating the merits of one place over another. They both loved Phad Thai, but each fiercely maintained that *their* favourite place did the best one. It was an argument they rehashed every time they ordered.

Archer took out his phone and pulled up a menu, walking over to hand it to Cordelia.

'Here, I have a feeling Davis is going to win this one,' he said.

Fionn opened his mouth to protest but just as Cordelia reached for the phone it started to ring, and she jerked her hand back, startled.

'I didn't think anyone had their phone off silent any more,' she said as Archer answered.

'Hi. Yes, of course I remember. Lovely to hear from you again,' he said as he walked out of the room.

Fionn immediately forgot about bickering with Davis, looking at him with raised eyebrows instead.

There was glint of excitement in Davis's eyes. 'Sounds official,' he said.

'He used his adult voice,' Fionn agreed.

Éabha was watching it all quietly, and Raven pulled out her phone, looking up the Thai restaurant.

'Here's the menu,' she said, handling it to Cordelia. Fionn stopped worrying about winning the Thai food battle, his mind already racing from the way Archer had tensed with excitement, his voice taking on his professional PSI tone.

They had a new case; he knew it.

Fionn wasn't surprised when Archer came back ten minutes later, brimming with barely contained excitement.

'Do you remember the cruise ship?' he asked.

Davis nodded immediately while Fionn wracked his brains. It sounded familiar, but how?

'After Hyacinth House,' Éabha said, her voice echoing the tiredness her slumped shoulders demonstrated. 'You got the call, when we were all celebrating not getting held liable for the house being burned to the ground.'

Archer nodded, and it all clicked into place for Fionn.

'I thought they'd dropped off the radar,' Raven said.

'They had,' Archer replied. He grinned. 'Until now.' He paused dramatically. 'They want us to fly out on Saturday. Urgently.'

Fionn could see Raven studying Cordelia out of the corner of her eye. Her girlfriend was clearly trying to keep an enthusiastic expression on her face, but she couldn't quite hide the worry shining through. Raven reached out and took Cordelia's hand silently, and Fionn looked away. He was intruding on a private moment.

'This week?' Davis asked, pulling his attention back towards the conversation.

'It's urgent,' Archer said. He looked around the room at the rest of the team. 'There've been a few ... incidents.'

Adrenaline shot through Fionn as the atmosphere in the room shifted. They were on to a big case here. He could feel it in his bones.

CHAPTER THREE

ÉABHA ARRIVED AT PSI HQ in the O'Sullivans' home in Kilcarrig the next day for their team meeting to plan the cruise-ship survey. The company had said to Archer that they'd send over a brief immediately, but the team didn't have a lot of time to prep before they'd have to fly out. Fionn lifted a hand in greeting as she walked in, barely looking up at her. The noise-cancelling headphones he wore and the way his eyebrows knitted together made it clear he wasn't ignoring her: he was just in the middle of something, probably an audio file he wanted to finish going through before the others got here. Éabha waved back and sat at her desk, leaning against the supportive back of her chair with relief. It was hard to be upright when she was fatigued, and today was another tired day. All she had done so far was shower and eat breakfast, but these days that was enough to begin to wipe her out.

It was only eleven thirty.

If she had the energy, she'd scream to the ceiling how much she hated this.

She glanced around the familiar office, at the loose ring of desks crammed into the centre of it, the armchairs that had been there back when it was the O'Sullivan's front room and not PSI HQ still shoved out of the way into the corners. Archer always said he was going to put them somewhere else, but never got around to moving them. The back wall was now lined with filing cabinets – a recent acquisition that had made Davis almost giddy with excitement at the organisational possibilities – while corkboards with various PSI cases decorated another, family photos still wedged between them. This was one of her favourite places in the whole world, the place where she had learned she could be herself and still be accepted. Her muscles started to relax, her jaw unclenching, as Davis came in and sat down at his computer, stretching his arms out in front of him before resting them on the desk. He frowned.

'Fionn, were you messing with my chair?' he asked irately, leaning down to pull on the lever and standing slightly up out of the chair. It was just the three of them so far. They were still waiting on Raven and, of course, Archer, who was physically incapable of ever being on time, to join them.

Éabha sneaked a glance at Fionn, who gave her an exasperated smile before answering. 'And risk the ergonomic safety of Davis Williams? Never.'

'Look, repetitive strain injury is a thing, OK? I spend most of my life at a desk,' Davis grumbled. 'I'm not dealing with carpal tunnel syndrome by twenty-five because you think it's funny to–'

'Davis. I did not mess with your chair to sabotage your efforts to have a posture that suggests you have a stick shoved somewhere extremely specific.'

Éabha laughed before she could stop herself, and Davis's grumpy face turned to her before breaking into a begrudging smile.

'OK maybe I was being a bit–' He broke off and uttered a string of curse words. 'WE ARE NOT THE PSYCHOLOGICAL SOCIETY OF IRELAND. STOP EMAILING US ABOUT CONFERENCES.'

Fionn and Éabha burst out laughing at his indignant expression. It felt good to laugh like this – she hadn't in a long time. The team rotated which of them went through the general enquiries email each week. This week it was Davis's turn, and he'd been plagued by emails from people mistaking PSI for the Psychological Society of Ireland. He'd been losing patience steadily all week and this was clearly the final straw.

'Oh, I have failed to respond to your email? And this level of attention to detail isn't acceptable? YOU CAN'T EVEN FIND THE RIGHT EMAIL TO CONTACT. HOW CAN YOU LECTURE ME ON ATTENTION TO DETAIL?' Davis ignored their escalating laughter, completely focused on his computer screen as he typed furiously.

'Wait, Davis, you're not actually replying with that, are you?' Éabha said, getting up out of her chair to bolt over to him. She wouldn't put it past him to actually say it.

She realised after two steps she'd made a grave error. Dizziness flooded over her and the corners of her vision blurred; ever since her disastrous encounter with Adrian, the ghost in the portrait, if she moved too fast or stood up too quickly, this happened. The doctor called it postural orthostatic tachycardia syndrome, or POTS. Lizzie called it the lingering effects of having your energy drained almost to death.

Éabha called it something that would have gotten her kicked out of her parents' house if they hadn't already evicted her.

'Éabha?' Both Davis and Fionn were on their feet as she stopped, reaching for Raven's empty desk to steady herself.

'I'm OK, just dizzy,' she said. Her vision narrowed to almost complete darkness, and she felt gentle hands guiding her to sit in a chair that had been pushed up behind her. She looked up to see Davis's concerned face studying hers.

'You sure you're OK?' Fionn asked, his voice behind her. He must have gotten the chair.

She nodded, but immediately regretted the action as the fuzzy static engulfing her brain intensified.

'Do you want some water?' Davis asked.

'No, I'm OK,' Éabha said again. She steeled herself for him to push back and start fussing, but Davis just nodded.

'You're not going to fall off the chair if I let go, are you?' he asked.

She realised his hands were still on her shoulders, not gripping her, but placed to support her if she needed it.

'I promise I will not end up on the floor,' she said, forcing a smile onto her face. Davis looked at her a long moment, then nodded and went back to his desk.

'Seriously though, you're not actually typing that are you?' Fionn asked him, moving the conversation on.

Éabha missed Davis's snarky response, focusing instead on breathing as the dizziness faded and was replaced instead by a warmth that was all gratitude. They weren't making a big deal of it.

Archer could take notes from them, a bitter little voice said. She shook her head. Archer was just being protective. He wanted to support her, to look after her.

It was just that his way of looking after her made her feel like she was slowly being suffocated.

But she was being ungrateful. 'Oh no, my boyfriend wants to look after me when I'm unwell.' *Get a grip, Éabha.*

She just wished his care for her didn't feel more and more like doubt in her.

They worked away for half an hour, Éabha insisting on taking control of the admin after Davis discovered two more emails for the Psychological Society of Ireland in their inbox and reached such apocalyptic levels of indignation that she needed to cling to her tourmaline bracelet to keep his emotions at bay. She even slid the tourmaline crystal earrings Lizzie had given her a few weeks ago into the single piercings in her ears. Éabha's ability to block emotions ebbed and flowed like her energy, and Lizzie's gift had been both thoughtful and practical, another line of defence against emotional interference.

That was the kind of support she needed: practical things she could choose to use or not use, depending on how she was feeling. Her physical health fluctuated so much day to day that her clairvoyant abilities did too; some days she barely needed even the bracelet, others she had the bracelet, the earrings and wondered if a helmet of tourmaline was a possibility.

As Éabha slid an earring in, Raven clomped through the door, dropping her leather jacket on the back of her chair and sitting on top of her desk instead of behind it. She swivelled to face Éabha, her legs dangling. Raven's deep purple amethyst pendant hung around her neck, resting on top of the black string top visible under her white shirt, which was unbuttoned most of the way down. Her silvery-blond hair was in her usual plait, and her heavy boots made a thunk when they hit off the wood of the desk.

'Could you make any sense of the reading Lizzie gave us to do?' she asked. Her tone was nonchalant, but the all-too-careful way she posed, a facade of indifference, made it clear she was worried.

'I got through, like, three paragraphs and my brain broke,' Éabha said.

'Phew, not just me then,' Raven said with a relieved grin.

Éabha echoed it back. She'd thought it had been her brain fog affecting her, making her struggle to process the reading. Sometimes when she was tired she couldn't make sense of words on pages, even forgot words mid-sentence as she was trying to speak. But if Raven had found it hard, too ... That felt hopeful.

'Magic class getting tough?' Fionn asked.

Davis bristled. 'It's not magic, Fionn, it's clairvoyancy, which actually has quite a few scientific bases ...' He trailed off as all three of them turned to look at him with varying stages of amusement.

'You were joking,' Davis said, a tinge of sheepishness in his voice.

'I have been known to do that occasionally, yes,' Fionn said cheerfully.

It was strange, having Davis leap to clairvoyancy's defence when he had been Éabha's biggest doubter. He hadn't even wanted her to join PSI. But the thing about Davis was, once he was on side, he was the most loyal defender anyone could ask for. And as soon as he had seen her gifts were real, he had immediately pivoted to not only defending her but wanting to study her, and prove to the scientific community that her gifts were real. He was always devising little 'labs', as he called them, for them to do together. But she never felt like she was the experiment. They were collaborating. After years of gaslighting from her parents, having someone so enthusiastic about irrefutably showing the validity of her gifts was a such a ... well ... a gift.

'Lizzie is on the theory portion at the moment,' Raven told Fionn. 'Which I understand is important, but also can be very … dense.'

'I was worried it was me that was dense, so honestly, this is a relief,' Éabha said.

The others laughed.

'Nope, we are as doomed as each other,' Raven said.

'Who's doomed?' Archer asked, walking in the door of the office.

Éabha hadn't heard the front door open, but even with her hearing aids in she only really heard it when things were completely quiet and the person – normally Raven, sometimes Davis if he'd been reading the comments about PSI on Reddit again – slammed the door shut behind them.

'Your girlfriend and me, as usual,' Raven said.

'Get a hobby,' Fionn said. Raven laughed, but Archer's face was serious.

'Are you all right?' He asked, striding over, his eyes focused on Éabha.

'Relax, Arch. It was just some particularly wordy clairvoyance homework,' Raven said. The usual snark in her voice softened as she looked at him, at the worry that tightened his eyes and set his mouth in a concerned frown.

Éabha knew that what had happened with Adrian, and The Lady before him, had rattled Archer. He needed to be the protector, and he held himself responsible for everyone in PSI. It was what she reminded herself of when he got overprotective, when she wanted to snap at him when he asked her for the sixth time in an hour if she needed anything. Archer's loveliest trait was his big heart, but it could be his most infuriating one, too. They all chose to be a part of this. They all knew the risks. Most of them had reminders of those risks: the burn scars on Archer's cheek and on Davis's arms and legs. The way Fionn's asthma still acted up and how he winced when he sat still for too long, the shoulder he'd dislocated still catching in its joint. Even Éabha's hair, once long and wavy and now in a short pixie cut after chunks of it burned in the Hyacinth House fire, was a constant reminder. And no matter how many times she told him otherwise, or Raven told him or Davis and Fionn told him, she knew he had never shaken off the feeling of responsibility for them being in that house.

She, thankfully, couldn't read minds, but she would have bet money that that was what Raven was thinking, what made her temper her usual sarcasm and not accompany the reassurance with an eye roll or raised eyebrow.

'So, boat stuff?' Fionn asked.

'Boat stuff,' Archer confirmed. He went to his desk and leaned against the front, looking around the room at the four of them sitting at – or in Raven's case, on – their desks.

'They've asked us to join them for a seven-day cruise in the Med on their ship *L'Imperiale*. It's a small cruise ship, very exclusive and luxurious. It has a capacity of a hundred passengers, and around fifty crew, depending on the sailing. Staff turnover has been … high, but they've guaranteed that a few of the staff who have been there since the experiences started are still on board and, in their words, "extremely eager to assist in any way they can".'

'Oh, they're spooked,' Raven said, sympathy clear on her face.

'Imagine being trapped in the middle of the sea with a ghost,'

Fionn shuddered. 'It's not like a building – you can't just leave.'

Éabha didn't need to imagine. She knew exactly what it was like to be trapped with a ghost, with no way of escape. She wouldn't wish it on anyone.

'We need to help them,' she said.

'That is kind of our whole reason for doing this,' Davis pointed out.

Archer glared at him, but Éabha laughed.

'I am aware, Davis,' she said lightly. 'I just mean this sounds like a really good case. Not just because I'm guessing that, if they're desperate enough to hire us, it means they have a seriously good reason to, which also means it's pretty likely to actually have a spirit.'

'We can't go in expecting anything,' Davis said quickly.

Fionn groaned. 'Please, no "unconscious bias," lectures, Davis. You know what she means.'

They had all heard enough about unconscious bias during the Merrion Hub investigation. Davis had convinced them to let a journalist, Audrey, shadow the team. He'd been determined to prove to her that parapsychology was real, and the two had bickered constantly. Audrey, however, had eventually been convinced, mostly by Éabha being kidnapped into a painting, which was pretty irrefutable proof. She and Davis ended up forming a pretty intense bond, and even dated for a brief while, until Audrey got offered a job in England and moved.

'We can hypothesise that there is a reasonable chance of paranormal activity,' Éabha said, grinning at Davis. 'Better?' She added with a raised eyebrow.

He nodded.

'And, if there isn't, these people must be really frightened,' she said. 'You'd have to be to complain to your workplace, especially when a lot of cruise work is seasonal. We can hopefully offer them some reassurance, at the very least.'

'I'd really like some more actual data, though,' Davis mused. 'Without it being a danger to anyone on the team, for once.'

'That would be nice,' Raven agreed. 'One ghost, no almost-dying, please.'

'Anyway,' Archer said, a slight edge to his voice. 'We'll be given free run of the ship once it doesn't interfere with the guests. They disembark most days, so there should be times when it's just us and the crew and maybe a few passengers floating around if they choose to stay on board. So I think we should go through the info they've sent us now, interview the crew immediately when we get on board, then break down the areas to run the equipment on, based on that, and we can go from there.

'Aye, aye, Cap'n,' Fionn said, saluting.

He took out a notebook and immediately started to write, muttering names of cameras and other equipment loudly enough that even Éabha could hear him. Davis, Archer and Raven starting to debate whether the possibility of guests being on the boat would interfere with any surveys drowned him out.

Éabha was getting tired, the noise and stimulation and concentrating on the admin draining her way more than she liked to admit, even to herself. But underneath the heavy weight of fatigue settling on her like an unwelcome blanket, she felt a flicker of excitement. A new investigation, one where she could show them all – and herself – that what had happened with Adrian hadn't changed her. That she could still do this. And maybe, just maybe, she'd stop seeing that flicker of doubt in Archer's eyes when he looked her.

CHAPTER FOUR

'OH, SO THIS IS, LIKE ... *fancy* fancy,' Fionn said, pausing on the dock to take in *L'Imperiale*. The ship loomed over them, its white paint gleaming in the warm French sunshine, incredibly different from the cold, grey skies they'd left behind in Dublin. The sea air, briny and refreshing and a complete contrast to the stifling atmosphere of the airport, almost lifted his spirits.

'I am already deeply uncomfortable,' Raven said, stopping beside him.

'I haven't packed nearly enough bow ties,' Fionn said, trying to joke his way past the sensation of heavy dread settling like a weight in his stomach.

'By which you mean any, right?' Raven asked, raising an eyebrow. Fionn nodded.

'Didn't think you were a bow-tie person. I'd have to rethink my entire opinion of you,' she said with a wink, before following his gaze back to the activity on the pier they were standing on.

It was a flurry of activity, of deckhands wheeling trollies stacked full of suitcases past them while their owners – their fellow passengers for the next week – strolled leisurely past, making their way to the gangway to board. Some of them took in their surroundings, the port filled with yachts neatly moored, a few about to cast off with their deck crew calling to each other and pulling ropes in what looked like incredibly complicated and impressive manoeuvres. Others barely glanced left or right, as though this was so familiar to them there was no wonder or interest to be found in it. No matter the attitude the passenger had, all of them were dressed in elegant linen suits and long, light dresses, no one with a hair out of place. Fionn could feel the seven a.m. Ryanair flight they'd gotten written all over him in every crease of his T-shirt, and couldn't stop himself looking down at his battered carry-on suitcase, with the scratches on it and the crooked handle that caught every time he tried to pull it up or put it down.

'I'd like to see any of them isolate a paranormal occurrence on an EVP or stare down a ghost in a burning building,' Raven said, nudging him with her shoulder.

'Come on, you two. Plenty more to stare at on board,' Davis said, ushering them along.

Raven went to follow him, silently taking the large suitcase Fionn had been hauling since they landed. It caught momentarily on the dock and Fionn let out a squawk as she yanked at it. 'My equipment! Be gentle!'

Raven gave him a sardonic look. 'It's cameras, in full protective casing, not a collection of radioactive chemicals.'

'You still shouldn't jostle them,' Fionn protested.

'Jostle is a great word,' Archer said, joining them. He was pulling his case with one hand, Éabha's with the other. She was trailing behind him, though she gave Fionn a forced smile when she met his eyes.

'I was saving you the trouble of carrying it on deck, but if you're worried about my *jostling*, you're more than welcome to take it back,' Raven huffed.

'Can we please stop bickering like a bunch of children?' Davis cut in. 'We're at work. Let's at least pretend to be professional until we get to the cabins.'

'Speaking of cabins, what's the craic with that?' Fionn asked.

'We have a three-person cabin and a two-person,' Archer said. He looked sideways at Éabha. 'It might be good if I can stay and help Éabhs–'

Éabha stiffened as he started to speak and sent an imploring glance to Raven.

That was interesting.

'I am not listening to Fionn snore for seven days,' Raven interjected. 'Sorry, Fionn.' She grinned. 'And we all know I'm too messy to share a cabin with Davis. He'd chuck me overboard within forty-eight hours.' She turned so Archer couldn't see her as she spoke, her body language still relaxed as she gave them a pointed look, inclining her head towards Éabha, whose discomfort had started to turn into relief.

'I know PSI is against prescribed gender norms but, in this case, I think a good old-fashioned two girls in one cabin, three boys in the other makes the most sense.'

Archer looked disappointed, but Davis quickly agreed. Éabha softly said she thought it would be for the best too, giving Archer's hand a comforting squeeze.

'Besides, this is work, not a romantic getaway,' she added.

Éabha always stayed in Archer's room when she slept over at the O'Sullivans', with Raven reclaiming her old room, Davis in what was almost officially his room now that he lived there most of the time, and the guest room unofficially Fionn's. Part of him wondered if he should ask Archer if everything was OK between him and Éabha. Archer didn't talk about his relationship much to

Fionn, and he wondered if Archer was afraid to. Ever since they'd fought about Archer cutting him out last spring, getting so lost in his new relationship with Éabha that he stopped making time for his friendship with Fionn and leaving him feeling lost and isolated, Archer had been trying so hard to make things up to him.

Fionn had told Archer a few times that he didn't want him to stop talking to him about those things – he just needed to make time for their friendship too – but sometimes it seemed like Archer was walking on eggshells around him. Fionn knew Archer felt bad about not being there for him when he'd figured out he was aro-ace, especially because his reaction when Fionn told him hadn't exactly been ideal. Archer was bisexual himself, and Fionn had overheard him telling Raven he felt like he'd really let another LGBTQ+ person down and, worst of all, it was one of his best friends. Archer's reaction hadn't been ace-phobic; he'd just been so lost in his own scenarios he didn't listen when Fionn had tried to explain what he was feeling. It had really hurt, yes, but Archer had shown through his actions he both wanted to support Fionn and accepted him as he was. That was all Fionn wanted. Except now Archer had gone from being oblivious to being too conscious and Fionn had no idea how to get him to just … relax and be Archer.

'We should find Captain Trudy Neale. She's our point of contact. She said she generally goes by Neale with the crew, though,' Archer said.

The five of them set off up the wooden ramp leading to the boat, the sound of the engines already filling the air. The gangway felt bouncy under Fionn's feet, and even the metal handrails on either side didn't make it feel much sturdier to him, especially because he could feel a vibration from the engines thrumming through them. He looked down at the sea as he walked, and even though the beautiful, clear, blue water should have looked inviting, he found himself swallowing hard.

'Don't worry, no one's ever fallen off the gangway, and you should see the state some of the guests come back from shore in,' a cheerful voice informed him. 'And the crew, for that matter,' it added conspiratorially. Fionn looked up to see a young man, maybe a year or two older than him, dressed in a crisp, white uniform with navy piping, smiling at him. His dark hair was neatly slicked back, and he had a tan that spoke of hours spent in the sun.

'PSI, right?' he asked Fionn in a quieter tone as the rest of the team came up behind him.

'Are we that obvious?' Fionn asked.

'Well, Archer did put a story up on Instagram this morning of you all getting on an airplane to go on a "secret survey" and none of you have changed since then, so it wasn't hard to spot you …'

'Aren't we supposed to be going under the radar, Archer?' Davis asked, exasperated.

'I didn't say where we were going!' Archer protested. 'Look, you try keeping your place in the algorithm without posting regularly. It's a nightmare.'

'So, are you one of our prospective interviewees?' Raven asked.

'I am, though, to be honest, I won't be as much help to you as some of the others on the crew. This is my first season on *L'Imperiale*. I'm Charles, by the way.'

If he had to guess, Fionn would say Charles was French, from the soft way he said his name: *Sharle*.

'Fionn,' he said, reaching out a hand to Charles.

The others introduced themselves one by one, stepping to the side as guests came up behind them and other crew members stepped forward to greet them.

'Neale asked me to keep an eye out for you. She's going to meet you at six p.m. in meeting room two to talk through everything. She asked me to apologise for not greeting you personally but, as you can imagine, onboarding day is pretty hectic and there are inevitably a few people who don't find things to their liking with whom she will need to smooth things over. Despite the fact that there is a full interior and hosting crew, they always want to speak directly to the captain. But I can take you to your cabins and get you settled. There's a welcome reception – champagne, of course – on the top deck, accompanied by a mandatory safety briefing that begins in thirty minutes.'

'Interesting combination,' Archer said.

'Yes, we have figured out the best way to get rich people to do things is to lure them with fizz,' Charles grinned. Then he glanced around nervously, as though afraid someone might have overheard him even though he still spoke in a low voice.

'Anyway, after the briefing, you are free to wander the deck or get some refreshments from the bar or whatever you want to do until your meeting with Neale.'

Fionn's stomach rumbled. A shower and a snack sounded ideal to him.

They followed Charles through long corridors aglow with soft lighting from ornate lamps fixed into the walls. The walls were navy, with detailing in shimmering gold, while the thick carpets were navy too, with delicate white spirals. The décor echoed the crew uniforms of crisp white with navy piping. Charles summoned a lift, which arrived swiftly. It was large and smooth, making no noise as it descended. They only went one floor down, but when Fionn asked if there were stairs, Charles looked at him in surprise.

'Of course, but guests don't tend to use them. Too much work,' he added with a smile.

Fionn had no idea how he'd find his way around. Every corridor was beautiful, but the same: decorated in deep navy blue with gold accents, the same navy-and-white carpet on the floor and they all had the same identically opulent decoration, which, he imagined, led to more than one guest who'd had slightly too much champagne needing to be escorted to their room. He was disorientated, and he was completely sober.

'There are five passenger decks. Deck eight is the observatory and stargazing platform. The pool is on deck seven, along with the late-night bar and dancefloor. Deck six has passenger cabins, the coffee lounge and a sun-bathing deck with plenty of loungers aft –' Raven's eyebrows knotted together at that and Fionn opened his mouth to explain but Charles beat him to it.

'That's towards the back of the ship,' he said with an understanding smile. 'Deck five – where we are now – has more cabins, the gym, spa and beauty salon, as well as a business suites and conference rooms in case people need to spend their holiday closing a business deal. The main dining room is on deck four, and there is another outdoor deck area with sun deck and reclining chairs aft. Deck three has the medical centre and security booth. There are members of staff stationed on every floor to assist guests when required.'

'So do you have, like, a hundred staff or do none of you sleep?' Fionn asked, reeling from the sheer amount of information Charles had rattled off so easily. He really hoped there was a map in the room or he'd definitely spend most of this survey wandering in circles. Charles laughed and looked around before answering. 'We have a max staff of fifty, but at the moment it's thirty-five and let's just say, lie-ins are a distant memory,' he said.

'Have you lost a lot of crew?' Davis asked.

Charles nodded. 'Fifteen so far. Neale's pretty worried about losing more. It's hard to find replacements at this point in the season.'

Davis nodded, as though storing that information away for later.

Fionn thought hard. 'Wait, if the guests are on decks eight to four, where are the crew?'

'Decks one and two,' Charles said. 'We divide the boat into guest areas and crew areas – having the guests deal with only decks eight to four makes it easier for them and helps them not to get lost. They usually only go down as far as the main dining room anyway – that's the last level with a sun deck to lie out on – but having the medical centre and security booth on level three – oh, and the crew mess actually – means someone will definitely spot them before they make their way down to decks two or one. Though there's always a few determined to get a glimpse of the engine room.'

They walked halfway down the corridor and Charles stopped at a door. 'Both of your cabins are on this level – deck five – to help you blend in as guests. This is the two-person cabin,' he said, looking around at them with an eyebrow half-raised, uncertain who to offer the key to.

'That's ours,' Raven said cheerfully, stepping forward, Éabha following behind her. Charles unlocked the door, handing each of them a keycard. 'Here are your keys to the room. There's a guest guide inside with a breakdown of what is on offer, when it's on and where it's located, as well as a map.' Fionn's shoulders sagged in relief at that.

'If the rest of you want to follow me–' Charles continued, walking three doors down and then opening another door. 'This is made up for three. The cabins here are designed to give more space than the average ship, so hopefully you'll all be comfortable. If you need anything, I'll be stationed on deck six, where you boarded, welcoming people for the rest of the afternoon. Just come and find me.' He handed Fionn all three keycards, smiling warmly at him. Davis and Archer thanked the steward and stepped into the cabin. Charles lingered.

'Do you do the interviews?' he asked Fionn.

'They're not really my strong point, but if we have a lot of people to talk to, I'll pitch in,' Fionn said. He didn't have Archer's easy way with people, and even Raven was better at connecting with people about this – years of shadowing her parents had taught her the skills she needed.

'So I'll possibly see you then, if not before,' Charles smiled. 'If you have any questions about the ship, I will be happy to answer them.'

Fionn perked up. 'I have so many, actually. Ships fascinate me. I was a pirate kid growing up, so the idea of sailing anywhere, even if a cruise ship is slightly different, is pretty exciting.'

Charles laughed. 'We have that in common. Come find me

when you have time. I'll happily answer any questions you have.'

'Thanks, Charles,' Fionn said, smiling at him. The cabin door shut behind him as he looked around, taking it all in.

It was far larger than he'd expected. There were three surprisingly spacious single beds in a neat line, a bedside table on either side of the middle one. All the beds were perfectly made, with starched, white linen decorated with navy stripes, and plump white-and-navy pillows. To the right of the door was a desk, a mirror hanging over it, and a shelf fixed to the wall beside the mirror. There was a door to the left leading to a bathroom with a shower, sink and toilet, decorated with sparklingly clean white and navy tiles. The towels were white with the vessel's logo – a navy anchor with the ship's name written underneath – embossed on them, and the customised toiletries all were stored in sleek navy containers with *L'Imperiale* printed on them.

'I'm on the left,' Davis said, dropping his laptop case onto the bed. Fionn claimed the right, while Archer kicked off his shoes and flopped, face first, onto the middle one. 'Oh, these are comfy,' he said delightedly, his voice slightly muffled by the pillow before he rolled onto his back.

Davis was already neatly unpacking everything from his carry-on while simultaneously talking about how hungry he was, stepping back and forth over the equipment bag that took up a huge section of the floor. Fionn had packed only the essentials, but even though the cabin was pretty spacious, it was still not the PSI office. He opened the bag and started going through it, checking that nothing had been damaged on the flight, and began pulling out voice recorders to check the batteries.

'Want a hand?' Archer asked.

'Nah, I have a system. Thanks, though,' said Fionn.

Archer stretched. 'In that case, I'll go check on Éabh– the others, see if they want to get food or have a nap before we meet Captain Neale.'

He went out the door and was back just a minute or two later.

'Éabha's napping, and Raven said she just wants a quick shower. Then she's up for some food. She said she saw in the passenger guide that one of the places on deck does pizza. I don't know about you guys, but–'

'Pizza sounds amazing right now,' Davis said, hanging the last of his long linen shirts in the narrow wardrobe.

'I would like to do a Raven and shower first,' Fionn said, putting the last of the voice recorders – all charged and working, thankfully – to the side.

'OK but hurry, I'm starving, and Raven promised she'd be quick,' Archer said.

Davis made an enthusiastic noise of agreement. Fionn saluted him as he walked into the little ensuite, closing the door behind him.

Ten minutes later, he had just pulled on his T-shirt when Raven's trademark *rat-a-tat* knock came at the door.

'Finally,' Davis said, as he opened the door.

'It was ten minutes,' Raven said, leaning against the door frame. 'And I told Archer you didn't need to wait for me.'

Davis turned to look at Archer with a betrayed expression.

'It was ten minutes,' Archer said, his delivery so similar to Raven's that everyone laughed, even Davis.

'Well, let's stop adding time now,' Davis said, striding out the door. He slowed slightly as they passed the girls' cabin. 'Éabha sure she doesn't want anything?' he asked.

'She was pretty tired. I said I'd bring her back a slice or something, but resting is a good shout so she's feeling on form for the meeting later,' Raven said. She paused, then looked at Archer even as she continued speaking to Davis. 'She's really not bad, not like some of the other days – she just needs a rest. Honestly, I wouldn't mind one either. I didn't sleep on the plane and it was an early start. Anyone would be tired.'

Archer's shoulders relaxed slightly as she spoke, and the little knot of concern Fionn felt for Éabha softened in his stomach. Raven was right – they'd had an early start and a long day already. Who wouldn't need a nap? This wasn't anything to worry about. Sure, Éabha got tired a lot, and anyone could see when she was struggling. But Lizzie was working with her, so hopefully she'd be back on her feet in no time. And probably the best thing they could all do was just not fuss over her. Even he could see the frustration building in her when Archer got too intense about checking on her. Éabha had always been good at hiding her feelings, but they all knew her tells by now, and the more tired she was, the harder it was for her to conceal her feelings. Masking was draining, and Éabha didn't have much energy as it was. But surely, with time, her energy would rebuild? Adrian couldn't have stolen it forever, could he?

CHAPTER FIVE

THE COMBINATION OF A SHOWER and three piping hot slices of pizza from an elegant kiosk on deck made Raven feel somewhat human again. She could never sleep properly when she knew she had to be up early, so she'd woken every thirty minutes throughout the night, convinced she'd somehow missed the flight, much to Cordelia's chagrin. Raven and Éabha had stayed at Cordelia's, while Fionn, Davis and Archer slept at Raven's apartment, so they didn't have the drive from Kilcarrig to the airport on top of an already early flight. Her apartment was a very small one-bed that she could only afford because friends of her parents had given her an extremely good deal on rent for it, and there was no way all five of them plus their equipment would have squeezed in there. She was amazed the three boys fitted as it was. Raven had woken Éabha up with a steaming mug of black coffee that the other girl had seized gratefully, taking long sips as she gathered her stuff and folded the blankets from where she'd been asleep on the couch. Cordelia stumbled out of her bedroom, her black shoulder-length hair rumpled and eyes bleary with sleep in a way that made her look so adorable that Raven felt a surge of resentment that this new survey made her have to be away from her girlfriend for a week.

It's just a week, Raven. Get it together.

'Take care of this one, OK?' Cordelia had said to Éabha, nodding towards Raven before hugging the other girl.

'I can take care of myself!' Raven protested.

'Physically? Yes. Emotionally ...' Cordelia said, raising an eyebrow.

Raven shook her head, swallowing her retort as Cordelia leaned down to kiss her. She and Cordelia had been together since last autumn, but her heart still beat faster every single time they kissed.

Raven was really going to miss her.

'There's supposed to be Wi-Fi on board so we can video call,' Raven had said after they broke the kiss. 'If you want,' she'd added hastily, trying not to sound too desperate. Cordelia looked at her, her face softening at whatever she saw on hers.

'I'll miss you too.'

Raven was all too aware that Éabha was perched on the arm of one of the deep, comfy armchairs in Cordelia's kitchen-cum-living room, scrolling through Instagram with one hand while drinking coffee with the other and pretending she couldn't hear every word.

Raven gripped Cordelia's hand, trying to put off the moment she had to let go of her until the last second, and looked up at her. She couldn't resist giving her another quick kiss goodbye.

'Let me know when you've arrived,' Cordelia said, then paused. 'Be careful, you two, OK?' Her voice was light, but her eyes were tight with worry.

'Aren't we always?' Éabha said drily.

All three of them laughed, but there was a forced undercurrent which made it clear – after two extremely close brushes with death apiece – that Éabha and Raven could be as careful as they wanted, but trouble always seemed to follow them.

Raven shook off the shiver that ran through her as she thought about that goodbye, adjusting the pizza box she was balancing on one hand so she could knock with the other, before swiping the key card and letting herself into the cabin she shared with Éabha. Éabha had arrived briefly on deck for the mandatory safety briefing – dutiful as always – before disappearing back downstairs immediately.

'I come bearing snacks. And it's forty-five-minutes until our meeting with Captain Neale,' Raven said, stepping inside. The cabin was dim, and she could just make out Éabha moving before she snapped on the lamp beside her roomy single bed.

'You're the best,' Éabha said, yawning and slowly shuffling herself up to lean against the deep mahogany headboard. Every movement was heavy and laboured, and her eyes had the tiredness Raven's carried after six back-to-back nightshifts in Origin, the bar she managed. They hadn't been thrilled when Raven requested a week of annual leave at the last minute, but thankfully she hadn't had to fight too hard for it.

'I'm glad someone is finally acknowledging it,' Raven said, placing the pizza box on the bedside table between their beds, followed by a can of energy drink.

Éabha pushed the covers back, slowly swinging her legs to the side of the bed before sliding down the edge of it onto the ground and reaching up to take the box off the table.

Raven stared at her.

'I don't want to get crumbs in the bed,' Éabha explained.

Raven snorted. 'You and I are two very different people.' But she still sank to the floor opposite Éabha, leaning against her bed.

'Thanks, Raven,' Éabha said softly, opening the box and looking down at the pizza inside it.

'It's literally free. We're all-inclusive as part of the job fee.'

'I mean for taking care of me in a way that doesn't make me feel like I'm being coddled.'

There was a pause as Raven wracked her brains for the right thing to say.

Éabha took a bite of the pizza, her eyes lighting up. 'Oh, is it just me or is this incredible?'

'Definitely not just you,' Raven said. 'They have an Italian chef who makes the dough fresh and a proper wood-burning oven. And that's not even a designated restaurant: it's a snack station. I'm very excited for dinner.'

She didn't know if she should acknowledge what Éabha had said. She wished Cordelia were here, to tell her how to navigate this. Raven had spent so long isolating herself from everyone around her, she was still rusty when it came to the whole emotional support thing, both giving and receiving it.

'I'm happy to go get it any time it's needed,' she said awkwardly, hoping Éabha would know what she meant.

'Hopefully we can go together next time, but that's good to know,' Éabha said. She smiled at Raven before taking another big bite of pizza.

CHAPTER SIX

ÉABHA'S HAIR WAS STILL DAMP when the boys knocked on their door. Even eating took it out of her when she was this tired, so she'd needed twenty minutes between eating her pizza and getting in the shower, then she'd needed to lie down in her towel the moment she got out. Hot showers made her feel dizzy and drained. After she'd mustered the energy to get dressed, in a long deep-green skirt and white top, she couldn't face the heat of the hairdryer. Her hair would be all over the place – actually dishevelled instead of her usual carefully mussed style – but she'd managed to apply enough concealer to hide the dark rings under her eyes, and some blush to take away the pallor of her cheeks. She'd always been pale, but now it was a dull pallor, not the porcelain complexion she'd had all her life. She slicked on some lip gloss, and studying her reflection, figured she looked pulled together enough that the damp hair would go unnoticed. Hopefully. She hated this – having to decide the cost of every choice and if it was worth paying. It was a constant weighing up of 'if I do X, can I do Y?' She'd needed to shower and eat, those were necessities. But drying her hair could drain her to the point that she'd struggle even more in the interviews. She wanted to show everyone – show Archer – that she could still do this.

So Éabha dredged up all the energy she could to greet the boys brightly as she and Raven stepped into the corridor. They'd decided all five of them would meet Captain Neale, before considering how to split into smaller teams to tackle the other interviews and begin planning the surveys.

Archer kissed Éabha hello, taking her hand as they walked down the corridor.

'Did you have a good nap?'

'I did, and Raven brought me that unbelievable pizza. And I had a shower. I am fully restored to humanity,' she said lightly.

'Yeah, I was going to bring you something, but Raven said she would since she was going back to the room anyway.'

'You both spoil me,' Éabha said, giving his hand a squeeze. Archer meant well, she knew that. And she was so lucky to have him. He could just be a bit ... much. Something like bringing snacks was genuinely helpful and she really appreciated it, but it was hard not to feel smothered when he did it alongside all the other things – like constantly telling her about how he'd seen an Instagram post on B vitamins or yoga or Vitamin D and had she tried those and oh, by the way, he'd already gone to the health-food shop and picked up the supplements for her. It made her feel like he thought she wasn't trying hard enough to get better.

'You deserve to be spoiled,' Archer said.

They were trailing behind the others, and he stopped to kiss her again, more deeply, his arms around her. All the tension, the worry, began to ebb from Éabha. She always felt so safe with Archer. Being with him was just pure comfort and a warm glow spread through her. When the kiss ended, she rested her head on his chest and hugged him tightly.

'Thanks, Archer,' she said.

'Any time, Éabhs. You know how much I wo-...' – She felt,

more than heard, him catch himself – '… care about you.'

'Are you two coming? Archer, I know you're really not good at timekeeping, but being late to a meeting when we're already on the boat is a bit much, even for you.'

Éabha pulled away to see Davis standing at the end of the corridor, his arms folded. Fionn and Raven were beside him, clearly trying not to laugh.

'Coming, coming,' Archer said good-naturedly.

They made their way easily to the meeting room they had been told to come to – of course Davis had already found it earlier so there was no risk of them getting lost or delayed en route. They filed in, all of them shifting into professional mode in a way Éabha could tangibly sense. It wasn't clairvoyance: she could see Fionn's back straighten, Archer's face grow serious, and Raven's expression become a mask of affable neutrality.

Captain Neale was already waiting for them. She was about Éabha's height, with short-cropped blonde hair. She wore the same crisp, white uniform with navy piping as Charles, but she had a lot of stripes – epaulettes, Fionn had told her they were called – on the shoulders of hers. Her captain's cap was on the table in front of her. She stood up to shake hands with each of them, briskly thanking them for coming, the muscles of her arms clearly defined under her white jacket.

'I'm glad you're here,' she said. 'With hindsight, I wish I'd had you out here before Christmas when my predecessor called you. I took over the captaincy very shortly after he'd enquired and, I'll be honest, it took a while to convince me – and therefore the owners – that it was worth doing. I thought the incidents were being exaggerated, and I think the owners were hoping it would all blow over.' She grimaced. 'Unfortunately, it only got worse.' She said it all very matter-of-factly, in an efficient tone that made it clear, though she would acknowledge her mistake, she wouldn't dwell on it. Éabha immediately respected her for it.

'Before we get into the details, I'd just like to confirm that we may record this?' Archer said.

'Yes, of course.' Neale replied. 'Once it is only for the purposes of your investigation and won't be shared with any outside parties.'

'Only the team will hear it,' Raven confirmed, setting a voice recorder on the table and clicking record.

Éabha always enjoyed seeing Archer and Raven in interviews. They worked together as a team, picking up on each other's train of thought as though they could read each other's minds. As far as any of them knew, that wasn't a gift Raven had, to the relief of them all. It was just the product of being siblings who had been – and were tentatively becoming again – best friends, alongside years of shadowing their parents when they were the original PSI.

They fell into the usual pattern, asking about the details they'd been given on the phone.

'It started with guests complaining about cold spots on the ship, lights flickering: things like that. But it has been escalating more and more. A few of the guests have had direct negative experiences that we can't explain rationally. The Ms Carmichael incident two weeks ago was the final straw.'

'Can you go back over that again, please?' Archer asked. 'It's good to hear it in your own words.'

Neale sighed. 'Ms Carmichael was last seen making her way out of the bar towards her cabin. There had been an ... incident shortly before then.'

'It would be helpful to know what happened,' Raven said. 'Any detail, no matter how small, can end up being beneficial to the investigation.'

'She took her shoes off on the dance floor, which we have a strict policy against for health and safety reasons,' Neale said. 'She was unhappy when we told her she either had to put them back on or she would be asked to leave. She left in a huff. With a half-full bottle of champagne in her hand, too. She passed a staff member stationed in the foyer, who saw her go down the corridor. Shortly after, they heard a scream and went to assist her, only to find the champagne, spilled and discarded on the floor of the corridor leading to her cabin, as well as her shoes a little further up. There was no sign of Ms Carmichael.' She paused, though Archer's rapid note taking did not. Neale took a deep breath, then continued, her voice steady as she reported, as though addressing an official hearing. 'We did a full search of the boat and eventually found her locked in one of the life-jacket boxes. She was distressed, disorientated and kept saying she felt the walls were closing in on her, and were going to crush her. She had also begun to have difficulty breathing, though that could have been from panic. Either way, it was lucky we found her when we did.' Neale stopped again, and the team waited silently for her to continue. 'She kept saying she had been intimidated by a crew member, and that she must have been knocked out because she woke up in there. She also threatened to sue, a lot. However, the uniform she described isn't one the crew wear, there was no evidence of assault and, while I hesitate to use inebriation as a reason to discredit a testimony, it is possible she blacked out. However, it is highly unlikely she climbed in there herself and the CCTV footage is … somewhat disturbing.'

'You captured the incident on camera?' Fionn asked. He leant forward eagerly, and Éabha felt a surge of hope. Fionn was amazing at finding either anomalies, or reasons for them, on audio and video.

Neale shook her head. 'Unfortunately, our CCTV footage didn't cover the ends of the corridor. We can see her on it, but not what she's looking at. It also malfunctioned for about a minute – the screen goes black, and when it comes back on, it just shows an empty corridor.' Fionn started slightly at that, his eyes lighting up behind his wire-rimmed glasses.

'Can we have access to that footage?' he asked.

'Fionn is our main technical analyst and has a lot of experience with video and audio footage,' Archer said.

Neale nodded. 'Of course.'

'We'll need the name of the staff member who asked her to leave, if they're on board. And the person stationed in the foyer. It would be great to talk to them,' Raven said.

'Almost all the staff are happy to talk to you,' Neale said. 'They're getting pretty uneasy, even the most sceptical of them. They could use some answers, or some reassurance.'

'Both of which are our speciality,' Archer said with a warm smile.

They continued to talk through the incidents, the itinerary for the week so they knew when the ship was likely to have a lot of guests on shore, as well as scheduled activities on board the ship, and any off-limits areas.

'Nowhere really, though we ask that you act like regular guests so as to not alarm the current ones, please,' Neale said. 'It's imperative that none of the guests know you're here to investigate a potential ghost. That also means no formal interviews with any of them – I'm relying on you to do your jobs discreetly. So for surveys, we would like them to be done with minimum disruption, at times that will draw the least attention.'

'While the guests are on shore is the ideal. It will allow for fewer variables for the data,' Davis said. 'Obviously, if not everyone chooses to go ashore, that could cause a few issues, but if we concentrate each survey on the smallest area possible, would it be believable to say it's off-limits for a few hours for maintenance?'

Neale nodded approvingly. 'That is definitely doable.' She huffed a sigh of disbelief. 'When I took this job, I would have laughed in your face if you'd said I'd be hiring paranormal surveyors to investigate the ship. But we have no other answers, and we're losing crew every cruise, not to mention that the guests are now possibly in danger.'

'Only the guests? Never the crew?' Raven asked, a thoughtful look on her face.

Neale shook her head. 'The crew have experienced some smaller stuff that has made them uneasy, but only guests have been … have had …' Neale paused, unable or unwilling to put it into words. They'd seen this before, where clients struggled to tell them everything because speaking the things out loud made them feel *real* in a way they hadn't quite before. 'The crew have reported a few strange noises, unsettling feelings, but none of them have seen … have experienced … I don't even …' she shrugged helplessly, the first time she had lost her air of confidence, holding her hands flat out in front of her, palms up. 'I don't even know what to call it. Whatever they've experienced, it's still enough for people to jump ship.'

'And there's no chance this was a crew member playing a prank?' Raven asked. She gave Neale an apologetic look. 'I'm sorry to ask, but if it's passengers that have exhibited … problematic behaviour, someone getting some very unsupernatural revenge by playing a prank that's gone too far is a possibility.'

'I asked the same question myself,' Neale said approvingly. 'But everyone was at their posts or has an alibi. I don't believe that it was a member of our crew.'

'And no one could sneak on board?' Davis asked.

'No. We have round-the-clock security and, despite what the blind spots and blackouts might make it seem, it would be impossible for someone to go unnoticed for any period of time. Plus there's never been any thefts or other suspicious activity reported.

Archer and Raven exchanged a glance, and Éabha felt a thrill of curiosity burning through her fatigue.

The O'Sullivan siblings had a theory, and she couldn't wait to hear it.

CHAPTER SEVEN

RAVEN HAD NO THEORIES. It was unlikely, at this stage – those would form as they interviewed the crew. She did, however, have some threads she wanted to pull on. Why had only the guests been physically targeted? Were there connections between the people who'd reported experiences? Why were they escalating now? Did the crew's reports have any merit or were they the result of the guests' reports?

The team left their meeting with Neale with many questions, another firm reminder to be discreet, and stacks of crew reports and customer feedback surveys. With a capacity of a hundred passengers per cruise, it meant that there were well over a thousand to comb through from the cruises that had already taken place that year alone. They were lucky to have access, though – as Davis pointed out when their faces fell at the piles of paperwork in front of them – the feedback could hold clues, something the person didn't realise was potentially a paranormal occurrence.

'I'll take the lead with these,' Éabha volunteered. 'I'll sit in on as many of the interviews as I'm needed for, but the energy can get overwhelming when I start to get tired. I know concentrating for long periods of time on top of staying open to other people's energies will start to drain me so I think we should pick and choose where I'm needed instead of me sitting in on all of them. If I take the forms, I can still do something useful while I sit out the others.'

'You don't have to do any of the interviews, Éabha,' Archer said quickly.

'No, I want to. I just can't do as many as I used to, but it'll go faster with both Raven and me sitting in on them.'

'But if it's making you tired, I really think–'

'I said I can do it, Archer.'

The snap in Éabha's voice made Raven wince. Archer flinched slightly, and Davis and Fionn fell silent. Even Éabha looked startled. She took a deep breath, reaching out a hand to hold Archer's.

'I said I can do it. I need you to trust me to manage my energy. I'm being careful, and it's why I'm stepping back on the number of interviews I do. I can focus on the paperwork. But having a clairvoyant in the interviews will be helpful at times, and Raven can't be everywhere at once.'

Archer nodded, and the moment of tension passed. Still, it was no surprise that when they were splitting into two groups of two for the initial few interviews, with Fionn sitting them out to work on the video analysis, Éabha immediately suggested that she and Davis team up, since 'Raven and Archer have such an established interview rapport'. Fionn could then take over for Éabha after he'd got the analysis finished, so she could work on the forms in the comfort of the cabin.

Éabha was correct, and it did make the most sense, but it was very clear it wasn't the only reason she suggested it. Raven felt a little pang at the look on Archer's face. But it was obvious that Éabha was frustrated when he'd pushed her, and it was fair that she would be upset with him for doubting her. She was being sensible about things – she was holding back where she needed to, to make sure she could do the other things. Archer needed to believe her when she said she could do something. Should she talk to Éabha? Or to Archer?

No, Raven. You just need to stay the hell out of it – it's your brother and your friend, and there's no winning in this situation.

She wished Cordelia were here.

Neale had given them a list of staff members who had reported incidents and who were willing to talk to them. She had also given them a list of staff members present when guests had reported things or who had interacted with them just before.

'I'll go through these and find any names on both lists – we should start with them,' Davis said.

'I'll go to the itinerary and start marking times it'll be good to plan surveys for, when guests are on shore or not using specific parts of the boat,' Archer added.

'Éabha and I will sort through feedback forms until we're ready to start interviewing,' Raven said.

'And I am going to the security centre to look at their CCTV set-up,' Fionn said.

Raven loved this part, when the team snapped into action. This was when they were at their most cohesive, most like a unit.

They stopped by her and Éabha's cabin to drop off the boxes of forms. The boxes filled the space quickly, and Éabha looked wryly at the others as they stacked them.

'We might need to do some light parkour to get out of here later.'

'You'd think they'd have heard about digital records,' Raven said, shaking her head.

Neale had requested they make sure to come to the formal meals and occasionally pop up using the facilities so that the guests didn't suspect anything. It was the first job on which Raven had ever been asked to eat free food and swim in a state-of-the-art pool before, and it was definitely something she could get used to. There was assigned seating at dinner. Neale explained that they changed the seating plan every night so that guests mingled and didn't get stuck with anyone irritating for more than a night. They'd suggested she split the team up into smaller groups so that they could chat to as many people as possible. Obviously, they couldn't directly ask questions about the investigation, since no one was to know why they were on the ship, but people might mention things in conversation that would help them.

'Dinner's at eight, so that gives us about an hour to get started before we need to spruce up and head down,' Davis said, looking at his watch.

'Should we aim to have a list of initial interviewees to give Neale first thing in the morning?' Archer asked.

'I really wish we didn't have to go to a formal two-hour dinner,' Fionn said. 'It'll be well after ten before we can even get started.'

'Late-night paperwork, how exciting,' Raven drawled.

'Obviously, don't stay up later than you can,' Archer said quickly, glancing at Éabha. 'It's been a long day and no one's under pressure to–'

'I mean, we have seven nights on this boat. We really do need to get a move on,' Davis said.

'Well, yeah, the rest of us–' Even Archer seemed to know he'd put his foot in it as Éabha bristled.

'Am I a member of this team or not?' she asked quietly. 'Because we split the load *as a team*.'

Fionn grimaced, looking up at the ceiling as though wishing he could crawl into it and disappear.

'Yeah, but if some of us aren't able to do as much—'

'Then they should judge that for themselves,' Éabha said firmly.

The tension in the room thickened until Raven could feel it coating her like tree sap.

'And we should all get started so we don't need to stay up until dawn reading over things,' Davis said, clapping his hands together. 'Right, Arch?'

Archer forced the corners of his lips into a curve.

'Right you are, Davis,' he said with false brightness. 'And that's our cue to leave.'

Davis and Fionn filed out the door, but Archer hesitated. There was already a wall of boxes between him and Éabha, and Raven could see him weighing up whether to climb over them to get back to her. Hesitantly, he blew Éabha a kiss, a smile lighting up his face when she blew one back.

'I'll see you at dinner,' she said. The words sounded like a peace offering.

When the door swung closed behind Archer, Éabha sighed, looking at the boxes. For a moment, Raven wondered if she should ask her if she wanted to talk.

Part of her was terrified Éabha would say yes.

Thankfully, Éabha cut in before she could ask. 'Let's dig in then,' she said.

CHAPTER EIGHT

THE PAPERWORK HELPED ÉABHA SETTLE HER MIND. She felt guilty for snapping at Archer, but he didn't seem to realise that every time she said she could do something, and he suggested she rest or told her she didn't need to do it, it felt like he was doubting her. That he didn't trust her to know her own limits. And even if she *did* push past them sometimes to do something, that was her choice. He didn't get to dictate how she handled this fatigue.

She knew he was trying to support her: she could feel it coming from him in waves. It was just sometimes it felt like he was suffocating her instead, and she didn't know how to talk to him about it. She'd tried, but he never properly heard her. Or he did, and would get better about it for a while, but his protectiveness quickly eroded it.

Éabha could also feel it, when he looked at her: the guilt, the worry. And she didn't have the energy to carry her own feelings and his too. No matter how many times she told him none of this was his fault, that her own choices had led her here, it didn't dam the flood of guilt that flowed from him. She didn't know how to make him believe her.

Especially now that it felt like he no longer believed *in* her.

Raven was quiet, going through page after page. Occasionally, she let out a snort and read out an outrageous complaint: 'towels not fluffy enough,' 'other people using the sauna at the same time as them', and it became a game for them, finding the most notionsy or petty complaints.

'"Staff make too much eye contact," OK, this has to be a joke,' Raven said a while later, waving a sheet of paper at Éabha.

'The terrifying thing is, I don't think it is.' Éabha scanned the page in front of her and snorted. 'Yep. "Waves too strong". Do they think the crew can control the *weather*?'

'No wonder the ghost finds the guests annoying,' Raven grumbled. 'I mean, if it turns out it actually *is* just a member of the crew locking drunk assholes in life-jacket containers, I can see how they were driven to it.'

Éabha looked at her, and Raven held up her hands.

'I'm not saying I'd do it! I'm just saying, as someone who also has to deal with entitled members of the general public on a regular basis, I get the appeal.'

Éabha laughed, shaking her head.

'Look, we can't all have your phenomenal powers of politeness and restraint,' Raven said.

Recently, though, it hadn't felt to Éabha that she still had them. She was so tired, and frustrated with being sick and scared about the future that it was hard to keep things in – and out, which was a whole other issue.

'Yes, because if we've learned anything recently, it's that repressing feelings is great for us,' she said instead.

'You've got me there,' Raven said. She looked at her phone. 'We should probably get ready for dinner. I can't believe there's a dress code.'

She might as well have said a 'pit of vipers', from her tone and the look of absolute disgust on her face.

Éabha giggled. 'It's a dress, Raven. You've faced worse.'

'Have I, Éabha? Have I?'

'Don't make me start pulling things from the trauma chest,' Éabha said, mock-wagging a finger at Raven.

It had started as a very grim joke – that everything they had been through was stored neatly in a chest, the lid firmly closed. They'd nicknamed it the trauma chest. Lizzie had sighed and folded her arms, exasperated, but Éabha thought that seeing her and Raven bond – even over something as bleak as that – had been enough to make her let it go.

'No, don't open that! There's not nearly enough room in this cabin,' Raven said.

They both laughed, and Raven got up and opened her bag, sitting on the bed to open it since that was pretty much the only available bit of space left in the room. 'One dress, coming up. Because the gender spectrum is enforced on this boat.'

'You can write an anonymous complaint on your survey on the way out,' Éabha said drily.

'You think I won't,' Raven said, pulling out a long-sleeved black dress.

'I know you will.'

Éabha went to the wardrobe, clambering over a few boxes to get to it, and opened it to take out one of the three dresses she'd brought for evening wear. The other guests would probably judge her for repeating outfits, but hopefully they wouldn't be paying enough attention to her to notice. She'd seen one woman in a large-brimmed sun hat board the boat with *three* suitcases. For a seven-night voyage. Shaking her head, she changed into a dress in deep forest green with small silver buttons down the bodice, and floaty, gauzy sleeves.

'Very "off to frolic in the woods with the fae",' Raven said. 'I like it.'

Éabha smiled at her in the mirror, as she smoothed concealer and foundation on, trying to hide the signs of tiredness from their early start and long day. At least her pixie cut was cooperating, and she didn't have to spend time – and energy – trying to style it. She studied her reflection carefully. She had done a good enough job of applying a mask. Turning away, she saw Raven standing there, pulling at the sleeves of her own dress.

This was the first time Éabha had ever seen Raven in a dress. She'd seen her in skirts once or twice, but Raven was almost always a jeans or shorts person. The form-fitting black dress had a small scoop neck and fell to mid-thigh. It had long sleeves, and she'd paired it with sheer black nylons, and black ballet flats instead of her usual heavy boots.

'Do I pass?' Raven asked. She actually sounded a little nervous. Éabha stepped over behind her and twisted her plait into a bun, pinning it neatly in place, then moved in front of her to pull a few tendrils loose to frame her face.

'With flying colours,' Éabha grinned. 'Ready?' she asked, trying to swallow her own nerves. She hoped the other people at the table would be nice.

Was it bad that part of her hoped they hadn't paired her with Archer? Even as the thought flitted across her mind, a hot stab of guilt knifed through her. She should be excited at the prospect of a fancy meal with her boyfriend. Even if they were undercover ghost hunters on a mission. She would be, tomorrow. But right now, she just needed space.

And they'd be cooped up together on a boat for the next seven days.

At least it had the capacity to hold a hundred, and that was just the passengers. Surely it wouldn't get *too* claustrophobic? Hopefully, soon they'd be so busy with the investigation that Archer wouldn't have time to fuss over her.

It would be fine.

It had to be.

CHAPTER NINE

'I CAN'T BELIEVE WE HAVE TO WEAR SUITS,' Fionn grumbled, tugging at his tie. 'It's like we're back in school.'

'Oh, come on. This is a bit different,' Archer said. He was wearing a deep-blue suit and adjusting a pink pocket square in the breast pocket of his jacket. A matching tie was secured in a perfect knot around his neck. The burn mark on Archer's cheek always stood out a bit more when he wore pink, but Fionn was glad he hadn't stopped wearing his favourite colour because of that. They all still carried something from Hyacinth House. It had been their first investigation as a team of five, and a baptism of literal fire. A lot of them had physical reminders; all of them had psychological ones.

Nearly dying would do that to you.

Davis stepped out of the bathroom in a grey suit, white shirt and pocket square with a neatly secured black tie, and his hair pulled back. He adjusted a pair of gold cufflinks on his wrists. 'What's Fionn complaining about?' he asked.

'Suits,' Archer said. 'He thinks he's back in school.'

'Nah, our uniforms did not look this good,' Davis grinned, looking at himself in the full-length mirror.

Easy for him to say. Davis already carried the few years he had on Fionn and Archer with ease: he never seemed to walk into a room and wonder if he should be there. Fionn frowned, pulling at the jacket of his plain black suit.

Archer sprayed on some cologne and checked his watch. 'We should go meet the girls,' he said.

Of course Archer would actually be punctual the one time that Fionn would happily be late.

Fionn didn't want to have to sit at a table and pretend to be fancy. His family had never had time for holidays – there was always work to do on the farm. They'd also had the mandatory monthly family lunches at his grandfather's, an opportunity for the patriarch to flay his chosen victim with his tongue for all their perceived flaws and failures. Besides, there had been a lot of hard years, and they'd never had money. Not like the O'Sullivans or the Williamses. Archer and Davis never made him feel like he was less, but other people had: the kids at school who'd sneered at how the soles of his runners were always worn through before he'd replace them, who'd pretended to sniff loudly and complained of a farm smell in the classroom when he walked in. It had stopped after a while, when it was clear he was under Archer's protection. Everyone loved Archer, and tolerating Fionn was a requirement for Archer's friendship. Not that Archer was ever rude or unkind to anyone – but everyone wanted to bask in his glow, and since he wanted Fionn everywhere he went, they had to accept that.

Fionn couldn't shake the feeling that, despite the suit, despite the cover story for how five people in their late teens and early twenties could afford this cruise without their parents, these rich people would take one look at him and know he didn't belong.

Archer was already out the door. Sighing, Fionn steeled himself to follow. Davis stopped him, putting an arm across the doorway.

'The trick is to walk in like you know you belong there,' he said, his voice low enough that Archer wouldn't hear. 'There are always going to be people who look around and decide that, for some reason, someone doesn't deserve to be there. Sometimes it's clothes, sometimes it's an accent and sometimes it's …' He trailed off.

Fionn knew what Davis had stopped himself saying: he had been the only Black person in his year at school, and the majority of his class in UCD was white. He'd never spoken to them about how that felt, and Fionn figured they weren't really the people to talk to. They would never fully understand, even if they did everything they could to support him.

'But if you act like *you* know this is where you should be, they'll follow suit. So shoulders back, head high and stop looking like you're expecting someone to kick you at any moment.'

'Thanks,' Fionn said. He straightened his back, and Davis gave him an approving nod.

'Come oooon,' Archer called from down the hallway. 'How am I not the one holding us up?'

'The world turns upside down,' Davis said wryly.

They caught up to Archer quickly, and the girls stepped out of their cabin just as they reached it.

Raven was scowling in the way that Fionn had come to figure out meant she was feeling awkward. She looked like a cat in a bath, like she was a second away from hissing and bolting. Even more than her usual cat energy, that was.

'You look beautiful,' Archer was saying to Éabha, his eyes soft as she smiled back at him, reaching up to straighten the corner of his collar.

'You look pretty great yourself.'

Éabha's hand slid into Archer's and they started walking down the corridor towards the lift that would take them to deck four, where the restaurant was.

Except on this ship, 'main restaurant' meant 'formal sit-down dinner in a ballroom'.

'Well, let's get this over with,' Raven sighed.

'You know it's dinner, right? Not your execution?' Davis asked, nudging her.

'My execution would be over more quickly,' Raven grumbled.

Fionn laughed, and Davis slung an arm over Raven's shoulder.

'Look, we just need to make polite conversation, eat some food and leave. Just ask them questions about themselves. People love talking about themselves. Besides, they might mention something helpful to the investigation.'

'They've been on the ship for, like, six hours,' Raven said.

'Maybe this ghost likes to let their presence be known quickly. We don't know.'

'This is alarmingly optimistic for you, Davis,' Fionn said as they made their way to the lift.

'It's from spending so much time with Raven,' he deadpanned.

Raven elbowed Davis in the ribs and, still laughing, they all got into the lift.

CHAPTER TEN

DINNER WAS LESS PAINFUL THAN DAVIS HAD FEARED. He'd put on a front because he could see that Fionn and Raven were baulking pretty hard at the prospect of mingling not just with the excessively wealthy, but with people who were comfortable moving through the world like it was made for them. He'd had no idea what to expect himself, but he'd relaxed slightly when he walked into the room and saw that not everyone was white.

First, an elegantly dressed woman with brown skin, wearing a champagne-coloured satin hijab that paired beautifully with her long midnight-blue dress, walked past him to her table, nodding in greeting when she caught his eye. Then as he and the team checked the seating plan for their table numbers, he saw a variety of surnames of different origins. Everyone in this room was most likely incredibly rich and privileged, but he was far from being the sole person in the room who wasn't white. He hadn't realised quite how anxious he was about that until the heavy weight in his stomach lifted.

He and Fionn were at one table while Archer, Éabha and Raven were at another. There were ten tables of ten in a sumptuous, high-ceilinged room. A large chandelier hung at the centre, casting soft light that made it bright enough to see easily without the harshness of overheads. In the corner, a tuxedoed musician sat at a grand piano, his quick fingers delicately playing music that was beautiful to listen to without being overpowering, allowing the hum of conversation to merge with the murmur of the songs dancing through the air. *Archer will be loving this*, Davis thought immediately. Archer adored classical music.

The staff moved so quickly and silently through the dining room he would have guessed that they were the ghosts. A menu with two choices for starter, three for main and two for dessert was already in place at each setting when they sat down, and a server offering wine appeared so quickly when they took their seats that Fionn started when he appeared beside him.

'No thank– oh, Charles, hello!'

'Hello, Mr O'Shea. Have you settled in to your satisfaction?'

Davis could see that the 'Mr O'Shea' threw Fionn for a moment and tried not to grin at the mischievous twinkle in Charles' eyes. The staff must have been told to treat them like all the other guests in public, which made sense.

Fionn had only ever been called Mr O'Shea by a teacher, generally when he was in trouble, so Davis could only imagine the effect this was having on him.

'Yes, it's been lovely,' Fionn said after a moment, playing along.

'Lovely, sir,' Charles said, moving to the person who had just sat down to Fionn's left to offer them wine, removing the larger glass of the two wine glasses when she chose white.

The dining room filled up quickly. Almost every table was full, meaning the ship was close to capacity. At Fionn and Davis's table were two couples and a group of four women who were travelling together, and Davis could feel himself relaxing as a few of them immediately initiated conversation. The woman beside him was in maybe her late thirties, with long brown hair that faded into gold at the ends – he was sure there was a fancy name for it; Éabha would definitely know – and a fuchsia dress. A necklace with a large, sparkling gem that he assumed was a diamond hung at her throat, and another large diamond shone on her hand alongside a gold band.

'The girls and I do a trip, just us four, every year,' she told Davis in a posh English accent. 'Talia and Prue both have kids, and Cecily is constantly travelling for work, so this is our one opportunity to have quality time together: no partners, no work, no kids, just us.'

She talked through the starter – a goat's cheese and beetroot salad with shaved fennel that Davis had to try not to wolf down – and well into the main before one of her friends – Cecily – interrupted, chiding, 'Cami, you know it's not polite to monopolise one person for the entire meal.'

Camilla – who insisted on Davis and Fionn also calling her Cami – was easy to talk to, in that all he had to do was ask her a question and she would monologue for at least five minutes and, when she exhausted the topic, he simply asked another. She hadn't asked anything about him, which had been a relief. On the other side of him, Fionn was deep in conversation with a man with black-rimmed glasses and an elegant woman, both in their early sixties. Well, he was mostly listening and just asking another question whenever there was a silence, but he was doing really well, and if he still felt uncomfortable, it didn't show.

Davis introduced himself to Cecily. She had a piercing gaze that made her slightly intimidating. She was warm and friendly but, as she explained what she did – a high-level broker for international clients all over the world – he knew she would have a core of steel.

She reminded him of Cordelia in that way, and not just because they both worked in real estate. It was that mix of warmth and ice.

'You know, not to stereotype, but it's amazing seeing two people as young as you appreciate something like this. I thought you young people were all in Ibiza or Majorca,' Cecily said.

Cami let out a loud laugh. 'Cecily, we're not even forty yet! You make it sound like he's decades younger than us,'

'Nearly two,' Cecily pointed out, making Cami groan and reach for her wine glass, draining the dregs, her ring glinting in the chandeliered light.

'Where is that waiter with the wine? I need at least one more glass to forget you said that.'

As though summoned, Charles appeared at her shoulder and filled her glass.

'Best not to let the glasses empty,' she said. She glanced dismissively up at him, then did a double-take. 'But someone as handsome as you can get away with a lot,' she added, smiling flirtatiously and placing a hand on his arm.

Charles smiled, the expression not reaching his eyes, dipped his head once and politely disentangled himself from her touch. Cami turned back to Cecily and blithely continued chatting, although Cecily was frowning now. Fionn had heard the exchange and turned to look. Davis gave him a slight warning shake of the head as he watched Charles leave – he could detect the tension in Charles' shoulders as he continued to circulate, and knew Fionn could too. A sudden sourness in his mouth chased away the taste of the delicious food in front of him, and for a moment he felt stupid for relaxing around these people. Cami had gone from being dismissive to almost predatory in just a few words, and Charles had had to smile at her.

Suddenly, Davis really wished the dinner could just be over.

By the break between mains and dessert, Camilla had lost interest in him and was gossiping loudly with Prue. Cecily caught his eye and twitched an eyebrow. Talia hid a smile behind her napkin, and he felt a bit better. He asked Talia about her kids and her job – she was a graphic designer, she told him at first, until Cecily admonished her for being modest and informed him that Talia worked with some of the biggest magazines in the UK. She had two children, aged twelve and ten, and her husband stayed at home while she went into London to work.

'He coordinates the childcare and manages the estate –' Davis interpreted this statement to mean 'hired the nanny and ordered the people who did the actual physical work on the estate around'– and I do the external work. I mean, obviously we have his trust, but I would go out of my mind in the country without a project to keep me entertained,' Talia said, flipping her hair over her shoulder.

Oh, these people were *rich* rich.

'And what do you do, Davis?' Cecily asked.

This was the part he'd been dreading. He didn't want to lie. He spent so much of his time defending parapsychology that not being able to be open about it grated. But this wasn't out of shame, or embarrassment, this was to aid an investigation. So he could do this.

'I've just finished my degree and I'm hoping to do a PhD,' he said.

'Oh, fascinating,' Talia said, leaning forward.

'Oh, it really isn't,' he said quickly. 'I mean, I haven't had my topic approved yet, so who knows what will happen.' He tried to swallow down the anxiety rising in his throat as he said that. This survey was helping to distract him from the fear of his exam results, of waiting to find out if he had a future in academia. He was in stasis right now, his fate in other people's hands, based on whether or not they believed his ideas had merit, and he hated it.

'You have so much time yet,' Cecily said encouragingly. 'I changed career at least three times before I was thirty.'

What would he be doing at thirty? Would PSI still be together? Would they be successful or would they have given up?

Would they have survived?

'Oh lord, we've given him an existential crisis,' Talia said. 'Quick, quick, change the subject!'

They all laughed, and Davis asked some more questions until squares of tiramisu or fresh fruit platters were placed in front of each person. Charles was once again serving their table, and Cami leaned in and said something in a low voice as he placed her plate in front of her. Davis didn't catch what she said, but the stiffness in Charles' stance as he once again smiled politely and moved swiftly away made him feel it wasn't a simple request for more water.

Camilla excused herself to go to the bathroom. She was a few steps from the table when suddenly the entire room was plunged into darkness. There was a thud, barely audible over the few scattered screams. The lights flickered back on to show Camilla on her knees. Several servers rushed forwards to help her up. Her face was red as she smoothed down her dress and, instead of continuing outside, she sat back at the table as conversations resumed all around them.

'Cami, are you OK?' Prue asked.

'Someone pushed me,' she hissed.

The table all looked at each other, and Davis felt Fionn lean forwards at the declaration, his attention snapping to her.

'Camilla, darling, there was no one near you,' Talia said. 'Are you sure you didn't trip when the lights went out?'

'Those Louboutins are pretty high,' Prue agreed.

'I've worn heels far higher,' Camilla scoffed. 'Girls, I felt someone push me.'

'I don't know what to say,' Cecily said eventually. 'There was no one near you, and the lights were only out for a millisecond.'

'You obviously weren't paying attention,' Camilla huffed.

The other three women exchanged mildly exasperated glances, silently sipping their wine before moving the conversation on.

Davis slid his phone out of his pocket. It had been fully charged leaving the cabin, but now was at eighteen per cent. Fionn turned his screen towards him, showing similar.

Dinner had just got very interesting.

CHAPTER ELEVEN

'SO THAT WAS A LOT,' FIONN EXHALED, flopping down on his bed in their cabin. It had taken all of Archer's restraint not to start asking questions the moment they'd left the dinner, but with other guests in the corridors, they had to be careful not to be overheard.

Archer watched as Davis took off his jacket and hung it on the coat hook on their cabin door before sitting at the chair in front of the small desk. He carefully undid his cufflinks, then methodically rolled up the sleeves of his shirt. Davis was working through the facts in his mind, analysing them, trying to come up with the 'angle of scientific enquiry', as he liked to call it. Archer had learned not to interrupt him, but it was hard to be patient. He, Éabha and Raven had been on the other side of the room, and none of them had experienced anything unusual before, during or after the momentary blackout.

The burn marks on Davis's forearms still showed. There weren't many, and they were not nearly as bad as the ones on his legs – Davis's cruise packing had consisted entirely of long, light trousers for the warm days, and while none of them asked about it, they all knew why – but every time Archer saw them it was still a reminder of what the team had gone through.

All the ways he had let them down.

It wouldn't happen again. Not this time. This time he would protect them. PSI had been his idea, after all. It was his company: he was responsible for them.

He looked away before Davis could catch him staring. Fionn undid his tie, unbuttoning the collar of his shirt too.

Archer's patience ran out.

'So what did—'

'We should wait for the girls,' Davis said mildly, his eyes still in that faraway place that meant various scientific protocols were whizzing around his brain.

He was, annoyingly, correct. However, they didn't have too long to wait; after a minute or two, Raven's knock came at the door and the two of them came in, changed out of their dresses and into hoodies and soft leggings.

Archer could see the tiredness on Éabha's face and it wrenched at his heart. He wanted to suggest she go back to bed, that she didn't need to be here for this. Didn't need to push herself to stay up doing paperwork. But then he remembered the mix of anger and hurt in her voice earlier when he'd said that, and he didn't want a repeat of that argument.

He was just looking out for her. He wanted to protect her, the way he hadn't before.

'You're looking at her like she's an abandoned dog at the side of the road, Little Brother,' Raven murmured, sitting beside him. She gave him a meaningful look.

When had Raven become an expert on Éabha? How was Raven, the person who was so bad at dealing with feelings that she'd avoided him for *years*, suddenly able to tell him what his girlfriend needed? Piping-hot jealousy surged up through him for a moment. Did Éabha confide in Raven now? Why was she pushing him away when all he wanted to do was help?

'OK, so,' Davis said, clapping his hands together. He'd obviously finished doing his internal scientific deep dive and was ready to come back and interact with the world.

He and Fionn filled them in on what they'd experienced during dinner, and Archer could feel the excitement growing. His mind raced as they talked.

'Do we need to start having recorders going during dinner? For possible EVPs?' he asked when they'd finished. His heart was beating fast, and he took a moment to calm himself. Electronic Voice Phenomena were the holy grail of paranormal surveyance, a rare occurrence. He was getting ahead of himself.

'We can't have them out on the table and they'd probably be muffled in a pocket,' Fionn pointed out.

'We could ask to put them *under* the table?' Raven suggested.

'What if someone drops a fork or something and sees it?' Éabha asked. 'I feel like there's a few people on this boat that would get paranoid about that – remember the man at our table that you asked one vague question about his business and he practically accused you of industrial espionage?'

'Good point, all we need is one guest kicking up a fuss and suddenly everyone is talking,' Archer said. He couldn't help but notice Éabha's proud smile – she was hard on herself about not having as much experience as the rest of the team, and he'd loved seeing her confidence grow month after month. They all believed in her; she just needed to believe in herself too.

'Besides, with the ambient noise it would be a massive headache to go through them every day,' Fionn said.

'Not to mention that recording people without their permission is extremely illegal. It would be a massive breach of GDPR, and we'd need every passenger's consent, which would involve telling them what we're doing and why,' Davis said, folding his arms and looking around the room with a raised eyebrow.

'Ugh, I'm such an idiot, I can't believe I didn't consider that,' Raven said, a flicker of annoyance crossing her face. Raven hated making basic mistakes and would be furious with herself for not thinking it through. 'I'm clearly more sleep deprived than I realised.' She bit her lip thoughtfully. 'EMF, though? Think we could subtly read one of the those under the table?'

'That's a thought,' Davis said.

'So, basically, for this potential encounter we have: the lights all going out for a moment, at least two phones being drained of battery, and a woman being pushed,' Archer said.

It was a start, but it left more questions than it answered. Why her? Why during dinner? Was it pointed or random?

'Maybe the ghost hates women in high heels,' Raven mused. 'Wasn't the other woman, Mrs Carmichael, wearing shoes she took off? The crew found them. And Fionn you said this woman was wearing ridiculously high heels.' Raven shuddered. 'Give me Docs any day.'

'They were very pretty shoes, though,' Éabha said dreamily. 'Even if I'd break an ankle.'

'OK, do we really think someone is hanging around a ship because of a vendetta against impractical footwear?' Davis sighed.

'Well, when you say it like that …' Éabha said.

'I mean, maybe the ghost doesn't like shows of wealth? Louboutins are expensive,' Archer said.

'She was wearing some fancy jewellery, too,' Fionn added.

'So was half the room, though,' Raven frowned. 'Why her? Why then?'

Davis wrote it all down and, after a little longer, they decided to call a halt to the discussions.

'We have a lot of reading to do tonight,' Archer said. 'Let's put this to the side and come back to it when we know a little more.'

'It feels like it's a possible paranormal reason, for sure,' Davis said. 'Though we can't rule out her losing her balance when the lights failed and trying to cover it up because she's embarrassed. And there's a lot of reasons the lights could have gone out. I'll chat to some of the engineers about how the boat is powered first thing tomorrow.'

This always gave Archer such a rush. The planning, bouncing theories off each other, the sense of purpose, the what ifs. They were hoping to do their first survey tomorrow, when the passengers were on shore at their first stop.

'I think we focus on the dining room tomorrow for the survey,' he said decisively. He hadn't expected anyone to disagree, and none of them did.

Éabha gave him a kiss on the cheek before she and Raven left to work in their cabin, and the lingering sensation of her lips on his skin made him smile as he started to sort through the documents in front of him. It was going to be a long night, but these were the kind of long nights he adored.

CHAPTER TWELVE

IT WAS ALMOST TWO IN THE MORNING when Éabha found it. Her eyes were blurring and she was about to admit she needed to call it a night – it was taking her a long time to read each word, and her brain felt like it was packed full of static. Raven kept yawning widely too, so she knew she wasn't alone in starting to struggle.

Éabha had just decided to call it quits after this cruise report – a document written up by the captain or first officer, summarising any issues that had arisen and how they had been dealt with – when she lurched forward.

Raven turned to look at her. 'Either you fell asleep sitting up or you found something.'

'Did you know a woman died on a cruise?' Éabha asked.

Raven swore. 'You'd think that would be something they'd have mentioned.'

'She fell overboard. They never found her body.'

'So a traumatic death and a very clear reason to want to hang around? Sounds like a possible ghost to me,' Raven said.

'Her name was Philippa Foster and she was on an anniversary cruise with her husband, right at the beginning of the season,' Éabha said, reading out the summary. 'They were taking a romantic walk on deck eight, where the platform is, to look up at the stars, when she leaned too far over the railings and lost her balance. Several people who saw them on their way out onto the deck said she was wearing high-heeled shoes that may have contributed to the accident.' She felt a spark of excitement. 'High heels!'

'Hmm, interesting,' Raven said. 'But you know what Davis would say here.'

'Confirmation bias,' they said in unison, then laughed.

'So we need to not fixate on things like the shoes this early. We could miss other things. Also, we need to see if any men have had experiences – because that's going to have an impact on that theory,' Raven continued.

Éabha deflated a little. Raven was right, and she hadn't sounded admonishing or judgemental when she'd said it. She was just gently reminding her. Raven doing anything gently was still strange to Éabha, but she admired how much the other girl was trying. She was still spiky and sardonic and didn't always get it right, but the effort was there. And no one just magically changed all of a sudden. It took work.

Even if sometimes Éabha felt like she'd changed irrevocably in a short amount of time. One day she'd been healthy and full of energy, then Adrian had pulled her into the painting and she hadn't been the same again. Might never be. She wanted to hope, needed to hope, that it would go, or at least get better. But more and more she was resigning herself to the fact that she needed to learn how to exist within the parameters she had now.

She hated that.

CHAPTER THIRTEEN

'WELL, THAT'S DEFINITELY SOMETHING TO ASK ABOUT,' Archer had frowned, looking at the report Éabha handed him. 'Especially the part where no one mentioned it at all.'

That had been six hours ago, only a few of those spent sleeping, and Fionn looked around the room at the bleary-eyed team. Raven and Éabha had burst in at half past two with the news of their discovery, and the team had descended into a flurry of activity. They'd all pulled a late shift, trying to narrow down the angles of how to approach this. It was important not to jump to conclusions, but learning about the death of Philippa Foster, a tragedy that hadn't exactly been brought to their attention, combined with a ghost that possibly had a thing about high heels, made it difficult to hold the theories in check. Despite their mutual exhaustion, Fionn could see that Davis was practically buzzing with purpose, while Raven had the expression that meant about eighty different thoughts were whizzing through her head.

'I Googled it and very little came up, which is odd. Stories like this normally make a big splash–' Fionn clapped a hand over his mouth, then removed it. 'I did *not* mean that as a pun.'

Davis groaned.

'I didn't!' Fionn protested, knowing his indignation was clear in his voice. He saved the gallows humour for his own life, not someone else's. And especially not the *end* of someone else's.

'I believe you,' Éabha said, standing up. She swayed suddenly and Archer leapt for her. As he did, Fionn's video camera crashed from the shelf and hit the floor.

It had been on the desk at the opposite end of the cabin from Archer and Éabha, the only people moving.

The team went silent, looking at each other as Éabha sank back onto the bed, Archer hovering nervously over her.

'I think you offended her,' Raven said mildly.

'I said I believed him!' Éabha protested.

'I didn't mean *you*,' Raven said.

'We can't–' began Davis.

'–make assumptions,' the rest of the team chorused, cutting him off. He folded his arms.

'We need to check there were no other causes.'

'It wasn't a sudden wave,' Fionn said, looking out the window to confirm his statement. The dark-blue sea was smooth and inviting, apart from the ripples spreading out from the boat as it cut through the shimmering water. 'The sea is calm. Besides, we'd have felt it.'

Davis nodded approvingly.

'The camera was several inches from the edge. It would have had to be physically moved,' Raven added.

'The temperature dropped by a few degrees,' Archer said, gesturing first at a thermometer, then at the gooseflesh that had broken out on his arms.

'I felt like my energy had been sucked. It wasn't the dizziness I get sometimes,' Éabha added. 'I can feel the difference now.'

Davis didn't question her on that, just tapped his pen thoughtfully. 'And Fionn had just made a pretty awful pun.'

'Accidentally!' Fionn said. A shudder ran through him as he

thought about it. What would that have been like, falling overboard, watching the lights of the boat getting further and further away as you were surrounded by inky-black water? He'd grown up watching terrible, low-budget shark films on the Sci-Fi channel, and scenes from every single one of them were flooding into his brain now. Were there sharks here? He needed to check.

And never go in the water.

'Éabha and I can go find Neale and ask her about it,' Archer said. He looked at Raven. 'No offence, but this is probably an interview that needs more of Éabha's light touch.'

'None taken,' Raven said.

'I'm going to go talk to Charles about last night – he's the only person on duty that we've already met, and he was on our table. He might have noticed something,' Fionn said. He didn't normally do a lot of the people work, but Charles had been friendly, and it would give him something to do before the survey. He'd already checked all the equipment, and it was ready to go. Besides, Charles had told him to ask any questions he had about ships, and he had so many. It would be nice to talk to someone new, someone who knew why they were here, and not have to watch what he said all the time.

'That's a good plan. Thanks, Fionn,' Archer said.

'I'll check in to see if we can do a survey in the dining room,' Davis said. 'I think focusing there after last night is a good idea.'

'For sure,' Raven nodded. 'If we get any evidence that this woman could be the spirit, I'd suggest we do the next survey on deck eight, but that's going to be tougher to pull off without someone noticing.'

'Maybe at night?' Éabha suggested. 'Ask to close it off after midnight, when everyone's likely to be asleep or occupied by the bar on level seven.'

'That seems fair to me,' Davis said.

They chatted through a few more logistics before splitting up. Fionn went to find Charles, awkwardly summoning the courage to ask a few crew before eventually tracking him down in a meeting room on deck five, sheets of paper spread across the table.

'Fionn!' Charles exclaimed, a welcoming smile on his face. 'You came to see me.'

'I hope I'm not interrupting?' Fionn asked.

Charles shook his head. 'I'm just recording some of the routes we're taking – I'm a junior navigator on board.'

'Navigator *and* server? They keep you busy,' Fionn said.

Charles shrugged. 'A crew member dropped out at the last minute, so a few of us are mixing roles. I hope I did OK – I'm not used to being a fine-dining server.'

'I never would have guessed,' Fionn told him. 'You handled everyone like a pro,'

'I'm used to dealing with guests,' Charles said.

'Even ones like the people at my table?' Fionn asked.

'Especially like those,' Charles said.

Fionn winced. 'That's a lot to deal with regularly.'

'Ah, you know, I smile, I move on. Sometimes guests have a glass of wine too many and get too familiar, other times they look through you like you're not even there.'

'Well, I think it's impressive,' Fionn said awkwardly. 'Besides, I'd have spilled wine on at least three people. You didn't even spill when the lights went out!'

'I am glad I could impress you,' Charles said, smiling at him.

'So, I wanted to talk to you about last night,' Fionn said. 'Do you mind if I ask you a couple of questions?'

'You think it was paranormal?' Charles asked instantly, leaning towards him.

'It could be, but we need more evidence before we say if it was or not,' Fionn said.

'I wish I could help. But the lights went out, the woman screamed, the lights came on and she was on the ground saying someone pushed her.'

'Did you hear or feel anything else? Nothing is too small or weird, I promise.'

Charles hesitated. 'For a moment, I thought I felt ... comforted. Like a supportive feeling? Which is strange, because I should have been scared – everything was dark and people were screaming. I don't know where it came from or why, just that ... I wasn't afraid.'

That was interesting. And directly at odds with Cami, who had said she was violently pushed.

'You think I'm mad,' Charles said ruefully.

Fionn laughed. 'Far from it. If I told you some of the stories we've heard, you'd be the one thinking I'm mad.'

'I'd like to hear them sometime,' Charles said. 'Maybe we can find some time when you're not investigating and I'm not working.'

'Yes, I'd love to hear more about the ship! We can swap stories,' Fionn smiled. He paused. Davis would murder him if he didn't ask about the woman. 'Do you mind if I ask you something else?' he asked hesitantly.

Charles's face lit up. 'Anything.'

Fionn paused. What was a not-awkward or weird way to bring this up? Archer would have known how to work it into casual conversation. Because somehow, he could even make 'so, when you lost a passenger overboard, how come no one mentioned that and it wasn't in any news outlets?' a not-uncomfortable conversation to have.

'We found a report from one of the cruises. About a woman who fell overboard?'

Charles looked away. 'I wasn't on the crew at that time,' he said.

'But people talk. Did anyone ever mention anything …' Fionn trailed off. 'Anything you tell me will stay with the team. No one outside of it, not even the captain, will hear what you say.'

'Apparently, they were a very nice and normal couple. She was polite and considerate, not like some of the other guests we get on board. He was one of those men who work a room, going out of his way to charm everyone around him. But Violet, one of the other crew members, said that she saw someone contradict him once and his face … apparently he was all smiles and affability until the person walked away, but then the look he gave them … Violet said she wouldn't want to cross him.'

'And no one knows how the woman fell overboard?' He asked.

Charles shook his head. 'The CCTV on those cameras … it wasn't there.'

'As in they weren't working or footage was deleted?' Fionn asked.

Charles shrugged. 'Deleted, or the cameras turned off. That can happen sometimes.'

'For long periods of time or shorter ones?' Fionn pressed.

'Normally shorter, maybe a minute or two. But on this night, it was several hours, I think. I'm not sure – that's just what I heard.'

'And does that happen a lot?' Fionn tried not to sound too urgent, as though it was a casual enquiry more than something that had set alarm bells ringing in his head.

'It has been happening more regularly, actually. We have no idea what happens. They all run on the same power, but it's only certain sections of the boat at a time.' Charles smiled at Fionn. 'You're good with this kind of stuff, no? Maybe you can figure it out.'

Already multiple theories were running through Fionn's head. He needed to get back to the room and start looking up some things to help narrow it down. With a jolt, he realised Charles was still looking at him expectantly, and he flushed.

'CCTV systems aren't my speciality, but I am good with cameras and video analysis. I have some things I need to look up before I can confirm any theories, though.'

'Well, I look forward to hearing them when we spend time together,' Charles said.

Fionn grinned. He hadn't made a new friend in a long time – he was an introvert, and between PSI, his job at the camera shop and helping out on the farm, he didn't have a lot of free time. He didn't *need* any more people in his life, but it was nice to know he could still meet new people and connect with them.

'I'll tell you then. I'd better get back to the team, but I'll talk to you soon. Thank you so much for your help.'

There were probably a million other questions he should have asked too, that Davis and Archer would gently – or not so gently, depending on Davis's mood – point out to him when he filled them in. But this was a lead.

'I look forward to it,' Charles smiled.

Fionn said goodbye and headed back to the others, one burning question in his mind: if the cameras had run out of power right when the woman fell overboard, that opened the possibility of them being drained by something paranormal.

And if they had been drained, that created another burning question – was the woman who fell overboard the ghost, or was she a victim of it?

CHAPTER FOURTEEN

ÉABHA AND FIONN SAT TOGETHER AT BREAKFAST, while the others went to another table. They were trying their best to circulate, to mingle with the guests and see if they could overhear anything. Breakfast was incredible, with a full buffet of fruits, cereals, fancy cheeses and charcuterie as well as freshly baked pastries laid out. Crew were also circulating taking orders for eggs, bacon, pancakes, waffles and a variety of other things.

Charles appeared the moment they sat down, fresh faced in an immaculate white shirt. All the crew were constantly 'on', with ready smiles, no matter how specific a request was – or the manner in which it was delivered. Charles appeared with their coffees so quickly Éabha thought he might be able to teleport or be telekinetic. Now *that* would be a clairvoyant skill she'd be delighted to have. No more having to get up to fetch the remote, or a new book when she wanted to read in bed. Charles took their food orders too – Fionn getting pancakes with bacon, while Éabha ordered some poached eggs and avocado on toast. The orange juice from the buffet was freshly squeezed and utterly delicious, though she couldn't help but notice that several of her tablemates had chosen to combine it with champagne for breakfast mimosas.

That seemed a bit intense for nine thirty, but then, decadence seemed to be most people's aim coming into this cruise. PSI, however, were there to work.

'How do you like your cabin?' Éabha politely asked the woman beside her. She and Fionn were sitting with two couples who were travelling together – 'old business partners', they had informed them, though they didn't say what kind of business.

'It's lovely,' the woman, Monica, said. 'I've been on cruises before that just really were not up to standard, but this ship, it's hard to find fault.'

'I'm sure we'll find a few by the end of the cruise,' one of the men said drily.

The four of them laughed, and Éabha saw Fionn give Charles a sympathetic look as he placed their food in front of them.

'I wish we could say the same for *our* cabin,' the other woman – 'Alexandra, never Alex' was how she'd introduced herself – said. 'The air conditioning must be faulty. The room kept becoming absolutely freezing.'

'I already asked Neale to get a tech to look at it,' Alexandra's partner said. Éabha had missed his name because someone was talking loudly behind her as he said it, and her hearing aids had picked up their conversation instead of the softly spoken man across the table. Alexandra gave him a grateful smile as she continued, 'And was it just me or was the weather particularly bad last night?'

'No, it was perfectly calm,' the man – she was reasonably certain he'd said his name was Miles, but he might have said Niall, so she was hoping to avoid having to say his name, just in case – from the other cabin said.

'I didn't notice anything,' Monica agreed.

'Well, several of my things went flying off the dressing table, and they were well away from the edges,' Alexandra said.

Éabha took a bite of her eggs, trying not to seem too interested.

'Maybe they were a bit closer than you realised after a few glasses of champagne,' Monica joked. Alexandra laughed, taking a long sip of her mimosa. 'I take my jewellery very seriously, darling, you know that.'

'Can't risk the diamonds,' Monica teased.

'She doesn't have enough,' Alexandra's husband deadpanned.

Éabha pretended to smile, her brain whirring, trying to think of a not-creepy way to find out which cabin they were in.

Luckily, she didn't have to. After breakfast – where they mostly talked amongst themselves and Fionn and Éabha just added a polite answer to a question when it was demanded of them – the woman beside Éabha took out her key card, still in its paper holder. And there, written on the front of it in big letters, was Cabin 4.

The cabin the woman who fell from the boat had been staying in. She felt the gentle pressure of Fionn's foot pressing against hers, showing he'd noticed it too and come to the same realisation.

Cold spots, things falling off flat surfaces, and a previous inhabitant lost at sea?

Sounded like a good lead to her.

CHAPTER FIFTEEN

'WE NEED TO ASK NEALE ABOUT the air-conditioning unit and if there's anything wrong with it,' Davis said immediately. Fionn and Éabha had filled them in as soon as they all got back from breakfast. Éabha had done more of the talking with the two couples so Fionn let her take the lead, but the jolt of excitement when he'd seen the woman's room number had been exhilarating.

'It would be better if we could go in, but I don't think they'll let us into a guest's room without more reason,' Davis continued. 'At least their engineer can rule out the air conditioning, and if there is an issue with it and they fix it, we can ask Neale to keep us updated on whether they report any other issues.'

'I don't think they're the type to stay quiet if there are,' Fionn said.

Archer laughed, but Fionn wasn't joking.

'You *really* love being around all these rich people,' said Archer, grinning knowingly at Fionn.

'It's my dream holiday,' Fionn agreed solemnly.

'I think they suck too,' Raven said, leaning in to whisper in his ear.

Fionn smiled at that. He knew Archer just thought Fionn simply didn't like rich people, but Archer didn't understand how completely, utterly, out of his depth Fionn felt. He wished he could eat with the crew, who knew exactly who PSI were and a lot of whom seemed to be just a few years older than him. He was reasonably certain that they would talk about things he was interested in and actually knew something about, or at the very least they wouldn't try to talk to him about the stock market.

That wasn't a bad idea, actually.

'I know we need to keep up the pretence of being guests,' Fionn said. 'But what do you think about me eating dinner with the crew at some point? If they'll let me? I think it would be a really good way to get some behind-the-scenes information. They'll talk freely.'

'Do you think they will with you sitting there, though?' Davis asked.

'They know I'm not a *guest*-guest,' Fionn said. He could feel the hope rising in his chest. It was a seven-night cruise – even one or two nights away from those uncomfortably formal dinners would make such a difference. It didn't matter how great the food was. He'd made it through one and he already needed a break – from both the people, and the suit.

'It's not a bad idea,' Raven said, echoing what Fionn had thought. She had her fingers wrapped around her purple pendant, and Fionn had a feeling she knew exactly how much he wanted this. 'And the rest of us can split into two groups of two, so no one would have to brave the formalities alone,' she added.

Archer shrugged. 'Run it by Neale. If it's OK with her, it's fine with me. I assume they eat before or after the guest meal, or in shifts, so find out when you need to be there.'

Relief flooded through Fionn. 'I'll go find her and ask about the air con while I'm there,' he said eagerly. He could see Raven biting back a smile.

'I'll come with you,' she offered.

They left the others in the cabin and went to find Neale.

'Thanks for the assistance,' Fionn said as they walked along the corridor.

'Honestly, I'm jealous I didn't think of it first,' Raven said. 'Though I think I'm a little more used to being around slightly inebriated rich people.'

'Are the Origin regulars this posh?' Fionn asked. He'd gone in a few times with Cordelia and it had seemed more hipster-y.

'Hipsters with money and a sense of superiority,' Raven confirmed. 'Not at this level, but enough to be annoying.'

'Everyone's annoying to you, though,' Fionn said.

Raven elbowed him. 'Keep the sass up and you won't get any more meal-avoidance assists from me.'

Fionn held up his hands. 'I promise, I'll behave.'

Raven had changed a lot over the last few months. She was still spiky and acerbic, but he could see she'd tried to soften herself more. She still gave them all grief constantly, but not in a 'hissing wildcat' kind of way. Now it was affectionate, teasing. He could practically see her looking around for an exit sign, panic on her face, any time someone expressed an emotion, but she didn't bolt through the door any more.

They were a proper team – and yes, they bickered and fought, but they had each other's backs.

Though considering they'd been through multiple life-threatening situations together, it would be impossible to doubt how much they cared about each other. Even when Davis was Davis-ing, or Archer was late to yet another meeting, or Raven was extra-irritable after a few late shifts at Origin in a row. Éabha was the almost-mild one, though he hadn't failed to notice her losing her patience – Éabha's version of it, which was 'a slight bit of frustration creeping into her voice' – when her energy levels were low.

They compared breakfast orders – Raven immediately saying she was going to try Fionn's bacon pancakes the next day – and kept their conversation casual as they went to find Neale. They needed to be careful. The ship was large, but there was a constant risk of being overheard at any time, and they needed the other guests to believe they were just regular cruise guests, the same as them. So all ghost talk had to be kept behind closed doors.

Fionn had been impressed by the size of the vessel, but even one day in, the corridors were starting to feel a lot narrower. The gentle rocking of the boat as he walked was a constant reminder that they were at sea, and even when he went out on deck, the expanse of sparkling blue water that stretched out in all directions was a reminder that there was no way off until they docked at Civitavecchia tomorrow.

Knowing there was very possibly a ghost wandering around too didn't exactly add to his comfort levels.

Neale was enthusiastic. 'Oh, my engineer has already been to the cabin,' she said when they asked her about it, pulling a sheet of paper out of a pile on her desk.

'That was fast,' Raven said. Neale smiled at her.

'It's a five-star cruise. A lot of the guests would consider us not psychically sensing the air-conditioning unit was potentially not working correctly as a failure, let alone keeping them waiting for the cabin to be checked.' She looked down at the page she was holding. 'Report says the cabin temperature was perfectly fine too.'

'Well, that's that ruled out anyway,' Raven said. 'While we have you, we have another request.' She quickly outlined Fionn's plan, while he stood beside her, bracing for the 'no', steeling himself to stay professional and not let Neale see how disappointed he was.

'No problem, I'll ask Charles to escort you down tonight, since you already met him when he was showing you around,' she said. Fionn kept his face neutral, trying not to show his surprise. He'd assumed he'd have to suffer through at least one more formal dinner tonight. Now, not only did he get a reprieve, but it would also be Charles bringing him. Charles had been so friendly and welcoming, and everyone he interacted with warmed to him. Personally, Fionn was relieved to have him as his escort, and from an interview perspective being with someone everyone liked would be helpful. People would open up more around Fionn if he was with someone they trusted.

Hopefully, if he found out enough good information, he could sneak away for a few more meals.

For the investigation, of course.

CHAPTER SIXTEEN

ADRENALINE COURSED THROUGH ARCHER as he led the others to the dining room as soon as the breakfast had been cleared for the day. Today was the one at-sea day of the itinerary, which made the necessity for this survey to be as inconspicuous as possible even higher, but they didn't want to wait until they arrived in Civitavecchia the next day. Part of him felt sad that he couldn't just join the passengers strolling up towards the pool deck or the spa facilities and spend the day lounging in the sun, hand in hand with Éabha, sampling the delicious food on board and taking in the scenery. He'd ducked out on deck briefly earlier and the cries of seagulls overhead, the feel of the sea air on his face – it all felt so refreshing, so exciting, he almost didn't want to go back through the door that would lead him to the interior of the ship.

That longing had been dampened when he'd met the team back at the boys' cabin, where the equipment was ready and waiting and the team were poised to begin. It felt like the survey was truly starting now – they had a specific thing to investigate, a possible lead on who the spirit was (if there was one, he reminded himself. Davis would be proud). They were just doing one of their basic surveys for now – just EMF readings and EVP, to see if they could pick anything up from the night before. Based on their results and their research, they'd start assessing whether they needed to try a stronger approach. Raven had her amethyst crystal on, and Éabha had taken off her tourmaline, but neither of them was actively trying to summon anything to them, which Archer was quietly relieved about. They said Lizzie had explained it as the difference between simply opening a door and actually inviting someone in. It was definitely best for Éabha to save her energy for when they needed it, and Raven seemed pretty OK with not actively seeking to draw spirits towards her until she had to. It hadn't exactly gone to plan either of the other times she'd done it. Maybe they'd be able to complete this survey without either of them using their gifts at all. He tried to shove down the warm glow of hope that rose in him at that thought.

Archer, Davis and Éabha waited in the centre of the dining room as Raven walked slowly around, EMF meter on. Fionn followed her with an infrared camera, scanning everything to see if any thermal imagery came up. When they'd covered the room, they rejoined the others in the middle.

'Nothing,' Raven said with a sigh, looking down at the EMF meter with a frustration that implied it had purposely done this to annoy her.

'It's been well over twelve hours since dinner,' Davis said. 'It would have been odd if there was any residual activity.'

Éabha placed her hand on the table where Davis and Fionn had been sitting.

'What seat was Camilla in again?' she asked. Davis pointed, and Éabha first ran her hand over the table in front of it, then placed her palm on the back of the chair.

'Fear. Hunger. A bit tipsy,' she reported. 'And she has serious issues with the woman with dark hair and green eyes she's travelling with.'

'Cecily,' Davis supplied.

Éabha withdrew her hand. 'I don't feel like she's lying, but I'm not getting much else. That's the top layer anyway – so many people have sat at this table, if I go any deeper it's just going to get confusing.'

Psychometry was Éabha's strongest gift, but even this brief foray into it seemed to sap her energy. Her speech slowed and she was struggling to get her words out. Archer had noticed how, when she was drained, she almost had to force the words out of her mouth, and sometimes it was like she'd forget mid-sentence what she was trying to say. He tried to help her out by stepping in and guessing how the sentence might end, but sometimes her lips would press together like she was irritated. She knew he was just trying to help, right?

'Charles had a pretty interesting take on what happened the first night,' Fionn said, shutting his camera off and drawing Archer's focus back to him. He paused, then looked at the others, his face scrunching with perplexity. 'He said he felt supported.'

'Physically?' Raven asked, frowning in confusion.

'No, emotionally. He said he just had this feeling, as though someone was being, like, "I've got you", protecting him or something.'

'While another person reported feeling violently pushed?' Archer said.

'And is still adamant about that,' Davis confirmed. 'We managed to "casually bump into" Camilla and her friends by the pool and strike up a conversation. She's certain she was pushed.'

'Even if her friends were either rolling their eyes or just sipping their champagne and zoning out,' Raven added.

'So two people with two very conflicting experiences with opposite emotional effects,' Archer mused.

'Charles said he noticed how comforted he felt because he should have been scared – the lights going out, people screaming, no one had any idea what was happening. But he just felt reassured and knew he'd be fine,' Fionn said, clicking repeatedly on the end of the pen he was holding as he thought. Davis stared at him pointedly until he stopped.

'It's a pity neither Éabha nor I were at the table,' Raven sighed.

'Maybe Éabha should sit at this table tonight. We could see if Neale can influence the seating chart?' Davis suggested.

Great, another thing for Éabha to expend her energy on.

'Raven can do that now too, right? Maybe she should have a go?' Archer said, as casually as he could, but Éabha stiffened beside him.

I'm just trying to protect you, Éabhs.

Raven bit her lip. 'I'm learning, but it's not a natural strength for me, not like Éabha. I'm good at sensing and moving energy …' – That was putting it mildly, thought Archer. She'd literally formed weapons from it and used it to fight a ghost – '… and hearing things. Éabha tends to feel and see the most strongly.'

'You're well matched,' Davis smiled. 'Almost a perfect balance of strengths.'

Both girls smiled at him, and then at each other, Raven arching an eyebrow as Davis spoke. Archer's heart sank. Logically, he knew the girls having opposite strengths was helpful for the team, but right now he just wanted Raven to say confidently 'I can do anything Éabha can'.

It would be so much easier to steer Éabha away from using her energy if she wasn't the only option. Instead, as the team packed up their stuff and made their way out of the dining room, instead of thinking about the interviews they had scheduled for the afternoon, or the questions they needed answered, all he could focus on was the gnawing anxiety growing deep in the pit of his stomach. Even looking ahead to where Éabha was chatting and laughing with Fionn as they turned down the opulent corridor, the sound of their feet muffled by the soft carpets, did nothing to ease his worries. He needed to finish this survey, not just for the job, or the crew, but so he could protect Éabha from pushing herself too far.

They just needed more information. Surely they'd be able to piece it all together soon?

CHAPTER SEVENTEEN

BY FIVE P.M. DAVIS AND ÉABHA were on their last interview of the day and he could feel her starting to flag beside him as they waited for the crew member to arrive. She took a long sip of her coffee and leaned back in her chair.

'Do you want me to do this one on my own?' Davis asked.

'No, it's the last one, I can handle it,' Éabha said.

Davis shrugged. 'OK.'

He could feel her studying him out of the corner of her eye, like she was expecting him to say something else. But Éabha knew her limits. If she wanted to stay, she should stay.

They'd commandeered a small meeting room for these interviews, not the business suite on deck five, but one used for the crew meetings on deck three. It was a lot less luxurious, the table a plain pine instead of the sumptuous mahogany, and the smell of food wafting down from the crew mess triggered a low growl from Davis's stomach. There were no windows, which felt claustrophobic, but at least they didn't need to worry about curious guests seeing them and wondering what was going on. Their key instruction – besides finding out if there was a ghost, obviously – was to stay under the radar, and Davis was not going to mess that up.

The door opened and a crew member stepped in. He was a Black man in his mid-twenties: if Davis had to guess his age, he'd say maybe twenty-five. He was tall and lean, his hair close cut and his white uniform perfectly crisp. There was a faint whiff of chlorine as he sat down.

'Sorry I'm a few minutes late; my cover at the pool was delayed,' he said, smiling. 'I'm Willem, one of the deckhands and lifeguards.' Davis wasn't great at placing accents, but at a push he'd have guessed Willem's was Dutch.

They introduced themselves, leaning across the table to shake Willem's hand.

'So, do you know why we're here?' Éabha asked.

Willem nodded. 'And glad of it too. Things have been getting progressively creepier around here.'

'And you think there's a paranormal reason for that?' Davis asked.

Willem hesitated. 'It feels mad to say it out loud, but I don't know what else could explain it. There's the stuff with the guests, the power outages, the CCTV being messed with ... and some of the crew have started experiencing things. Weird noises, cold spots, unusual smells.'

'Unusual smells?' Éabha asked.

Willem nodded. 'I smelled it once. It's floral. Kind of like women's perfume. But I was in a room with no fresh flowers, one that hadn't had detergent or anything sprayed in it recently. It made no sense.'

This was a new piece of information.

'And it's not just me,' Willem added quickly. 'A few others have too. A couple of them have left now, but there's still some left: Rob, Violet, Federica, Carlos ...' he trailed off as Éabha took the names down. They'd check if the others had interviewed any of them later.

'Were you on the ship when Mrs Foster fell?' Davis asked.

Willem nodded. 'That was a tragedy. She was really lovely.' He paused, then hurriedly added. 'Not that it wouldn't have been sad either way, it's just … you don't always get people who talk to you like you're a person, you know?'

Éabha nodded sympathetically. 'Do you remember anything specific about that night?'

'I wasn't on duty,' Willem said. 'I was woken by the man-overboard alarm, got dressed and rushed up to the deck. This ship takes a while to stop so by the time we had we'd already moved on a bit. We deployed boats with spotlights to try to find her, but … You wouldn't last long, not in these waters, not after a fall like that.' He leaned forward, his voice low. 'Do you think the ghost had something to do with it?'

Davis and Éabha exchanged a glance.

'Or that she *is* the ghost?' he asked, his voice rising slightly.

'It's too early to say anything conclusive,' Davis said.

Willem gave him a knowing look.

The rest of the interview went smoothly. Willem was friendly and eager to help. There was no trace of scepticism in him. When he left twenty minutes later, Davis and Éabha waited until the door shut behind him before they spoke.

'The perfume was new,' Davis said.

Éabha nodded thoughtfully. 'It was good he could tell us who else had smelt it. It'll be interesting if they all got the same scent.'

'Or if there's anything similar about where they smelt it,' Davis added.

'These interviews are giving us more questions than answers though,' Éabha frowned.

Davis couldn't help but agree, even if part of him enjoyed the challenge. The two of them gathered up their notebooks and equipment, shoving them into gym bags to hide them on the walk back to their cabins. They'd both dressed in athletic gear, so that if they bumped into any other passengers, it would look like they had just been to the gym. They didn't see a lot of people, but they were still careful to discuss ordinary topics as they walked past other guests.

'See you at dinner,' Éabha smiled when they reached her cabin.

'I can't believe Fionn managed to bail out on the second night,' Davis said, shaking his head.

He knew Fionn hadn't been comfortable last night, but this ploy to avoid the dining room for an evening was inspired. And genuinely a very good idea for the investigation too.

'I think Raven's jealous she couldn't join him,' Éabha laughed. 'I'll see you soon.'

She swiped her keycard and disappeared into her room, while Davis made his way the few doors down to his own cabin, his mind whirring. There were so many questions about this case, and they had six nights, including tonight, to answer them.

He wasn't getting off this boat until they'd solved this mystery.

CHAPTER EIGHTEEN

'THANK YOU FOR BRINGING ME,' Fionn said to Charles, trailing him down a narrow staircase to the crew mess. He'd been so excited about his genius plan to avoid the formal dinner that he'd forgotten a key part – he would have to go by himself. None of the others would be there to take the lead, allowing him to mostly observe. He'd need to initiate and steer the conversation.

'Everyone knows what we're here to do, right?' he asked Charles, his stomach churning. He really wanted to find out something useful tonight, to justify this deviation beyond simply avoiding the formalities. He definitely didn't want to accidentally put his foot in it, that was for sure. Davis would never let him hear the end of it.

'They do,' Charles confirmed, opening a door and ushering Fionn through it, down a long, narrow corridor that had the smell of cooking wafting down it. 'With varying degrees of enthusiasm.'

'Yeah, we get that a lot,' Fionn said.

He couldn't blame them. It must feel a bit out there to have your workplace hire a team of ghost hunters, especially if you didn't believe in ghosts.

The quiet of the corridor was shattered the moment Charles opened the door to the crew mess. There were thirty-five crew on board, and about twenty of them were crowded into the mess. There was loud conversation, laughter, heat and the clinking of cutlery, an almost instantaneous onslaught of sensory overload. Some of them were still in uniform, either the starched white with navy piping or the white polo neck and navy shorts of the deck crew, while others were in jeans and T-shirts or tank tops.

Fionn looked at Charles, who grinned at the apprehension Fionn knew was written all over his face.

'Don't worry, we don't bite,' Charles said.

Multiple crew members called out to Charles as he steered Fionn towards the buffet, which offered hot food like lasagne, chicken and chips, vegetable pasta bakes and vegetarian samosas laid out under heaters while beside them was a station with a range of salads. Fionn couldn't help but notice that a few eyes lingered on him with long, sceptical looks, turning and whispering to the people beside them with smirks. He could feel himself trying not to shrink inwards, reminding himself that of course there would be a number of people baffled or irritated by the team's involvement. He pushed his shoulders back, focusing on what Charles was saying.

'I'm afraid it's self-service down here,' Charles said, leading him to the cutlery station.

'This is amazing,' Fionn said enthusiastically, eagerly reaching for a spatula and sliding a large slice of lasagne onto his plate.

Charles looked at him with amusement. 'You don't like being waited on?'

'Not at all,' Fionn said. He caught himself, and added quickly, 'I mean you're all very good at it.'

Charles threw back his head and laughed, earning them a few curious looks.

'But yeah, I just … I'm here to work too, you know?' Fionn said. 'It feels awkward sitting there being served like one of the paying guests. This is way more comfortable.'

'You need a break from being undercover?' a voice behind him said teasingly.

Fionn turned to see one of the deck crew, a girl around his height with muscular arms and short hair who he'd seen mopping the decks earlier, grinning at him. She was out of her deck clothes, in denim shorts and a tank top that revealed an intricate tattoo of a purple flower on her bicep.

'It's very hard being incognito,' he told her solemnly.

She laughed and he felt a flush of pleasure.

'I wish part of my job involved three-course meals and using the pool,' she said.

He blushed. Did he sound ungrateful?

'Oh, I know how lucky I am,' he said quickly. 'I just feel awkward when it's under false pretences, you know? I have to sit there at every meal and lie about why I'm on this cruise, while also finding a subtle way of asking if anyone thinks they might have seen a ghost.'

'Listening to them talk about stocks and trading without even being able to have a glass of wine would be tough,' she agreed. 'I'm Violet, by the way.'

'Oh, Archer and Raven chatted to you earlier, didn't they?' he said, recognising her name immediately as they sat down at a long table. Violet sat into a chair on one side while Fionn, followed by Charles, slid onto a bench on the other.

'They did. I'm very much Team Ghost, by the way. As in, I think there is one. I'm not condoning the ghost's actions.'

'Though I can empathise with some of them,' another voice chimed in, dropping into a chair beside Violet. It was another of the deck crew, a tall man who was about twenty-five or so.

'Willem,' he said, shaking Fionn's hand. 'So how exactly do you find a ghost?'

It was such a relief to be able to talk freely. Fionn told them about PSI, about how the team dynamics worked and how they generally went about an investigation. A few people passing by obviously caught snatches of their conversation, and while a few seemed to slow with interest, even smiling at him, he heard a few scoffs and 'utterly ridiculous the captain's entertaining this' comments. The comfort of the friendly group around him, Willem and Violet and Charles's genuine curiosity and belief, made it easier to shut those comments out.

'So that's why you're here? To see if anyone gives anything away?' Violet asked, playfully leaning forward onto the table and raising her eyebrow dramatically.

'I'm here to avoid wearing a tie, to be honest,' Fionn said. 'But don't tell Archer.'

The others laughed, and Charles elbowed him gently. 'I can't believe you didn't dress up for us.'

'I will next time,' Fionn said. They laughed again.

This was nice, making new friends, connecting with people. Maybe in a different life he'd have done this – sailed, seen the world.

He'd chosen ghosts though. And he was happy with his decision. When he wasn't almost dying.

'So, let me justify coming here,' he said. 'What are your theories? Honestly.'

'I think it's a load of bullshit,' a loud voice said from behind them.

The other three stiffened, exchanging glances. Fionn turned to see a man in his late twenties standing over him, his face hostile. His straw-blond hair was slicked back neatly, and he still wore his white steward's shirt which stretched across his muscular chest. The stripes on his shoulders denoted that he was high up the chain of command.

'Some faulty wiring and a few drunk guests covering for themselves with a ghost story, that's all it is,' he scoffed.

'And what about the other things that have happened?' Willem said, indignant.

'Why would someone choose to haunt this ship?' Slicked Hair shot back, rolling his eyes and starting to turn away.

'Maybe if they fell overboard and no one found them?' Fionn suggested, keeping his tone casual. He was channelling Davis, his cool logic and neutral tone with just a hint of pointedness.

Slicked Hair stopped abruptly, his eyes narrowing as he studied Fionn, saying nothing.

'You really are good at your job,' Violet said tapping on the table in delight.

Slicked Hair turned away properly this time and put his tray forcefully down on the next table down from them, his cutlery rattling against the plate. Violet and Willem's backs were to him, but Charles sat up a little straighter beside Fionn, his eyes on Slicked Hair too. The steward sat with his back to them, but everything about his body language said he was still listening. He could have been a bit more subtle about it, but he was making Fionn's job easier by not being.

'Were any of you on the boat when it happened?' Fionn said.

'I wasn't,' Charles said.

'I was,' Violet said, shuddering. 'It was awful.' Willem nodded emphatically.

'We radioed for help and searched for her while we waited for the coastguard to arrive. But it was too late – we never found her,' Willem said, adding, 'I told Davis and Éabha about it earlier.'

'I heard the CCTV broke,' Fionn said carefully. Violet and Charles looked at each other, then Violet leaned in. 'Not broken – gone. Like it had been erased,' she said in a low voice.

'I didn't know that,' Willem said.

That was interesting. It could be paranormal, but it could just as easily be mechanical – or sabotage.

Slicked Hair was still listening intently. His shoulders were taut, and while he held his fork in his hand, he hadn't taken a single bite of the food in front of him.

Best to change the subject, not seem too interested.

'So, Willem, have you ever experienced anything?' Fionn asked. 'Besides the perfume?'

Willem shook his head. 'But my roommate has. Hang on, I don't think you've talked to him yet.' He turned and bellowed 'ROB' across the room. A small, slight man with light-brown hair came over.

'It would have taken you two seconds to get up and fetch me instead of deafening the whole room,' he said cheerfully as Willem introduced him to Fionn.

'He wants to hear about that night,' Willem said.

'Ah yes, so, I was on night watch with …' Rob spoke in a low voice, leaning in, and jerked his head to indicate Slicked Hair. 'We were in the security booth, monitoring the CCTV screens and keeping an eye on the cameras for late-night drunk passengers trying to go look at the stars. It was especially important after … well, you know. So, we're sitting there and the room goes icy cold, out of nowhere. Then I smell something strange, something floral. I think it was perfume. Definitely not my cologne, or …' He jerked his head towards Slicked Hair again. 'Then all the monitors start to flicker, one after the other. All except the one showing the part of the deck where the guest fell off, the one that stopped working the night of the accident.

'Now I, being the brave specimen of a man that I am …' – the others snorted at this – '…was unfazed, but old Slick over there? White as a sheet. Won't admit it now, of course, but I saw him. And then, I swear, I heard a voice. Right beside my ear, like someone was whispering into it. I nearly jumped out of my chair, it was so close. And the room was dead silent before then too. Despite that, it was hard to make out, but it was definitely a woman talking, and she was saying two words over and over. I could only figure out one, though.'

'What was the voice saying?' Fionn asked. His heart was starting to pound, and he struggled to keep his face and voice neutral.

'"Find", then something I couldn't make out. If you ask me, it was Phillipa Foster. And she was asking us to find her.'

CHAPTER NINETEEN

'FIND ME,' RAVEN REPEATED AND SHIVERED. Fionn had been waiting for them in the boys' cabin when they got back from dinner, flushed with the knowledge he'd gleaned. She was happy his gamble had paid off and he could stand over his suggestion to eat with the crew. She'd felt his emotions when he'd suggested it, and how deeply uncomfortable he was in the fancy five-star service world of the cruise. He had to be desperate to suggest doing what was essentially a bunch of interviews on his own, when he normally was happy to focus on the equipment and let the rest of them do the talking.

'Technically, he just heard "find" and then drew conclusions himself,' Davis pointed out. 'It could be a spirit that lost something on the boat and wants it back.'

'Or the woman who lost her life and was never seen again,' Raven said.

'Rob said during the encounter he smelt something. A woman's perfume, he thought,' Fionn said.

'Rob is one of the names Willem gave us,' Éabha said, double checking her notes from her earlier interview.

'Two of the other crew members have smelt it as well: one in the security booth too, and another when she was cleaning a cabin,' Fionn said. He paused dramatically before adding, 'Cabin four.'

'*See*,' Raven said pointedly.

Davis frowned and she held up her hands. 'I'm not saying it

definitely is. I'm saying it's reasonable to believe it is pointing us in that direction.'

'Slick is hiding something,' Fionn said.

'Who?' Éabha and Archer said in unison.

'Sorry, I didn't get his actual name. He's tall, burly with blond, slicked-back hair. He was really confrontational about PSI but then sat at the table behind us, eavesdropping. It could be he's embarrassed about being scared that night, or …'

'You think he might know more than he's letting on?' Davis asked, clicking the end of his pen as he thought.

'I think it would be worth someone else speaking to him,' Fionn said. 'Not me, he's already suspicious of me. But definitely a shields-down clairvoyant should try and get a read on him.'

'OK. Do you think he'd respond better to "sweet and pretty" or "I will drop-kick you off the boat if you lie to me?"' Raven asked.

'Which one am I?' Éabha asked innocently.

'Drop-kick, obviously,' Raven said.

'I think Éabha is a good shout,' Fionn said. 'Maybe Davis and Éabha? I don't think he's someone that can be charmed by Archer.'

'You say that like I'm not charming,' Davis said, stretching.

'Oh, immensely. But I think sweet-and-innocent Éabha and scientific-logic-you will work better. He seems like a guy with an ego.'

'You're better at reading people than you want to admit,' Archer said.

Fionn's face lit up at the compliment.

'So tomorrow Davis and Éabha go find Slick, as Fionn so charmingly calls him,' Raven said. Fionn kicked her, and she kicked him back as she continued, 'Then Archer and I can keep going with our planned interviews, and Fionn, do you want to sort out equipment?'

'Sure. And I'll find Slick's photo in the crew profiles for you, so you know who to look for.'

'I think, if we're comfortable, we could aim for a séance tomorrow night,' Archer said. 'We have good reason to believe it's Philippa Foster, and we can see if our evidence tomorrow supports it. If it is, we might as well try summoning her. The worst that could happen is we're wrong and she doesn't turn up.'

'Wow, these are much lower worst-case scenario stakes than we're used to,' Éabha said.

Everyone laughed, but Raven could see the worried look in Archer's eyes even as he joined in.

'Does this mean we can actually sleep tonight?' Fionn said, yawning.

'Oh, sleep,' Éabha said. 'Big fan of that concept.'

'Yes, everyone go get a good night's rest,' Archer said, his eyes lingering on Éabha. 'We need to be on top form for tomorrow.'

'Aye, aye,' Fionn said, saluting him.

Raven and Éabha said their goodnights and made their way to the cabin. Éabha was pale and tired, and flopped face first onto her bed.

'You brush your teeth and stuff first. I need to muster the energy to do mine,' she said, her voice muffled by her pillow.

When she came out of their bathroom, Raven saw how slowly and laboriously the other girl had to push herself up. She said nothing, though. Éabha would ask for her help if she needed it.

'Goodnight,' Éabha said a few minutes later, crawling into her bed and flipping off the light.

'Time to find a ghost tomorrow,' Raven said cheerfully.

The silence told her Éabha was already asleep.

CHAPTER TWENTY

THE MORNING WENT QUICKLY. After breakfast, Éabha and Davis managed to track Slick – his actual name, they'd learned, was A.J. – around eleven. The rest of the guests were still in the process of disembarking at Civitavecchia, and Davis couldn't help shooting a few envious glances. This port was the one that allowed people to visit Rome, and as much as he loved his job, the thought of spending the day wandering the narrow, twisting streets of Rome, stopping for a café or gelato before wandering past the Colosseum or the Forum was unbelievably tempting. The port below was a bustle of noise and movement under the already hot sun, so they found a quiet space to pull A.J. aside.

Davis knew from the moment the conversation started that he would be difficult. A.J.'s face immediately switched from a charming 'what can I do for you' smile to almost open hostility as soon as Davis asked to talk to him about his experience in the security booth.

'Rob been talking bullshit again?' A.J. asked gruffly. 'What a surprise.'

'We'd love to hear your version of events,' Éabha said sweetly.

A.J.'s eyes lingered on her, on her wide, blue eyes, gentle smile and flowery dress. It was a good thing Davis was doing this interview, not Archer, because the way A.J. leaned towards Éabha, deepening his voice and eyeing her up made Davis want to step between them. Éabha could handle herself though. Archer wasn't jealous, but he was protective of Éabha, increasingly so since the horrors of the Merrion Hub.

This could have ended very badly indeed.

Éabha met his gaze, still playing innocent and unthreatening. People tended to underestimate her, which was objectively very funny, considering she could sense intentions and emotions and knew exactly what was going on under the surface at all times. Watching people try to lie to her was always very entertaining.

'Not much of a version to share,' A.J. shrugged. 'We were on late watch, Rob got edgy, freaked out, then decided to say I felt it too, to save face.'

A.J. had an American accent Davis couldn't place, and the broad, well-built steward leaned against the wall with such nonchalance it felt forced.

'You didn't hear anything unusual?' Éabha asked. 'Or notice anything out of the ordinary? Nothing is too small, really.'

'Only unusual thing was working with someone convinced they were hearing voices,' A.J. said. 'Amazing he still has his job. But not only is Rob still here, people actually believe his bullshit.'

'He's not the only one who seems to have experienced things,' Davis said, making a show of checking the file he was holding. A.J. started to lean forward and Davis quickly snapped it shut. Not to hide the people's names – he was far too experienced to actually carry those around with him – but to hide the fact that there was nothing of note in that folder. He wasn't lying, per se, just implying, to see what A.J. would say. Maybe he'd point them in a new direction.

'Look, there's a whole thing about sailors being superstitious. I guess even cruise ships aren't immune,' A.J. said.

'I suppose it's easy to jump to conclusions, especially after there's been accidents on board,' Éabha said, in her most sympathetic tone. 'I heard about that poor woman who fell overboard. That must have been hard on the crew. Did you work here then?'

A.J. stiffened, his face hardening for a moment and eyes darting up and down the corridor. It was just a split-second, and then he was relaxed and nonchalant again, leaning casually against the wall.

'I did,' he said.

'And did you–'

'Look, I'd love to chat, but I was due in the security booth five minutes ago, and there's really nothing I can tell you that would help. Rob got freaked out in the middle of the night. It happens to a lot of people. And unfortunately, he dragged me into it to make himself feel better.'

'Thanks for your time,' Davis said. He shook A.J.'s hand. Éabha, her wrist now devoid of its usual tourmaline bracelet, followed suit. A.J. turned and strode down the corridor and into a stairwell. Éabha's face had stayed completely neutral as she shook his hand and continued to stay so as she and Davis walked down the corridor in the opposite direction. She waited until they got into the lift and the doors had closed.

'He's hiding something,' she said. 'I could feel it.'

CHAPTER TWENTY-ONE

RAVEN WALKED BRISKLY ALONG ONE OF the lower-level corridors of the ship, looking for Neale. Raven hadn't been on deck seven or any of the outdoor areas all day, and she was eager to find the captain quickly and clear things up for the séance so she could get up and out into the fresh sea air and vibrant Mediterranean sunlight. Even though *L'Imperiale* felt bright and spacious, the lighting always at the perfect level, it was artificial. Stifling. She didn't know how the crew did it for months at a time. How did they not start to feel the walls close in around them?

That was a possible reason for what the crew had reported. Not the guests, though their reports were different in nature anyway. But the crew's reports – the chills, the sensation of being watched, of hearing voices they couldn't make out – those could all be symptoms of being too long below deck, with almost every interaction a high-maintenance guest demanding something new from them. A few of crew had said in their interviews that they were required to provide service so efficient they pretty much needed to be psychic, and that the word 'no' wasn't supposed to be in their vocabulary, except in exceptional circumstances. Long hours, claustrophobic surroundings, high-pressure work and a profession that, historically at least, was superstitious?

It could lead to a lot.

But Raven had this nagging gut feeling it wasn't that.

It was hard now, balancing the logical, parapsychology-trained side of her brain with clairvoyant intuition. She second-guessed herself a lot, even though she was almost always proven right.

Like how, right now, she knew from instinct that someone was watching her.

She also knew that, when she turned around, the corridor would be empty.

Just as she did so, the lights began to flicker. The two furthest away from her, on either side at the far end of the corridor, went first. They both flickered briefly in unison before extinguishing. Then the next pair followed suit. And the next. And the next.

Flicker.

Extinguish.

Flicker.

Extinguish.

Advancing towards her. Slowly plunging her into darkness.

She would not run.

She planted her feet, taking a deep breath. Her mental shields were up, but she sent probe of energy out from behind them, trying to sense what was ahead.

The last thing she saw before she was engulfed in darkness was the cloud of her breath in the now-icy air.

She stood, waiting.

'How can I help you?' she asked out loud. Her voice echoed hollowly in the corridor, but she was relieved it sounded steady. She waited, ears straining in the pitch-black gloom, hoping she would be able to hear a response over the sound of the blood pounding in her ears. She was kicking herself for not having a voice recorder on her.

Silence.

'I'm here to help you. But you need to give me some clues. Who are you? Why are you still here?'

Silence.

Then, right beside her ear, a single, rattling breath that sent icy shivers down her spine, goosebumps erupting over the skin of her neck.

'Find it,' a voice said, laced with an urgency that bordered on desperation.

Raven stood there in the darkness for a minute, trying to calm her racing heart, waiting to see if the ghost had anything else to add. She used those moments to breathe deeply, steadying herself, slowing her heart rate and feeling the frigid air start to warm again. This helped; focusing on the practical aspects, taking logical note of what was happening. Losing herself in the familiar protocol that had been drilled into her since she was young. When she was certain the ghost would say nothing more, she clicked on the torch light of her phone, noting that the battery was depleted, though fortunately not fully drained. She made her way down the corridor to the door at the far end, trying to force herself to walk steadily, but painfully aware of how fast she was striding, boots heavy on the plush carpet underneath her feet. Just before she reached it, the door opened, bright light spilling in from the connecting corridor, a figure silhouetted in it. Raven stopped short, biting back a yelp of surprise.

Raven?' a familiar voice said.

'Neale!' Raven said, her voice still miraculously steady as she started to walk towards the door again. 'Just the person I was looking for. Also, it seems every lightbulb in this corridor has died at almost the exact same time.'

Neale looked around. 'What an unusual coincidence,' she said.

Her tone and the casual nature of her response made it clear there were people nearby. 'Thank you for letting me know.'

'I have a few questions about excursions. Would I be inconveniencing you terribly if I asked for a quick chat?' Raven asked.

She stepped through into the brightly lit corridor, hoping the effects of her encounter weren't clear on her face. As she'd guessed, two well-dressed charter guests were disappearing around the corner, having clearly just been discussing something with Neale before she opened the door.

'Of course, right this way,' Neale said, gesturing to one of the business lounges. The door was open and the room empty.

Raven followed her into the lounge, where she sat heavily into a chair.

'Do I want to ask?' Neale said bluntly.

'Probably not,' Raven said. She took a deep breath. 'The team and I would like to use the dining room after the dinner service for some investigation purposes. Is that possible? We'd need to be sure no guests interrupted or were near enough to hear anything.'

'That can be arranged. We'll keep everyone in the bar. That's where they tend to go anyway.'

'Great,' Raven said. 'You wouldn't happen to have LED candles on board, would you?'

Neale's gaze was stern as she studied her. 'Do I want to know?'

'Probably not,' Raven said again.

'Will it be a danger to my guests or this vessel?' Neale asked.

'I would be pretty confident that it won't be, but obviously things like this are never one hundred per cent.'

That was an understatement. Though she was reasonably certain this ghost didn't want to murder them, and 'reasonably certain' was actually the most confident she had ever been.

'You can have it from half past midnight,' Neale said. 'I need to let the guests leave at their leisure after dinner and give the crew time to clear everything.'

'That's perfect.'

'And we only have real candles.'

Raven's stomach clenched for a moment as, in her mind's eye, she saw a burning house, Archer and Davis trapped behind a wall of fire, Fionn and Cordelia hauling her through smoke-riddled hallways as she weakly tried to fight to go back.

That fire hadn't been from candles, she reminded herself. The Lady had triggered an electrical fire. And there were enough electrics on this boat that if the ghost wanted to do it, it wouldn't need a bunch of candles.

That shouldn't have been a reassuring thought, but for some reason it calmed her.

'That would be great. Where can I get them from?'

Neale assured her they'd be ready after the dinner service.

'And a fire extinguisher too, to be on the safe side, please,' Raven added.

Neale looked at Raven for a long moment, consternation flashing across her face for a moment before she nodded. 'That's sensible.' There was a long pause before she asked, 'Do you feel like you have a lead?' It was the most hesitant Raven had ever heard her.

'We're hopeful, but we don't want to make promises and let you down. We'll aim to have a more thorough report in the morning,' Raven said, trying to soften her voice.

Neale shook her head. 'Over fifteen years working on cruise ships and yachts, and I'd really thought I'd seen it all. But this …'

'Tell me about it,' Raven said. 'I feel like I've seen more in less than a year than I expected in a lifetime.'

Neale laughed. 'Imagine all the things you'll have seen by the time you're my age.'

Raven laughed with her, though a little anxious tug nagged at her. With how this year had gone, if they kept encountering ghosts like their previous ones, would she even make it to Neale's age? Would the others?

Raven kept her face neutral, chatting through a few logistics before leaving the lounge. The lift up to the top deck was spacious and smooth but still seemed to take an eternity, her foot tapping impatiently the entire way. The moment the doors – with gilt edging, because even the lifts were fancy – slid open, she burst out onto the top deck, the beams from the late-morning sun already hot. She leaned against the railings, closing her eyes and letting the sea air on her face, the wind in her hair, the tang of the briny ocean and the warmth of the sun ground her.

She was with her team. She was safe. And she would keep them safe.

This would just be a normal spirit, someone they could help pass over smoothly and then collect a large pay cheque and a glowing recommendation from the ship.

It had to be.

But even the raucous shriek of the gulls overhead couldn't drown out the memory of a low, urgent voice whispering 'find it' in her ear in the darkness.

CHAPTER TWENTY-TWO

ARCHER COULD SEE THE EXHAUSTION etched on Éabha's face as they prepared to leave the meeting room. They'd done another round of crew interviews – nothing new or exciting had come up, which made him feel like they'd used up Éabha's energy for no reason – and so after a few hours, they'd finished up to go and get ready for dinner. As they walked along the corridor to the cabins, he couldn't stop noticing how her shoulders were slumped and her eyes were heavy, almost unfocused. There was none of the brightness that normally shone from their shimmering blue.

'You should rest,' he said gently, taking her by the elbow.

'I was planning on it,' she said.

'You don't need to do the séance tonight,' he said. 'I'm sure Raven can handle the clairvoyance part–'

'Raven hasn't led one yet and it's something she should prepare for, not just have it sprung on her,' Éabha said firmly.

'She led the one in the Merrion Hub,' Archer said quietly.

'The one where she almost died?'

He was just trying to look out for her. Why did she act like he was insulting her?

'Archer,' she stopped, looking up at him. Two guests passed by, and they fell silent, waiting until they were out of earshot. 'I told you I can do this. It's safer with two of us.' Éabha rested her hand on his arm, squeezing gently. 'I know what I'm doing,'

'I know you do,' Archer said, covering her hand with his. 'But I can see how tired you are. You shouldn't overdo it.'

'I can be the judge of that,' she said.

She didn't get it, did she? They could all see how hard she was pushing herself. Even on her good days she still wore out easily. If there was a spirit – one that had already drained her in order to knock the video camera off the shelf – what would happen in a séance? She had so little energy left: what if this spirit took the last of it? A flicker of worry snaked up his spine. And what if that took the rest of the team with her? They could all end up in danger.

He had thought he'd lost her once before and couldn't face that again. He couldn't be responsible for losing her. Or for anything happening to the others because he couldn't make the tough decisions.

She was studying him, her brow furrowed. 'You don't trust me,' Éabha said flatly.

'I do,' Archer protested. 'I know you'd never lie. I just worry you'll push yourself too hard because you don't want to let anyone down. And I don't want you to have to spend three days recovering from doing a séance when you're already tired.'

'Isn't that my choice to make? The only way I can figure out how to live with this is if I test it. I might sometimes overdo it, but I'd never put anyone in danger. Raven and I have been putting together a plan to make sure of that. We were going to explain together at the pre-séance meeting.'

Envy rose like bile in his throat for a moment. He used to be the person Éabha bounced ideas off. Now it was Raven. It was because she could actually help, because she had the same gifts, he knew that, but it made him feel so … useless.

'Oh,' he said.

'I know I can't always judge beforehand how much energy I'm going to use on something, and I get why that is concerning to you,' Éabha said. 'But I've gotten really good at knowing when I'm approaching my limit. And I've promised Raven the moment I feel my energy start to cross into warning-light zone, I'll let her take over. I'll have my bracelet and earrings to hand too, so they'll go on immediately, cut me off from the spirit if she's there. We're feeling pretty confident about it, but we need to test it.'

'What if the test goes wrong?' he asked.

'Then that was my choice, my mistake, not yours. You're not responsible for me, Archer.' She looked at him steadily. 'I would never do anything to endanger this team.'

It was a solid plan, and Raven wouldn't agree to it if she didn't believe in it. He wished that was enough to quell the roiling nerves filling his gut.

'I can't see you get hurt again,' he said, putting a hand to her cheek.

She closed her eyes, leaning into his touch for a moment, before stepping back.

'And you think I don't worry about you? I watched you almost burn to death, Archer. We've both taken risks in this job and will continue to as long as we're part of PSI. I need to know you support me.'

'Always, Éabha,' he said, his voice thick with emotion. Did she know just how much she meant to him? How important she was – would always be?

Her gait was slow and heavy as they walked back to the cabins. Archer asked her what she thought of the food so far, just to break the silence more than anything, and there was a long pause before she said, 'I'm really sorry, but I can't process words right now. I just need to lie down. I'll be OK after a few hours' sleep. I think I'll rest through dinner and join you at midnight when the dining room is cleared.'

Her voice was slow, and every word seemed to cost her. He had seen her like this before, when even basic answers were too much for her. She needed to be in the dark, alone and in silence, until she had rested enough. Was six hours really enough for her to be OK for the séance? And she wouldn't have had dinner either. What if she thought she was able for it and she wasn't?

'You'll get me for the séance?' she asked him at the door. Her words were laboured, her hand heavy on the door as she swiped the card. 'I'll be OK,' she said, squeezing his hand. 'I just need a rest. And I'll let Raven take over the moment I get any warning signs. Just come get me when the team is ready, OK? If I don't answer, let yourself in and wake me up.'

Sometimes sounds didn't wake Éabha up straight away; as she was hard of hearing, they had to be really loud to wake her if she was deeply asleep. Touching her would wake her instantly, but she wasn't overly sensitive to noises. The alarm on her phone was so loud in the mornings to make sure that she heard it that the first time it had gone off, he'd startled awake, falling out of bed with a heavy thud. Éabha's frantic apologies had quickly changed to peals of laughter once she'd confirmed he was all right.

'OK,' he said, kissing her cheek.

She disappeared inside, the heavy sound of the door closing echoing the weight gathering in the pit of his stomach.

Six hours later, the image of her exhausted face was still front and centre in his mind as he and Fionn sat in their cabin, organising the equipment.

'Still no Éabha?' Raven asked, when she and Davis joined them in the boys' cabin, after checking the arrangements with Neale one last time.

'Arch is going to get her at the last minute, when we're sure we're ready. She needed a rest,' Fionn said, stacking some EVP recorders into a bag.

Raven nodded thoughtfully. 'That was a good call. We've had a few late nights and some busy days since we got here.'

'And we have a pretty solid theory now,' Davis said, smiling.

'Let's hope that turns out to be true. And that this séance is less dramatic than our other ones,' Raven said.

'You and Éabha are evenly matched for séances, right?' Archer said, trying to be casual. He was still hoping Éabha would change her mind about going ahead with their test and sit this one out. Maybe if Raven agreed she could do it by herself it would be easier to steer Éabha in that direction ... he'd feel less guilty about trying to do it if Raven said it would be OK if Éabha didn't come at all.

'I guess, if by evenly matched you mean we've both nearly died during one?' Raven said, sarcasm underlining every word. Éabha had been possessed by The Lady in the first one, and Raven nearly trapped in a painting in the second. 'Éabha definitely has read more and learned more from Lizzie, though. And she has more control over her energy; I'm still getting the hang of mine. We don't exactly have rogue spirits to practise on between surveys. It's definitely better that she takes the lead and I step in if needed.'

Raven was probably just being modest or doubting herself. It would be fine if Éabha wasn't there.

Archer didn't let himself consider why he was so desperate to convince himself of that.

The team readied themselves, picking up bags of equipment. Raven outlined her and Éabha's plan for the séance, Fionn listening intently, eyes serious behind his glasses while Davis nodded approvingly. 'It's the most controlled way you can test it and, so far, this potential ghost definitely seems the least homicidal out of the ones we've faced.'

Even Davis was on side. But what about the risks? What if Éabha misjudged, or– anxiety made his chest tighten and he tried to keep his face neutral. Hopefully, Raven hadn't started bringing her walls down yet so she wouldn't sense how strongly he was freaking out internally.

'I'll get Éabha and meet you there,' Archer told them.

'Oh, Arch, can you drop this in too?' Raven asked, gesturing at a black backpack. She'd changed out of her dinner dress into her survey clothes in the boys' cabin, to avoid waking Éabha before she had to get up. Raven complained about having to dress up, but he'd seen how carefully she folded away her dress and delicately placed it into the backpack she was now handing him. Which meant either his big sister cared more about what rich people thought of her than she was willing to admit, or she'd enjoyed wearing it more than she'd ever say out loud. Ever since she'd come back into his life, she'd kept surprising him in different ways.

Raven handed Archer her room key. 'Just in case you need it,' she said.

The others waved and walked off, and he turned to go back to the girls' cabin. He knocked on the door, the bag heavy in his hand as he waited.

No answer.

He knocked again.

What if something was wrong?

The seconds ticked by and there was no answer. Worry started to gnaw at him, a creeping concern that made him swipe Raven's door key. Gently, he pushed the door open.

'Éabha?'

It took a few moments for his eyes to adjust in the dim light. Éabha was fast asleep in bed, curled on her side, her hair tousled and mouth frowning as though she was having a bad dream. Even in the weak light he could see the dark circles under her eyes.

How could she still look that exhausted when she was asleep?

He quietly put Raven's bag on the floor, took a step towards her, and hesitated.

She'd told him get her, to come in and wake her up but, looking at her now, it just didn't feel right.

She'd push herself too hard if she came.

Quietly, ignoring the shrieking voice that yelled 'traitor' at him, Archer left the room and closed the door.

CHAPTER TWENTY-THREE

RAVEN TRIED TO CALM HERSELF as she helped Fionn and Davis set up candles in the now-deserted dining room, but even focusing on methodically lighting candles didn't help push away the writhing sensation in her gut.

It would be fine. Éabha would be with her this time, not on the other side of a portrait with her life depending on Raven not messing up. Éabha was going to lead it. All Raven needed to do was be there and take over if Éabha's energy got too low. And even if she *did* have to take over, Éabha would still be there to help and tell her what to do if she needed assistance.

Easy.

So why was the dread rising up in her?

Yes, both séances the team had attempted before had ended in them nearly dying. But they had been on the back foot those times. This time they were prepared. Calm. Ready. Completely different circumstances.

And if no one got possessed or sucked into an inanimate object, it would be their most successful séance to date.

It was a low bar. Surely they could meet it?

Not for the first time, she wished Cordelia were here.

She took out her phone, tapping out a message and pressing send before she could talk herself out of it.

I miss you, love you.

Her heart lifted as she saw 'typing' appear under Cordelia's name.

Is everything OK? Are you about to do something reckless?

The response made her sigh, warm affection filling her as she typed back quickly.

Can't I tell my girlfriend I love her without there being a life-ending threat nearby? she asked.

You can. But considering your track record, you'll forgive me if I have some trust issues.

Raven couldn't suppress her snort of laughter. She could hear Cordelia saying that, see the arch of her eyebrow as she did, a sardonic look that Raven could only wipe away with kisses.

How she missed her. The only person who always called her out on her bullshit, who made her softer, more open.

'Stop flirting and get back to work.' Davis's voice pulled her away from her phone. He smirked and she elbowed him in the ribs as she went past him to light the last few candles.

'Look, given how our séances have gone before, I reserve the right to say my goodbyes,' she said. Her tone was flippant, but one look at the boys said they saw through it.

Dammit, she'd really lost her edge once she'd started telling people how she felt.

'You two have got this, Raven,' Davis said seriously. 'These are very different circumstances to the last ones.'

Sometimes Davis said something that made her realise how alike their thought processes could be. It made sense, considering they'd grown up together – Davis was basically her second brother.

'You've got this, Raven,' Fionn echoed. 'We're all here with you. And no one's life depends on it this time, which is an added perk.'

'That is a bonus, all right,' Raven said.

She and Éabha had prepped a lot for this. They'd been studying with Lizzie and Raven finally had some sort of control over her gifts. It would be fine.

And she'd have her friend beside her, leading it, guiding them both, and they'd have their team supporting them.

The door opened and they all whirled, for a moment afraid that a late-night drunken guest had ignored the 'closed for cleaning' sign and tried to come in anyway.

A circle of candles was pretty difficult to explain.

Luckily, it was just Archer.

Just. Archer.

'Where's Éabha?' Raven asked, trying to sound more casual than she felt.

'She told us to go ahead without her,' Archer said. 'She's still exhausted.'

Raven's stomach sank and she didn't miss the look Fionn and Davis exchanged. Éabha was the clairvoyancy prodigy. Raven didn't exactly fill anyone – herself included – with the same degree of confidence.

'She said Raven is more than capable of leading it,' Archer added.

He looked off, his eyes sliding from Raven's as he spoke. The way, since they were kids, he had looked when he was lying or hiding something.

He obviously didn't share his girlfriend's confidence.

It stung, a little.

But then how could she expect them to believe in her when she didn't believe in herself?

She rolled her shoulders back, pulling herself up to her full height of five-foot-two, which admittedly wasn't objectively impressive, but she had intimidated six-foot-tall drunk bankers out of Origin. A ghost wouldn't be a problem.

Besides, Lizzie had told them, over and over, that emotions impacted everything. She needed to put her doubt aside and focus.

'Right, lads, our clairvoyance expert has spoken,' she said, clapping her hands together. 'We've gone over this a million times with Lizzie; after the second round of "multiple team members nearly dying" she made it a priority, can't begin to think why.'

Fionn laughed.

'This isn't a big showdown. We just want to have a chat, find out some information. Emphasis on EVPs, so Fionn, do you have the voice recorders all set up?'

EVPs had always been Raven's favourite: sitting in the dark, asking questions, ears straining for a response. Going back through the audio files and sometimes finding something even clearer than they'd expected. The thrill of that discovery.

Now she didn't just listen for answers, she felt them too. She had an extra sense, which technically was an advantage, but it was always when she used their traditional ghost hunting tech that she was most at home. It was comforting. Familiar.

The team snapped into survey mode. This wasn't even really a full séance, more a half-survey/half-séance. A fact-finding mission. The ghost had shown it could be hostile when provoked – and if it was who they suspected, Raven didn't blame her for wanting to shove a few people around the place – so they needed to be careful, but this wasn't The Lady level, not Adrian level. Hopefully.

And Éabha would never have told Archer to go ahead without her if she didn't truly believe Raven could do it.

A small, warm glow rose in Raven. She and Éabha hadn't exactly got off to a strong start – Raven's fault, mostly, though Éabha had definitely demonstrated she wasn't all sweet passivity. But the other girl had become a very good friend to her. She was the only person who truly, fully understood what this was like, and her confidence in her meant a lot.

Even if she really, really wished Éabha had come.

But she'd seen Éabha push through some pretty bad days, and if the other girl didn't think she was able for it, she must be severely exhausted. It was good she wasn't forcing herself past her limits.

They quickly finished setting up the room, with candles lit, a protective circle of salt and crystals on the floor surrounding the team. Cameras were set up around the room on tripods, and each team member had a voice recorder. Fionn placed two EMF readers at opposite sides of the circle.

'OK, so we're going to use her name, right? And if no one shows up, we know our theory isn't correct,' Davis said, already sounding offended at the concept that a theory he believed was correct might not be.

'Yep,' Raven said.

She checked her hair was still firmly in its plait, more to give her hands something to do than because she thought it needed it. They stepped into the circle of candles and salt, Fionn eying the flickering flames warily.

'I can't believe we have to use real ones,' he said. 'While on a very flammable boat.'

Archer gestured at the multiple fire extinguishers he'd placed around the circle, just outside the salt. 'We have precautions in place. It'll be fine.'

Slowly, Fionn peeled his gaze away from the dancing flames. 'Of course,' he said, a flicker of uncertainty in his voice.

Raven had a sudden flashback, to a coughing Fionn on his hands and knees outside Hyacinth House. He and Cordelia had pulled her from the burning house, while Davis and Archer were trapped inside, Éabha trying to help them. Fionn and Cordelia had saved her life, but she'd immediately tried to run back in, Cordelia holding her back as she screamed and screamed until Davis and Éabha had appeared in the doorway, a barely conscious Archer in their arms. She'd been focused on the house for the long, agonising minutes before the others had appeared, but she'd heard Fionn's sobs as he'd coughed, struggling to get to his feet. He would have run back in himself, despite the dislocated shoulder, despite the fact he could barely breathe, if he had had the strength to stand up. He would never have forgiven himself for leaving the others inside, even though he'd saved Raven's life by doing so, if Éabha and Davis hadn't managed to drag Archer out. She knew that instinctively, because she would have been the exact same.

Fionn dealt with everything through humour and avoidance, but that made it too easy for the rest of them to forget how deep the scars from Hyacinth House ran for all of them, Fionn included.

'OK, everyone into the circle,' she said, ushering them in through the gap she'd left then closing it with the remaining salt. 'And don't–'

'–break the salt,' they all chorused.

Archer flinched at the memory of what had happened last time the salt circle was broken. By him.

Raven pretended she hadn't noticed even as a pang of sadness surged through her. Would they ever be able to conduct a séance without reliving past traumas?

The four of them sat, legs crossed, at different points of the circle. Raven inhaled slowly, her fingers finding her amethyst pendant for comfort.

'Let's take a few deep breaths together,' she said, the fingers of her left hand still holding the pendant. 'Clear your mind of any worries, anything you're thinking about needing to do after this. This is about us, in the here and now. Breathe in ...'

She was relieved at how easily the familiar opening sequence came to her. Lizzie had had them both memorise and practise it, but she'd never led the team in it. As she breathed, she consciously lowered the brick wall in her mind, the shield, and started to send out her energy. She could see it in her mind's eye: a purple glow forming around her, that she pushed out and away from her, probing the space around her. She could leave it like this, as one solid piece radiating from her, or shape it into tendrils, reaching out for specific things. It was something she excelled at: manipulating and shaping her energy. She could use it as an investigative tool, or a weapon. For now, it was merely investigation, to see what energy was in the room besides her own. She hoped that was all she would need to use it for. One by one, she became aware of the energies of the three boys: Davis, focused and determined; Fionn, his apprehension softening with each long exhale; Archer, a lingering sense of guilt still hovering around him. Thinking of breaking the salt circle at Hyacinth House must have affected him more than she'd thought.

Raven finished the breathing exercises, opened her eyes and looked at the team.

'We ask that we are joined in the circle only by those that mean us no harm,' she said. 'We come in good faith, to listen and to understand, and ask that only spirits with the same intentions join us.'

Raven took a long pause, the sound of her own breathing mixing with the others. They breathed in tandem: slow, steady inhalations, a rhythm set by the exercises. It grounded her, even as she became aware of the silence outside the circle, creating a blanket of stillness as though the world outside the circle had paused.

'We ask that the spirit of Philippa Foster join us in the circle and speak to us, if you mean us no harm.'

She left a long pause, her energy alert, waiting for the sense of anything other than the energies of the team.

'Philippa Foster, we ask you to join us. We wish only to understand, and to help if we can,' Raven said.

Another long pause.

Nothing.

Maybe they were wrong? Maybe Philippa wasn't the ghost?

She tried to shove down the momentary spike of doubt that pierced through her. She needed to keep her emotions steady.

Luckily, repressing emotions was what Raven did best.

'Join us,' she repeated.

Then she felt it. The pull, the clear sign that something was trying to siphon her energy, and saw all around the circle the flames of the candles begin to dance and flicker. She put up enough of a shield to stop the draw on her while still keeping her energy aware.

She felt a little surge of pride at how naturally that came to her.

The energy shift warned her that it was about to happen. The others did not have the same foreshadowing. So when the figure of a woman, rippling and faint, appeared in the centre, not even Davis managed to avoid jumping.

'It's about time,' the woman said irritably.

CHAPTER TWENTY-FOUR

'THANK YOU FOR JOINING US,' Raven said, biting down her retort that it was the ghost who had taken three invitations and five minutes to actually appear.

The woman arched an eyebrow at her, and Raven wondered if she could tell what she was thinking. It was definitely Philippa Foster; she looked exactly the same as in her photograph. She was wearing the long, red gown and high heels she'd been wearing the night of the accident – Raven had seen them in CCTV stills from earlier in the night.

'I'm sorry, I've been trying to get someone's attention for months,' the woman said. Her voice echoed slightly, like she was on the phone with bad signal, but every word was clear and, besides that slight echo, sounded completely normal. 'Being murdered can make you a bit tetchy.'

'Murdered?' It was Archer who spoke, just as Raven processed the woman's statement. Realised fully what that meant. The spirit turned to face him, and Raven shot him an admonishing look. Only one of them was supposed to speak.

'Yes, murdered. I know the crew – and my ex – would have you believe that it was a tragic accident.'

'Your ex was on the boat too?' Raven asked, confused. The file had said Philippa was travelling with her husband.

'Well, I didn't get to divorce him on account of being dead, but I feel that if your husband murders you, you should at least get to call him your ex in the afterlife,' the woman snapped. The echo in her voice grew stronger and her form began to rise up off the floor, her hair flying back as though blown by an invisible wind and she glowed brighter. As she did, the flames on the candles rose up, a surge of heat coming from them.

Raven needed to calm her down.

Though in fairness, if she had been murdered and everyone said she'd simply had too much champagne and fallen off a boat, she'd be a pretty angry spirit too.

'What can we do to help?' Raven asked quietly, keeping her voice calm and hoping it was the right question.

Philippa settled again, her hair floating back down around her face, the glow fading.

'Show people the truth,' she said. 'Please. I don't want to be here, but I can't move on with everyone thinking he's some wonderful man who suffered a tragedy. *He* was the tragedy.'

'OK ...' Raven said slowly, her brain whirring. 'And how do we do that?' She winced, hoping it wouldn't set off another ghostly tantrum. 'It's just that the CCTV is gone, and while *we* believe you, the police won't believe *us* if we tell them a ghost told us. We need evidence.'

'He bribed a crew member to delete the footage. One of the ones with access to security. I ... I don't know his name.'

If Raven didn't know better, she'd say Philippa looked embarrassed.

'I tried to learn everyone's name, but we didn't cross paths before ... and then afterwards ... things get hazy here. I don't always have energy to ... and I need to hide from ...'

She was rambling now and starting to fade in and out of view, her voice growing softer as she did. Raven needed to get her back on track before she disappeared.

'That's OK,' Raven said. 'Describe him to us. Is he still on the boat now?'

Philippa nodded. 'Slicked-back blond hair. An attitude he never shows the guests, but the other members of the crew.'

That sounded familiar.

'My husband – ex-husband – bribed him. But the man kept a copy of the CCTV, either as collateral or, I guess, if he needed more money down the line. He hid it, on the boat.'

'Where?'

'In my old cabin,' Philippa said grimly, her mouth curving up in an angry smile. 'I guess he liked the drama, or irony. There's a loose skirting board in the cabin, next to the bedside table on the right-hand side – pull it out and you'll find a USB stick taped to the back of it. I've been trying to get at it, or get attention, but all I've managed to do is scare a bunch of the crew and a couple of cruise guests. Oops.' She shrugged, a weirdly human gesture for someone who was basically transparent.

There was absolutely no sincerity in the 'oops'. Raven liked her. It was strange dealing with a non-violent spirit for once, one with a relatable personality. Philippa was focused on getting the truth out, and while she'd taken some steps to get their attention that had resulted in a fair few freaked-out people, she hadn't tried to physically harm anyone, even the crew member she knew had helped cover up the murder. She spoke in a way that showed she was used to getting what she wanted, but not in the same entitled, rude way other guests on the ship spoke. Plus, she hadn't tried to possess or kill her, which was a first.

'We'll get it,' Raven said.

'Thank you,' Philippa said, the warmth of her gratitude flowing into her energy and mixing with Raven's. She turned slowly, scrutinising each member of the team as she pivoted. Raven studied her as she did, and realised with a jolt that her feet didn't rest on the floor, but millimetres above it. 'I mean it: thank you. I'm sorry for being a bit dramatic. It was the only way to get you all here.'

'You are the chillest spirit we've ever encountered,' Raven said. She paused. 'Though maybe you could stop pushing people at dinner time? And locking the guests in enclosed spaces?'

Philippa's brow furrowed.

'Oh, that wasn't me,' she said, fear growing in her eyes. 'It must be the other one.' She shuddered, wrapping her arms around herself. 'I'll be so glad to move on. He scares me.'

An icy dread spread over Raven. Her eyes darted to Archer, then Davis. Fionn was only visible through the haze of the ghost herself, so she couldn't see his expression, but the others were clearly trying hard not to burst out with a bunch of questions.

'What other one?' Raven asked, trying to keep her voice steady.

'The angry one. He was here long before me. He used to leave me alone, I guessed he thought that I'd already got what I deserved,' she said. 'So I wasn't too afraid of him at first. But he's become more terrifying the longer I've been here. He's unravelling … Be very careful with him.'

'Do you know who he is?' Raven said.

Philippa tightened her arms around her torso like she was holding herself, her shoulders hunched as she shook her head. 'I hide from him. He's started hunting me down, stealing my energy. I didn't know that was what he was doing at first. I think he forgets about me sometimes, and I can build my energy back up when he does. He's started doing it more and more and there's this feeling ... I can't explain it. But every time I see him, he's more ... uncanny. He feels less ... less human. When I can manifest, I've been mostly in the security room or my cabin, trying to get someone to find that damned USB stick. Apart from when you all arrived, and I tried following you around for a bit. But it's when I manifest that he remembers I'm here. And tonight took a lot from me, he probably remembers me now. I need to hide. Please, you'll help me, right?' Philippa was becoming agitated again, a restless, crackling energy starting to emerge from her like static as her anxiety grew.

'We will. We can't get it tonight. It's too late and there's guests in the cabin. But it will be first thing in the morning, as soon as the guests go out for the day,' Raven said.

'And you won't tell anyone that could let that man know you're onto him?'

'We'll go to Neale and Neale only,' Raven confirmed.

Philippa relaxed visibly.

'Thank you. You have no idea how much it means to know they won't get away with this.'

The spirit's voice choked up and Raven could see glistening tears starting to run down her face.

'We're here to help you,' Raven said awkwardly.

Emotionally supporting spirits was, in some ways, even more complex than trying not to be murdered by them.

'Thank you,' Philippa said. She turned slowly again, as though taking in their faces one last time. 'So young,' she murmured. 'You're all so young.' Then she whipped her head to the side, looking at the wall as though she expected someone – something – to come through it. Waves of pure terror crashed from her and Raven solidified her shields so she didn't drown in it.

'I need to go,' Philippa said. 'I can feel him, the other one ... he's sensed something's happening.'

Raven cast her senses out further and she could feel it too – an angry, curious energy coming from the depths of the boat.

'End it so he doesn't come and investigate,' Philippa whispered urgently, her eyes wide. 'I can't let him find me. And I don't think he'd be as happy about your presence as I am. Please, find the USB stick. Let me move on.'

'We will,' Raven said. She needed to formally dismiss the spirit. Taking a deep breath, she started.

'Thank you for joining us in our circle. We bid you farewell.'

Philippa shimmered slightly before blinking out of existence. Raven hoped she had somewhere to hide, that they hadn't kept her there too long. She leaned forwards and blew out the main candle, keeping her senses on the angry, curious energy coming from the bowels of the ship. She felt its attention turn from them and fade, and she blew out a breath.

'Well, that was ... not what we expected,' Fionn said, looking around at them.

'A second spirit. How did we not guess that?' Archer said, shaking his head. 'It's why some people saw a man in a crew uniform, while others smelt perfume. Two spirits. So simple.'

'I'm actually embarrassed we didn't hypothesise it,' Davis said, folding his arms and scowling with disapproval. It wasn't directed at the team as a whole, though; Raven knew that. Davis was annoyed with himself. He was always telling them they needed open minds and not to fixate on one theory. He'd be fuming he hadn't considered the possibility of multiple spirits on one ship. They all stood up, shaking the stiffness out their legs after sitting for so long.

'So: prove a murder, find another ghost. That's a unique to-do list,' Fionn said.

'I think we may have undercharged for this one,' Archer said, running a hand through his hair.

'At least the breakfast pastries are great,' Fionn said. 'And besides the whole "prove my murder" task and the dramatic "there's another, angrier ghost bopping around" reveal, she was pretty nice. She didn't try to possess anyone or drop heavy things on our heads. A clear frontrunner for "nicest ghost we've met".'

Archer chuckled. Smiling, Raven lifted a candle to blow it out. She could feel her energetic walls snapping back into place while the others kept discussing Philippa's revelation. Without the spirit to focus on, the others' emotions were starting to rise up and swamp her own. Fionn's excitement, Davis's annoyance, both underpinned with exhilaration. She caught a brief sensation of what felt like guilt from Archer just as her walls snapped firmly into place, shutting absolutely everything out as she took off her amethyst pendant. It was a relief not to be able to feel everything around her.

It meant, however, that just a few moments later, the sudden sound of a voice behind her made her almost drop the candle she was about to blow out.

'Sounds like an interesting case. You'll have to fill me in, since no one bothered to wake me.'

As one, the team turned to see Éabha standing in the doorway. There was silence as Éabha's words hovered in the air between them.

CHAPTER TWENTY-FIVE

ÉABHA GLANCED AROUND the room. Archer was no clairvoyant, but even he could feel the shift in the energy as the silence lingered.

'You did the séance without me?' she asked. She looked at Raven, every word underlined by hurt. 'I thought we were doing this together.'

Raven looked confused. 'Archer said you …' She broke off, glancing over at him. Archer could practically see the pieces slotting into place in her mind.

'Archer said that I *what?*' There was a hard edge to Éabha's voice now.

Raven hesitated, looking over at Archer again as though waiting for him to interject. He opened his mouth to speak, then shut it again.

'What did Archer say?' Éabha repeated.

Raven stared at him. Her reluctance to reveal that he had told them what was now clearly a total lie would have warmed him under any other circumstances, his big sister protecting him again.

'He said that you'd told him you needed to keep resting, and to do it without you.'

Archer whipped his head around to stare at Davis as he spoke. His friend wasn't looking at him, only at Éabha, his arms folded and his jaw set.

'After I repeatedly told you I could do it,' she said flatly. 'That we had a failsafe if at any point I realised I couldn't.'

'I was worried. I was protecting you—'

'No. You were making my decisions for me,' Éabha cut across him, scowling, her arms folded tightly across her chest, blue eyes pure ice. 'How is that any different from what my parents did to me?' Her voice caught. 'I had years of them controlling me, of them deciding what I could and couldn't do. I can't ... I won't go through it again.'

Her words pummelled him like an avalanche of rocks.

'Éabhs, that's not fair, that's not—'

'No, what isn't fair is you not listening to me. Not trusting me when I tell you I can do something. You were the first person who believed in me, Archer. And you've broken my heart by showing me that you've stopped.'

How was Éabha not getting this? He was helping her. Protecting her, the way he had failed to before.

'I *do* believe in you, Éabha. But you're pushing yourself too much. I couldn't let you put yourself in danger yet again for an investigation.'

'That was my choice to make, Archer! You don't know what I can or can't do. You have to trust me to know my own limits. And if I push myself too far, that's on me and no one else, but nothing gives you the right to take that choice away from me!'

'I'm the leader of this team and I have to make decisions for the good of it. If something goes wrong with you, it endangers the entire team. Has it occurred to you that none of us want to go through what we went through last spring again?' The words burst from his mouth before he could stop them.

Éabha recoiled. 'What *you* went through? I'm sorry, I missed the part where you were dragged into a portrait and drained of your life's energy by a narcissistic, evil spirit. One who also took my freedom to choose away from me.'

The parallel felt like a punch to his stomach. It wasn't fair, not at all.

'Do you know what it was like seeing you trapped in that portrait? I was losing my mind! I didn't know if I could save you. And I couldn't. Without Raven, we would have lost you. *I* would have lost you.' His voice cracked as he finished speaking.

For a moment Éabha softened, looking around the group. Archer's eyes followed hers as she took in Davis, his face impassive, Raven's eyes flitting between himself and Éabha as though watching a tennis match, Fionn apparently finding something very interesting at his feet while simultaneously trying to melt into the wall behind him.

'I understand that was difficult for you, Archer. For all of you. But you had no right to make that decision for me. Or for the rest of the team. I wasn't being reckless. I told you I could tell if my energy got too low, and I told you Raven and I had developed a plan for what to do if that happened.'

The weight of exactly what he'd done landed on him all at once and all the air left his lungs. If he didn't make this right, it would crush him.

'Éabhs, I–' He took a step towards her but she moved back, raising a hand in front of her.

'No. I can't. I need–'

'Please,' Archer said, his voice cracking again. He took another step towards her. He needed to hug her, to hold her, to tell her how sorry he was. To explain that he knew he'd made a mistake, but that his heart was in the right place – in her hands. Where it had been almost from the moment she'd walked into the PSI office and asked to join the team.

'I said STOP, Archer!' Éabha yelled. 'Will you please just listen to what I am *telling* you I need, not what you *think* I need?'

The ferocity in her voice stopped him in his tracks.

'Éabha, he really was trying to help,' Fionn murmured.

Archer turned to him gratefully as Éabha spun around to look at him.

'It wasn't right—'

'No, it wasn't,' Davis interjected harshly.

'—but Archer wasn't trying to undermine you,' Fionn continued.

'Well, he did,' Éabha said. She looked back at Archer, and the mixture of anger and sadness in her eyes made him want to fall to the floor and weep. 'You did.'

She turned to walk away. 'I need some time.'

The door closed firmly behind her, and Archer was left with only the damning silence of the rest of the team staring at him.

CHAPTER TWENTY-SIX

DAVIS WAS TRYING VERY HARD not to scream in frustration.

They had one ghost whose murder they needed to expose, another ghost – the one responsible for the angrier, scarier experiences people had had – to identify and deal with, and Archer had decided to make the team do a séance without their most experienced clairvoyant despite her saying she was well enough and wanted to do it.

Davis was used to his logic tempering Archer's emotion. But the temptation to grab his friend and shake him, while asking what exactly his thought process had been, was almost overwhelming. Archer had looked around at the expression on everyone's faces, mumbled something about needing some air and left. Hopefully not to find Éabha – she had made it all too clear she needed space from him.

'What's the protocol for informing people of a murder when your source is a ghost?' Fionn asked, glancing from Davis to Raven and back again.

Normally, Davis would want to have it out with Archer, but he knew right now they all needed to cool down. He also wanted to ask the others what the fuck they thought Archer was thinking, but Fionn's question was a good one.

'Neale knows what she hired us to do. We can tell her what we know, she can make an excuse to check the cabin and then I guess she goes from there in terms of turning it over to the police?'

'It should be enough for Philippa to move on, at least,' Raven said.

'And then we can figure out who the hell the other one is,' Davis said. He didn't try to hide the frustration in his voice. He was annoyed with himself for not even considering the possibility that there was more than one ghost. It was so simple, so obvious. He ought to have thought of it.

'We should figure out who's going to talk to Neale,' he said instead.

'Archer and Raven,' Fionn said promptly. Raven gave him a look that made it clear she would prefer to be nowhere near that conversation.

'What?' Fionn protested. 'Archer's the CEO, and Raven led the séance: you're best placed to explain.'

'You are, unfortunately, right,' Raven sighed.

'Is Archer going to be in a state to have that conversation?' Davis asked. 'His judgement is clearly lacking right now.' There was a bitterness in his tone, and he knew he should probably temper it, but he was angry and needed to let it out somehow. Archer had no business cutting Éabha out of the séance without her consent. And he'd pushed Raven into a position where she had to lead one, for the first time, with no back-up or time to prepare herself.

Raven had done a really good job, but it could have gone wrong so, so easily.

They were a team. And yes, Archer led them, but he didn't get to make decisions for them.

Éabha's *face* ...

Fionn looked at his watch.

'It's two o'clock. Neale's up from about six, right?'

'Yeah, I think so,' Raven said. She blanched. 'Wait, does this mean …'

'That you and Archer should find her first thing before the guests are up? Afraid so,' Fionn said, clapping her on the shoulder.

'I just wanted some sleep,' Raven said, dropping her head into her hands. Davis tried to hold back a smile – this was the closest he'd ever seen Raven go to being dramatic.

'Look, if you're up at six, you can casually let Neale know that a guest was murdered and a crew member hid the evidence and still have time to video call Cordelia before breakfast,' he said cheerfully.

Raven's face brightened. 'Yeah, I can talk to her before–' She broke off, clamping her mouth shut, a faint blush rising on her cheeks.

Raven was flustered.

Oh, this was hilarious. Enough to momentarily take Davis's mind off everything.

'It's OK to admit you like your girlfriend, Raven,' he said.

She rolled her eyes at him. 'I'm aware, Davis,' she said snarkily.

Raven was definitely flustered.

'Cool, so: report that there was a murder, tell Neale where the evidence is, casually mention there is, in fact, another, angrier ghost on board that we still need to find, chat to your girlfriend, have some coffee and a croissant,' Fionn said. 'All in a morning's work.'

'That only *I* have to do while you two sleep in,' Raven grumbled.

'From the look on Davis's face right now, I really don't think we should be sending him anywhere with Archer,' Fionn said lightly.

Davis glared at him, but he knew Fionn was right. They needed to keep things together professionally, or at least appear that way to the client. And they had a lot to deal with now. He needed to not get into it with Archer. Distance would be good.

If only they weren't sharing a cabin.

'He meant well, Davis,' Fionn said. There was no teasing in his voice now, just uncharacteristically earnest gentleness.

'He lied to everyone and put us all in danger.'

'I didn't do *that* bad a job,' Raven said, folding her arms. She smirked, like she was trying to lighten the mood, though there was a tightness around her eyes. Davis didn't know if it was from the Archer situation or actual worry about how the séance had gone.

'You did great, Raven, seriously. But it wasn't fair to put you in that position with no notice, and no back-up. What if Philippa hadn't been so agreeable? And what if the other ghost had turned up too? You'd have had to face them both on your own.'

Raven frowned. 'You have a point,' she said, almost reluctantly.

Raven was still making up for having abandoned Archer for years. And the rest of the team – it had hurt him as well when she cut them out. They'd practically been siblings. Davis knew that made her hesitant to call any of them out sometimes. And she never fully sided against Archer even when she didn't completely agree with him.

'I don't think it was fair of him to make Éabha's decisions for her, but I understand where he was coming from,' Raven said. 'Just … consider me neutral on this, OK? I need to be there for everyone. And right now, I just want to get the whole "murdered ghost needing us to find evidence for her" thing out of the way.'

'Is it just me or are the jobs getting more complicated the more we do?' Fionn asked.

'I mean, no one has tried to kill us,' Raven said. 'That's a nice development.'

'No one has tried to kill us *so far*,' Fionn said.

Raven opened her mouth to retort, then snapped it shut.

No one could say Fionn didn't have a point.

'Tomorrow we need to dive back into the files, see if we can find anything,' Davis said. 'I have a few more crew chats lined up too. Éabha and I can work on those.'

'Probably best to split things up for a while,' Fionn said.

The mood shifted, the awkwardness seeping back into the room. Davis had no idea how he was going to deal with Archer. Normally, whenever they clashed, they'd have it out, give each other space to cool off, have it out again, and inevitably reach some sort of peace deal.

How could he get space when Archer was sleeping less than two feet away from him? And they were on a mega yacht heading out to sea?

Davis knew the ship was over a hundred metres long, but it was starting to feel claustrophobic.

CHAPTER TWENTY-SEVEN

RAVEN HAD HAD SOME STRANGE conversations in her lifetime, but 'a ghost told us she was murdered on your ship and here is where the evidence is hidden' was definitely a new one. She'd met Archer, who was pale with dark circles under his eyes and looking like he hadn't slept for even a moment, outside his cabin just before six o'clock. When Raven got back to the cabin the night before, Éabha had been in bed, curled up on her side, cocooned in blankets. Raven had asked her if she was OK and she'd said yes, she just needed to sleep, but Raven had definitely heard the other girl's muffled sobs later in the night. She'd lain there, agonising over whether to say something, but had no idea what to say to Éabha. So, instead, she'd stayed quiet until eventually exhaustion from the séance and the long day took over. It had seemed like she'd just shut her eyes when her alarm went off again.

Neale's face was hopeful when they found her at her office, though her expression quickly fell when she saw their expressions. Shutting the door behind them, they'd sat and quickly explained everything.

'Well, at least there's one easy way to find out if this is true,' Neale said grimly. She called in a steward and asked him to prep one of the deluxe cabins.

'We'll tell the guests we're upgrading them as the air conditioning is causing issues for them and we want to apologise for that,' she said. 'Then, once they've agreed and we've moved their things for them, we'll check the skirting board. If there's something there …'

She pulled at her stiffly starched sleeves. 'Well, we'll deal with that. It's a port day, so I'll be able to notify the authorities at Ajaccio if necessary.'

This felt surreal.

The guests moved quickly, grumbling slightly but mollified by assurances of the superiority of their new luxury cabin with a private section of deck.

'Thankfully, someone dropped out last minute,' Neale told Raven and Archer as they accompanied her to the cabin. Raven's heart was pounding wildly. What if the spirit had been wrong? Or lying? If they pulled out the skirting board and nothing was there, would that make Neale doubt PSI as a team?

Raven didn't need to worry. Neale jimmied out the skirting board and there, taped to the back of it, was a USB stick. Neale swore, and Raven felt a rush of relief. Archer barely reacted at all – he was on autopilot, his brain clearly completely elsewhere.

Probably replaying last night over and over again.

They hadn't mentioned it on the way to Neale. Raven didn't know what to say, to be honest. She wanted to shake him, to ask him how, if even *she* could see that his constant fussing over Éabha was pushing her away, he couldn't. But she also wanted to give him a hug, to tell him it would be OK.

Would it, though? Éabha had looked so hurt and angry, and her quiet sobs had made Raven's heart ache more and more with each one. She was devastated. And, for all his good intentions, Archer had been the one who'd done that to her.

Raven loved her brother, and in so many ways she thought he was the better of the two of them. But he'd messed up. She wanted to fix it for him, step in and help to make up for all the times she'd let him down in the past. But this was something he'd need to fix himself.

She didn't know how to talk about it without saying the wrong thing, making it sound like she was judging him or admonishing him. Davis would be no help – he was furious. Davis was very rigid in his moral compass, and this was something he'd definitely judge Archer for. Fionn, though she was happy he was supporting Archer, wouldn't be one to ask him the hard questions.

And Éabha, most likely, wouldn't be speaking to him any time soon.

So that left her. She could see all the sides and she hated it. Was this what happened when you tried to be emotionally aware?

Part of her missed just running away when things got hard. It had been so much easier. Even though she'd been miserable the whole time. Even though she'd let everyone down.

No, it was time to make up for past mistakes. She'd find a way to support everyone and bring the team back together. Somehow.

She needed to call Cordelia. She'd know what to do. Or at least looking at her beautiful face would make Raven smile for a while.

'We'll take it from here,' Neale told her gravely, clapping her on the shoulder and startling her out of her reverie. 'We need to find out what's on this, and if it's what we think it is, confirm with evidence which crew member hid this. And get the police involved.' She exhaled heavily. 'I really hope I am not about to go and watch a murder,' she said, looking down at the slim black USB stick in her hand. 'I'll let you know the results soon,' she added.

They left the cabin and Neale made sure it was firmly locked behind them.

'I was so happy to get this job,' she said to them with a rueful smile, before adding, 'I'm sorry to ask, but can you make sure to all show up at breakfast? And just a reminder not to mention anything about it outside the cabin. I swear, the walls have ears on this ship, and we can't risk anyone finding out about this.'

They assured her that they would be the soul of normality, then returned to their cabins in silence. Raven's brain was stumbling over everything: the argument, the fact that they might have just uncovered a murder, the way they still had another, angrier ghost to find. She'd felt his energy on the lower decks. She didn't want to get his attention. She shivered, and the fact that Archer didn't even notice showed just how lost he was in his thoughts. They stopped outside his cabin and Raven tried to think of something supportive to say.

Nothing good came to mind.

'I'll see you at breakfast, Little Brother,' she said eventually, reaching up and patting his shoulder. It was the best she could do. It definitely wasn't enough. The way his eyes looked through her, before he nodded and opened the door to his cabin, made her heart want to break. She walked the few doors down to her own cabin, bracing herself to go back inside.

They'd all work it out. They had to.

CHAPTER TWENTY-EIGHT

'OK, I HAVE NO IDEA HOW I'VE never asked you this before,' Éabha began, twirling the straw in her iced coffee. Davis put his book down and looked over at her. She had shown her face at breakfast for the shortest possible period of time, picking at some scrambled eggs she didn't have an appetite for at all and letting Fionn and Davis carry on a conversation around her until she could leave. Archer and Raven had told Neale their information, and Raven's grim nod when she arrived at breakfast confirmed they'd found what they'd expected. They had to wait to hear what Neale found on the USB stick, and what that meant, before they could plan their next move, so Éabha had taken advantage of the unexpected free time to get an iced coffee and sit out on deck. She had been touched when Davis arrived a few minutes after her, holding his own iced coffee and a book, and settled down beside her.

Davis was sitting in the sunshine, long legs stretched out in his linen trousers. The burn scars from Hyacinth House were strongest on his legs, and Éabha couldn't help noticing that even in the Mediterranean heat he never wore shorts. She had no idea if he was a shorts person or not – maybe this was how he'd always been? But a little part of her told her that the long, light trousers and linen shirts were as much a self-conscious choice as a fashionable one.

Éabha had perched in the one shady spot on that part of the deck, the early morning sun already strong. Her pale skin went red the moment she set foot in the sun no matter how much SPF fifty she applied, and she already felt so emotionally raw she had no desire to add burnt skin to the equation. But she'd needed to be outside, with the salt air filling her lungs and the cool breeze refreshing her. Every now and then she looked longingly onshore at the new city they'd arrived at overnight, at the white-sand beaches and bright Corsican buildings of Ajaccio, wishing she could abandon ship for even just a few hours.

'Go on,' Davis said, raising an eyebrow at her. She looked around to double-check there were no guests in the vicinity.

'Did you always believe in ghosts? And the work PSI does? It's just, you're obviously sceptical about a lot of things, and we didn't exactly get off to a smooth start …'

Davis chuckled at that. 'That's a polite way to put it – I was a dick.'

Éabha grinned at him. 'I was choosing to be nice.'

'Ever the PSI sweetheart, Éabha.'

'*Anyway* – I know you kinda grew up with this, so maybe that affected it but I'm just so curious: did you have to be convinced? Or were you all in from the beginning?'

'So I was definitely embarrassed about my parents being paranormal investigators. Like, they're doctors, you know? And because I was young, they wouldn't show me any of the evidence they found. So they couldn't prove to me it was real.' He smiled. 'You can imagine how well I took that.'

Éabha definitely could, and she felt a twinge of sympathy for his poor parents.

'My mum and dad weren't as forthcoming with the details as Archer and Raven's parents. And while they loved the work, it wasn't their full-time job. They didn't mind that I wasn't into it, and they just laughed it off when I tried to debate them. But Archer …' Davis smiled fondly. 'Archer believed so strongly, you know? And it meant so much to him that I believed too. That I would want to investigate with him.'

It was one of the things Éabha loved about Archer – his infectious enthusiasm. He was the heart of PSI, the glue that bound them all together. That had brought them all together, really. He had recruited Fionn and Davis. He had responded to Éabha's message and fought for her to join. He was the reason Raven had come back. It all led back to Archer.

'So, he convinced me to break into his parents' office with him. He wanted to show me the proof, and I … well, you know me. I couldn't resist the promise of data. So we broke in and went through the files and the audio and I just … I knew it was real. Not just that, though: I was *fascinated*. It opened up all these other questions about the world and I knew it was something I wanted to keep studying. Arch still uses it against me when we argue – he'll be like "well, you also didn't think parapsychology was real" and I'll ask him how exactly that applies to whether pineapple belongs on pizza but …' Davis trailed off, the fond smile that had appeared on his face fading into sadness.

They sat together in silence for a few moments.

'Sometimes he needs to remember that just because he's been right before doesn't mean he's always correct,' Davis said eventually.

Éabha *hmmed* in agreement, her own thoughts starting to whirl again. She sipped on her coffee, more for something to do so she didn't have to respond. Davis went back to reading his book and she pretended to read hers, though her eyes stayed fixed on the same line over and over, her mind completely elsewhere.

She had thought she'd felt her heart break before, when she'd packed up her room and left her parents' house for the last time. But that ache was nothing compared to the twisting pain of her heart being wrenched apart at the realisation that, of all people, Archer had lost faith in her. Deep down, part of her had been preparing for her parents to reject her. She'd clung to the hope that it wouldn't come to it, that they'd finally understand her and accept her for who she was. But in the depths of her heart she'd known the moment she started working with PSI that she'd set herself on a path that would most likely end with them disowning her. She'd chosen her truth over their lies, and the price was her relationship with her parents.

She hadn't seen *this* coming, never thought for one moment that Archer would stop believing in her. Archer, the first person to embrace her gifts. The person who opened the door to PSI, who went with her to her first meeting with Lizzie, who'd held her while she cried the night her parents kicked her out. They'd been a team, supporting each other, caring for each other and, even when they'd made mistakes, they'd never turned away from each other. Until now. All of this – whatever Adrian did to her, the effects it was still having, the fears that this was her life now, forever, scared her so much that when she thought about it for too long, anxiety rose up until she felt like she was drowning. She needed to believe there was a way through it, to live with this. *She* needed to believe that she could do this. Her plan had been solid, she knew that. But Archer so clearly doubted it, doubted her, it was hard not to let the seed of scepticism take root. It was so hard to hope and, intentionally or not, he had crushed that hope underfoot. And now ... now she couldn't quieten the voice that whispered she was broken, useless. And always would be.

She kept staring at the pages of her book, willing herself to concentrate on it, to lose herself in the words instead of her own heartache. But she couldn't stop replaying the moment she'd walked into the dining room and realised the team had done the séance without her. Remembering the confusion on their faces as they'd looked from her to Archer. How the heavy-weighted blanket of betrayal had enveloped her. It was all she'd been able to think about last night, as she buried her head in her pillow, willing the soft material to soak up the tears and stop them falling. As her tears had finally started to slow, another sensation had kindled within her: a blazing fire, rising up through her body. How *dare* he? He knew just how many decisions had been dictated to her. How controlled she had been her entire life by people who had lied to her. How she had been taken and trapped and drained by Adrian. She had told him she could do this. That she had chosen to do this. And he had decided he knew better anyway and stepped in. Stepped *on* her, on this fledging sense of autonomy she was trying so hard to cultivate.

Almost immediately, her inner placating, peace-making voice tried to dampen the fire – *he was probably just worried. You're being unfair to compare him to your parents* – but the fire roared in defiance. Anger was not an emotion Éabha felt comfortable embracing. There had been so many times she'd wanted to give in and scream and rage, but always there was a lid on her emotions, always she shoved them down. She'd spent so many years in her parents' house biting her tongue, stifling who she was and suppressing what she wanted, and instead moulding herself into what they wanted her to be. When inside, part of her had been screaming, banging its fists against the walls that trapped it deep inside her. She'd hoped the fresh air on the deck, the space and warmth and sea breeze would cool it. But it was still there, a roiling, twisting flame that would not be quenched. And Davis's unspoken support, how he had quietly come to find her – and not so quietly defended her last night, as she'd figured out from the small details Raven had given her – made her hope that her outrage was justified.

She stretched out on her lounger, extending a leg into the sunlight that was already growing in heat and feeling it warm her.

Maybe it was time to let the fire burn.

CHAPTER TWENTY-NINE

'OH BABE, SOUNDS LIKE YOU'RE in the middle of a whole situation,' Cordelia sighed, her face sympathetic in the phone screen. Raven leaned back against the cool wall of the stairwell. She'd snuck away immediately after breakfast to call Cordelia, desperate for her calming insight, and to be able to have an open conversation without worrying she was going to upset someone.

'You have no idea,' she said. 'Everyone's taken sides and I'm in the middle trying to stop them all losing their minds. I have no idea how to keep the peace. Until recently, I've been the one causing the problems, not fixing them.'

'Well, isn't this a much nicer place to be?' Cordelia said. 'Emotionally,' she added with a smile, when Raven stared at her impassively. 'You spent until March of this year feeling guilty for pushing people away and avoiding things. Now you're right there in the thick of them.'

'How is it still *this* terrible?' Raven wailed.

Cordelia laughed the throaty laugh that made Raven wish desperately for some way to preserve it every time she heard it.

'Because everyone can be hard work sometimes, but when you love them, they're worth it.'

'Why are you so sensible?'

'Because one of us has to be.'

'Why don't you come here and do the emotion-negotiating then?' Raven asked, only half-joking. A pang of longing shot through her.

She wanted nothing more than to have Cordelia here, to sit with coffees in their hands and platefuls of the tiny pastries Cordelia loved so much and just talk until they figured this out together.

'Because you're in the middle of the Mediterranean and I have work,' Cordelia said. 'Besides, this is good practice for you.'

'I don't want to practise,' Raven grumbled.

Cordelia laughed.

'At least give me some advice?' Raven begged.

'Always,' Cordelia said soothingly. She paused. 'Though you do still need to tell me exactly what happened. I only got a hushed voice note of the CliffsNotes version.'

'Yeah, it's kinda hard to get the privacy to talk in detail,' Raven said. 'Hence why I'm currently in a random stairwell that one of the crew informed me has weirdly good Wi-Fi.' She turned the phone so Cordelia could see, then turned it back to herself and pulled a face. Cordelia laughed again and Raven felt the last bits of tension ease from her body.

'So tell me: what's going on?'

Raven told her, about the weird tension between Éabha and Archer, how he had lied to them about the séance, and how Éabha had arrived to find the truth, blown up at him, and been furious since. Raven left out the details of what they'd discovered, paranoid that someone might enter the stairwell and overhear at the worst possible time. The team drama wasn't classified; one of the crew covering up a murder was.

'Davis is fuming with Archer and fully on Team Éabha, while Fionn is more "yes, Archer messed up, but it came from a good place" and leaning Team Archer. And then I'm here like … I have no idea what to say. Because honestly, he's my brother and I love him, but I totally understand why Éabha's pissed. I'd be raging. He's trying so hard to protect her that he's smothering her and even without using ...' she hesitated for a moment, mindful of Neale's warnings about ship's walls having ears and waggled her amethyst pendant at the screen '... you know, I can feel her wanting to bolt. But also, he's my brother and he loves her, so I'm not going to throw him under the bus.'

Cordelia inhaled deeply. 'Wow, I know ships can feel claustrophobic but you're taking it to a whole new level.' She paused, thinking carefully, her black hair gleaming in the faint sunlight shining through the window of her apartment. 'For what it's worth, I think you're handling it well. Just keep listening to Éabha and validate her feelings without judging Archer. And as for Archer ... it sounds like this is coming from a place of fear. Have any of you talked to him about it? About the why?'

'We all know why,' Raven said, shrugging. 'He's protective and blames himself for last spring.'

'OK, yeah,' Cordelia said, a tinge of exasperation entering her voice. 'But have you *talked* to him about it? Let him tell you that himself?'

'Um ... no.'

'Maybe that'd be a good place to start?' Cordelia said gently.

'What are you, a real estate agent or a therapist?' Raven grumbled good-naturedly.

'You literally called me begging for help.'

'It was more of a plea,' Raven countered. She paused. 'I miss you.'

She didn't know why her heart beat that bit faster when she admitted it. As though it was a weakness to say it, or something embarrassing.

'I miss you too,' Cordelia said. 'But look, it's just a few days more.'

'Every boat day feels like three regular days,' Raven said.

Cordelia smiled, her eyes soft as she looked at her. 'Check in with the others about if they want to talk. Be there for them when they want to because they will, eventually. And focus on the investigation when you want to clear your head.'

'What would I do without you?' Raven asked.

'Let's not find out,' Cordelia said. She hesitated. 'And Raven? Look, I can tell there's some other stuff you can't tell me about right now, but please be careful, OK? Éabha's not at full strength and you're still new to this. Don't take any unnecessary risks, OK?'

'You say that like I'm not always careful,' Raven said lightly.

'Given the events of, like, four months ago,' Cordelia said, 'you'll forgive me if I haven't quite gotten over them yet.'

Ah yes, the whole secretly-planning-to-offer-herself-to-Adrian-in-exchange-for-Éabha thing. Between that and the almost-burning-to-death-in-a-house-fire thing, it was a miracle Cordelia even spoke to her, never mind loved her.

'I'll be careful,' Raven said. 'I promise.'

Cordelia let out a *hmph*, as though she didn't quite believe her.

'How are the new apartments selling? You happy with how it's going?' Raven asked. More than anything she wished she was curled up on Cordelia's couch, drinking a cup of coffee and listening to Cordelia's dramatic re-enactments of her day. Instead, she was stuck on a boat, unable to so much as briefly step onto land even when they were in port, with her team split in two and an angry ghost with an apparent propensity for locking guests in terrifyingly small spaces.

At times like this, Raven started to question her life choices.

When they hung up, nearly an hour later, her heart felt so much lighter. She practically skipped back to her cabin. Just before she reached it, she was intercepted by Neale, who quietly updated her: they footage was exactly what they'd expected, and the police would be summoned to arrest A.J. They were hoping to have it all go under the radar with the guests. And to be sure of that, they didn't want PSI doing any survey work until after dinner.

'Can you behave like regular guests for the rest of the day?' Neale asked, running her hand through her short blonde hair as she glanced around again, checking there were no guests nearby. It was the most ruffled she'd appeared so far. 'Just use the day to visibly act like the other guests – hang out on deck, use the facilities. Nothing that could imply there's anything going on.'

'Sure, we can handle that,' Raven said. She and Éabha would need to try to check in on Philippa, see if this was enough to let her move on, but they could do that from their room. She was curious – and a little worried – about the other spirit. They needed to get to work as soon as possible, but if their employer asked them to take a day off, who was she to argue?

They could all definitely use it. She went to her cabin first, where Éabha visibly relaxed when she told her. Next, she went to the boys' cabin, and even Davis didn't seem upset that the team could separate for the day. Fionn and Archer decided to head for the gym, and when Raven returned to her cabin, she and

Éabha decided to take a swim in the fancy on-deck pool in the afternoon. Raven had wondered if that might be a bit too much exertion for Éabha, especially before a night survey, but it had been the other girl's idea. She'd also suggested Raven take the lead on summoning Philippa, with Éabha there for support, and the other girl's confidence in her sent a rush of warmth through her. Clairvoyancy came naturally to Éabha in a way it didn't to Raven, and she really admired her friend and her ability to embrace her gifts so fully. When Raven thought about clairvoyancy and her goals surrounding it, it was always Éabha who came to mind, Éabha whom she wanted to emulate, to stand alongside. Raven might have successfully pulled off the séance the night before, but she and Éabha were stronger together, and it was Éabha who was integral to the team as a clairvoyant.

So when she and Éabha settled cross-legged on the floor of their cabin, a circle of salt around them and their crystals in front of them, she had to swallow down her nerves. She wanted to do a good job, make her friend proud of her. As séances went, it was the easiest they'd ever had, even more than the night before. Philippa appeared immediately when Raven called for her, appearing in the centre of the cabin.

'I saw,' she said immediately, beaming around the room gratefully. She looked slightly confused when she saw Éabha, but was obviously too polite to ask who she was. 'Do pass my gratitude onto the rest of your team, won't you?'

She sounded like she was sending her compliments to the chef. They'd only proved her bloody murder. Raven had to stifle an exasperated smile. Philippa was harmless, and definitely the nicest ghost she'd met so far. The first one to actually thank them, with tears in her eyes, for their help.

'Do you feel ready to move on?' Raven asked. She tried to keep her voice soothing and gentle, but neither of those came easily to her and she cringed a little, wondering if she just sounded like a bad imitation of a psychic in a film.

'I mean, I'd love to see him go to prison,' Phillipa said, smiling dreamily. 'But I've wasted enough time on him as it is.'

Raven breathed a sigh of relief. She didn't want Phillipa's moving on to be dependent on a court case that could take years, especially if her husband – ex-husband – was as powerful as he claimed. People like him tended to find a way out of these things. Best for Phillipa to take this as her job done and move on.

'Be careful,' Phillipa said. 'The other one, the angry one – he's unravelling.' She turned, looking at them both carefully. 'And you're both very young.'

Was that ... worry in her voice? A ghost actually cared about them?

This survey really was having a lot of firsts.

'We will, thank you,' Raven said, swallowing hard. Phillipa's concern had caused tears to prick at the corners of her eyes, and she didn't quite know why.

'Goodbye,' Phillipa said, fading slowly in front of them. Raven could feel it, the moment she crossed over. A deep instinct that told her Phillipa wasn't just invisible, she was gone.

'Goodbye,' she said. She looked up and met Éabha's eyes, which were glistening with tears.

'We actually helped someone,' Éabha said. Then she laughed,

a bright, startled sound that Raven hadn't heard in a while. 'This feels good.'

'It does,' Raven agreed, the warmth still glowing in her chest.

'You did really well,' Éabha said.

Did she know how much those words meant to Raven? Could she tell? As she thought that, the other girl leaned forward and put her bracelet on.

Oh, she could tell.

At least this meant Raven didn't have to use her words.

It was good that she was now two for two on leading successful séances, but the reality was that Philippa was an exceptionally nice ghost. The other one, that would be different. They'd need Éabha. And while Raven had every sympathy for Archer's protectiveness towards Éabha, she had to agree with Davis. They needed to trust Éabha to know her own limits: she'd had people make decisions for her all her life. They couldn't start doing that to her, too. If they did, they would probably lose Éabha for good.

CHAPTER THIRTY

THE LATE AFTERNOON AIR WAS BALMY, the harsh heat of the Mediterranean sun offset by the cooling breeze of the sea air wafting over the ship, when Éabha followed Raven out onto the deck, trying to look confident in her fancy boat robe that covered her swimsuit. The robes were long and unbelievably soft, and while the luxury of them felt amazing, she still wasn't used to strolling along the corridors in them. But it was what all the other passengers did – to and from the pool and spa, glints of gold and platinum from expensive rings, watches and necklaces flashing in the lamplight or the bright sunlight of the deck. Apparently even bikinis needed jewellery to complete their look. And since the team needed to blend in, they had to follow the lead of the other guests.

Almost every deckchair had someone lounging on it: women with elegant swimsuits and chilled glasses of rosé, and men with expensive sunglasses, holding icy beers. Hardly anyone was in the pool, seeming to prefer posing alongside it. Éabha couldn't see anyone actually looking at them, but she felt eyes on her as she and Raven made their way to deposit their things on a long, low bench beside the pool.

'Well, if it isn't my favourite guests.'

The familiar voice seemed to come from above them, making Éabha jump, until she looked up and saw Willem grinning down at her. He was perched in the lifeguard's chair in crisp, white shorts with a navy-blue stripe down the side, and the navy crew polo-neck T-shirt with the ship's logo on the breast.

'I assume I am your number one,' Raven said drily. Éabha giggled as she spoke.

'Of course,' Willem said, jumping down from his high chair and winking at her as he landed.

The team had unanimously agreed Willem was one of their favourite people on the crew. Raven and Archer had done a second interview with him after Fionn's crew dinner and even Raven had instantly liked him. He was friendly, enthusiastic, didn't act like they were insane for being paranormal surveyors and he was great for ship's gossip when they bumped into him. Between the team feeling so weird at the moment and having to make polite conversation with the other guests, the brief interactions they'd had with him had been a breath of fresh air.

'So does anyone actually use the pool?' Éabha asked him, only half-joking.

'It's mainly for preening around, apparently, but a few people do get in, especially just before they leave to get ready for dinner. So they're not seen with wet hair for long,' he told them, his voice low so no one overheard.

'We're about to cause a scandal then,' Raven said. She shrugged off her robe to reveal a black one-piece swimsuit, then turned and dropped the robe on the sun lounger, her back looking oddly bare without her trademark plait falling down it. Éabha had helped her coil the long braid into a knot on top of her head – 'like a ballerina' she'd said, before dissolving to fits of laughter at Raven's expression at the comparison. 'Yes, because I am known for my grace and athleticism,' Raven had deadpanned back.

Éabha slid her own robe off her shoulders, folding it and placing it on a sun lounger. She'd left her hearing aids in the cabin, afraid she'd either lose them or forget to take them out before she got into the water. She was normally very careful – the times when she was younger and had accidently got into the shower with them in had trained her well – but she didn't have the best faith in her memory right now, not when she was tired. She tried not to hug her arms around herself, revealing her self-consciousness. Instead, she took her tourmaline bracelet off her wrist. She held it in the palm of her hand for a long moment, reluctant to let it go and take away the extra assistance it gave her in shutting out emotions, before putting it with her robe. The rich women around the pool, half of them dripping in expensive jewellery to accessorise their poolside fashion, would probably sneer at how cheap it looked on its simple cord, yet for her it was more valuable than any of the diamonds winking in the late-afternoon sunlight. Hopefully, they weren't playing close attention, because between her inexpensive jewellery and the fact that they could probably tell she'd got her blue bikini in Penneys – if they knew what Penneys was, of course – they'd probably petition to have her thrown overboard.

'So how are things–'

'You,' a voice interrupted them, the snap of the accompanying fingers the only thing sharper than the interruption. 'Where's my champagne?'

Éabha saw Willem's eyes shut briefly as he took a deep breath, before plastering on a polite smile and turning. Behind him, a man was gesturing back at a pair of sun loungers. One, his presumably, was empty, while beside it a woman who seemed to be in her late-twenties was scrolling on her phone, a wide-brimmed hat obscuring most of her face.

'Sir? Is there a problem?'

'Yes, you're standing around flirting instead of doing your job.' The man, who looked to be in maybe his fifties, was speaking to Willem in a slow, condescending tone like he was speaking to a five-year-old. 'I ordered champagne for my girlfriend and me from you several minutes ago. I see no champagne, but I do see you.'

'I am the lifeguard today. My colleague Alex is doing poolside service,' Willem said politely.

Éabha could feel the tension roiling off him, and she resisted the urge to pick up her tourmaline bracelet from where she'd carefully placed it on her robe and put it back on.

'I ordered it from you,' the man insisted. A more hostile edge had entered his voice, as though even the slightest hint of a correction from Willem was a grave insult.

'I'm sorry for the confusion, sir, but it would have been my colleague, who I think I see returning now.'

The man, Éabha and Raven all turned to see another crew member approaching, holding an ice bucket, a bottle of champagne and two glasses.

'Well,' the man blustered. 'It's about time. And you need to work on your tone when addressing guests – that was very abrasive.'

Éabha studied the arriving crew member as he approached the sun loungers. Alex was someone she hadn't met in the course of the interviews. He was short where Willem was tall, broad where Willem was lean. The only similarity was their skin colour. Her stomach churned with discomfort at the realisation. She looked at

Raven, the same understanding spreading over the other girl's face.

The man went back to his loungers, barely looking at Alex as he poured and handed the champagne to him. The man did not thank him.

'I'm sorry you have to deal with people like that,' Éabha murmured to Willem.

'What a prick,' Raven added in a low mutter.

Willem shrugged, looking around to make sure no one had heard and giving Raven a warning look. None of the other guests seemed to have registered that anything had happened, and the man and his companion were too busy sipping champagne, the interaction clearly already gone from their minds. 'You get used to it. The pay is good and the longest you have to put up with anyone is seven days, so …'

Éabha looked over at the man, just in time to see him knock over the bottle of champagne as Alex turned to leave.

'YOU IDIOT,' he bellowed.

'That wasn't his fault,' Raven said. She stepped forward, as though she was going to confront him, but Willem put his arm in front of her.

'Don't, please. You'll only make it worse. Alex will bite his tongue, apologise, go downstairs, tell Neale what happened, she'll commiserate with him about having to put up with this and then when we're off duty, he and I will do a shot and make a toast to the expensive things we'll buy with the money from this voyage.'

'You have a lot more self-control than I do,' Raven said. 'I thought the hipsters in the bar I manage were bad; they have nothing on these people.'

Alex mopped up the champagne as the man made loud, pointed comments to the woman beside him about how the quality of the service industry had really deteriorated.

'I'll go and offer him a complimentary something or other,' Willem said. 'Then maybe by the time you're out of the pool, he'll have shut up.' He gave them a tight smile and strode over, while Éabha and Raven took it as their cue to get into the pool.

The cool water enveloped Éabha and as she sank into it and she couldn't help smiling at the refreshing sensation of it, but the roiling emotions from that scene still clung to her.

'Walls up, E.,' Raven said, leaning in close to speak softly into her ear as she trod water beside her. 'I know it's harder without the bracelet, but walls up.'

Éabha closed her eyes, focusing on building the mental walls in her mind, brick by brick, and the emotions dulled. She and Raven took full advantage of having the pool to themselves, Raven swimming determined, steady lengths while Éabha alternated between paddling and floating, letting the water wash over her.

They were just getting out when Mr Champagne from earlier stood up and walked over to the steps to the pool, barely glancing at them as he descended into the water. He started swimming in broad, confident strokes. Éabha had just wrapped her towel around her when an icy cold gripped her, running down the length of her spine. She looked over at Raven, who had whipped her head around to study the pool.

'You feel it too?' Éabha asked in a breathless whisper, her chest tightening with anxiety.

Raven nodded, her eyes darting around the pool. 'It feels *pissed*.'

That was an understatement. The depths of the rage were terrifying. Éabha leaned down and, fingers trembling, grabbed her bracelet and shakily slid it back on her wrist, breathing a sigh of relief at how it tempered the emotions. She shut her eyes, once again visualising the brick wall, making sure there were no gaps.

'There,' Raven said.

Her voice was forcibly calm and Éabha's eyes snapped open, looking to where Raven was nodding. A man was prowling around the edge of the pool, his eyes fixed on the lone swimmer gliding through the water. He was wearing navy coveralls and a cap, and he seemed a little fuzzy around the edges. The cap was low over his face, and between that and the tilt of his head, she couldn't make out any of his features. No one else seemed to notice him. Éabha couldn't tell if it was just indifference or if they couldn't see him.

'There you two are,' Davis's voice came from behind them. They whirled to face him. 'I wanted to check if you want to go over stuff before or after dinner?'

'Can you see him?' Raven interrupted, her voice low and urgent. She took Davis's arm and turned him towards the pool, to the pacing, blurred man and his prey obliviously doing laps of the pool.

'See who? The guy on the sun lounger with the red T-shirt?' Davis asked, describing a man behind the ghostly figure.

The figure had come to a halt now, and as he looked down at the swimming man, the tilt of his head revealed an expression of pure fury. His rage was pulsating, pushing up against Éabha's barriers, though thankfully not breaking through.

'No. Not him,' Raven said grimly.

Davis shivered. 'I did not expect it to be this cold ... Wait, what am I missing?'

'He's here,' Éabha said.

Davis swore softly, staring at where the girls' gaze was fixed as though he could will him into sight.

'Do you have any equipment with you?' Davis asked.

'Yes. It's tucked in the pocket of my swimsuit,' Raven said, her voice dripping sarcasm. 'Does it look like I have a bloody video camera or EMF reader on me right now?'

Davis opened his mouth to retort. He didn't get a chance to though, because Éabha interrupted him with a scream.

CHAPTER THIRTY-ONE

DAVIS DIDN'T REALISE HE'D STEPPED in front of Éabha until he was there. The moment she screamed, instinct took over. Realistically, Éabha and Raven were more protection to him than he was to them, since they were both powerful clairvoyants and he couldn't even see the ghost they were looking at.

But he could see foaming water surrounding the man who had suddenly ducked under the pool's surface. See him briefly rise up again, clawing at the side of the pool, before disappearing again. As though he had been shoved back down.

Willem dived into the pool, swimming swiftly to the man's side. He surfaced, the man in his arms, his face confused as he and the man disappeared back under.

'The ring,' Raven yelled, rushing to the edge of the pool where a life ring hung. She tossed it to Willem, pushing past the woman in a large hat who had thrown her phone aside and was kneeling by the side of the pool, her arms reaching out towards the water, crying 'Roy' over and over again. Alex jumped into the pool, swimming to the other side of the man – Roy – who seemed to be struggling against an invisible force, something that held him down even as he desperately tried to rise up.

Willem pushed the life ring into Roy's grasp as Alex supported him from the other side. Roy's arms wrapped around the ring, only to be suddenly wrenched away, like a marionette's. Roy cried out in confusion and fear. Alex tried to hold him up as Willem got the ring to his hands again, only to be jerked away again, as though something had pulled him back. Roy's head went under the water again, one hand still weakly reaching for the edge of the pool. Davis was dimly aware of the screams, of someone running to get assistance. He had never felt so powerless, not even when he had been trapped on the other side of a wall of flame in a burning house. He couldn't even see what was happening, what was *really* happening, to try to intervene.

Raven, however, could: she ran around to where Roy was scrabbling at the pool's edge and launched herself at an invisible something alongside the pool – to the horrified guests it probably looked as though she'd tripped. Her arms wrapped around thin air and she landed hard on the tiled edge, looking up in pain and frustration. Beside Davis, Éabha had her eyes screwed shut, one hand reaching towards the pool, beads of sweat on her forehead and her tourmaline bracelet dropped to the ground beside her. Raven looked over at her, then at the empty space in front of her, and closed her eyes too.

A moment passed. Then another. Then another.

Roy resurfaced, no longer held under the water. He was limp and face down.

Willem and Alex hauled him from the water and, as the tall lifeguard started to give CPR, Neale and a medic rushed out onto the pool deck. The few guests still on the deck hovered, trapped in the uncomfortable combination of needing to know what was going on but not wanting to gawk at a tragedy happening in real time. Or maybe they did, that macabre need to witness despair. The same way everyone on a motorway slows down when passing an accident – to witness the gory details.

More staff arrived, ushering people away. Raven picked herself up and walked back to Davis and Éabha, her face twisted in anger even as tears shone in her eyes.

'I couldn't stop him,' she said.

'*We* couldn't stop him,' Éabha corrected her. She reached out a shaking hand to Raven, but the other girl turned away.

'I need … I need to …' Raven said, a tremor in her voice.

She needed to break down, and not in front of all these people. Davis knew her well enough to know that. Éabha was trembling violently, her forehead coated in sweat and a pallor showing on her pale skin. Davis reached out and took the hand still extended towards Raven and squeezed it gently, as Raven sank onto the edge of a sun lounger.

'You should sit down too,' he said softly to Éabha.

'We should … we should give them space.'

Across the pool, the medic slid a hand over Roy's eyelids, closing them, and the woman in the large hat let out a wail. Éabha recoiled as though she'd been shoved, and Davis picked up her tourmaline bracelet, handing it to her silently. Éabha slid it on.

Willem sat on the ground beside the medic, shaking his head. Davis could just make out what he was saying.

'I was trying to lift him, but it was like there was a huge weight pushing him back under the water. It doesn't make any sense. Alex and I were trying to hold him up. I swear, something ripped his hands off that lifebelt. I can't explain it.'

The medic wrapped Willem in a towel, then a robe, talking about shock, when suddenly Willem's head shot up. He looked right at Davis, Éabha and Raven and shook the medic off, rising shakily to his feet and striding over to them.

'You know what happened here,' he said.

It was not a question.

Raven was slumped, her elbows resting on her knees. Davis could see the effort it took for her to raise her head, to look Willem in the eye, as she said, 'We do.'

Davis drew Willem to one side. 'I know you've been through a lot, you're still processing,' he said gently. 'But if you could tell us, in your own words, what happened, before your brain has a chance to start rationalising things, that would be really helpful.'

Willem nodded, and Davis took out his phone.

'May I record to share with the team? No one but us will hear it unless you explicitly consent at a later date.'

Willem nodded again.

Davis wished Archer were here. He was the best at dealing with the emotions, with the people. Willem was soaked, terrified and clearly going into shock, and Davis had no idea how to get the information they needed without causing him more upset. He'd just seen a man die in front of him.

They all had.

Could they have done something to stop this? Could they have figured this out sooner, and prevented this? Was this their fault?

'It's not your fault,' Éabha murmured, leaning in to Davis to keep her words just between them. He turned to look at her.

'I can feel the guilt radiating from you, even through the bracelet.' She shrugged. Her voice was weary, pure exhaustion lacing every word. 'But you can't think that way. We didn't know this would happen. You couldn't have done anything to stop it.'

'You mean "we",' Davis said.

Éabha didn't answer.

He could almost physically see Raven pulling herself back together, her shoulders strengthening and the emotions disappearing from her face as she willed her tough facade into place.

'Can you tell us, in your own words, what happened?' she asked Willem, her voice calmly professional, something he'd seen her hide behind before.

'No detail is too small or strange,' Davis added automatically. It helped, having a script to follow. To stop his brain from dwelling on the details, from starting to process the fact that they had just seen a man die. Recognising that the ghost they had been brought here to find had killed him. Understanding that they hadn't … they hadn't been fast enough and– He snapped his thoughts out of their spiral before they could suck him down, focusing instead on Willem, on the protocol, on the familiar routine of the investigation.

'I heard Éabha scream, and saw the swimmer disappear under the water. I thought maybe he'd got a cramp or was having a heart attack. I dived in and swam to him, and I was trying to bring him to the surface but … it was like there was a force holding him down. It wasn't the weight of someone unconscious; it was fully like he was being shoved down. Like I was fighting against more than water. That part of the pool is too deep to stand in, so I had to keep pushing off the bottom and trying to rise up and whenever we hit the surface, something pressed him down again. Then someone threw a life ring in, and I was trying to get the man to hold onto it. And then Alex was there, and he was trying to hold him up too, and the man was reaching for the ring ...' He looked up at them, his expression hollow. 'I could see the fear in his eyes. He was fighting, but whatever was happening was stronger ... I swear, something ripped his hands off that life ring.'

Éabha shivered hard beside Davis and Raven cast her eyes down at the ground again.

They had both seen it. But what exactly had they seen?

'Then, suddenly, all the resistance was gone. We got him back to the surface no problem. But he was limp, and unconscious, and I tried CPR, but it didn't work.' Willem's voice cracked. 'I tried to save him. I really did.'

Neale came over, her voice compassionate. 'Willem? We want to take you downstairs, let you get dry and dressed. Is there anyone you want to talk to?'

'Mia,' he said immediately. He looked at Davis. 'She's my girlfriend. I would really like to call Mia,' he said. His voice still shook.

Neale nodded, gesturing for him follow.

'Willem,' Raven said. He turned to look at her. 'You did everything you could.'

'We all did,' he said, then slowly followed Neale back below deck, still clutching the robe tightly around him.

'We need to talk to Alex,' Éabha said. Her teeth were starting to chatter and her words were slow, like each one took effort.

'No, we need to go back to the cabins, get the two of you warm and dressed, and get Fionn and Archer,' Davis said firmly. 'They need to interview all of us. I don't have a lot to say compared to you, but it's protocol. They might have a question I've missed because I'm too close, because I was …'

Useless.

He'd been useless. His mind raced, thinking of what they needed to do, who they would need to speak to. It was easier to focus on the practicalities – what the next step should be, how to look after the other two – than to think about what had just happened.

Someone had died.

And they hadn't been able to do a thing to stop it.

CHAPTER THIRTY-TWO

'I JUST ... FUCK,' FIONN SAID, exhaling heavily.

He was sitting on the floor of the cabin, his back against Archer's bed. Davis had just finished telling them what he had seen at the pool, playing back Willem's interview for good measure. The silence was thick in the room as the recording finished, the three of them sitting in silence. The moment Davis told them the ghost had appeared and someone had died, Archer had sprung off his bed and gone to bolt for the door to check on the girls. Davis had stopped him, firmly telling him that they had said they'd have showers to warm up and get changed before meeting them back here.

'Give them a minute to breathe,' he said softly.

Archer had bristled, then deflated. Fionn had barely concealed his sigh of relief – the tension in the cabin between Archer and Davis had been high ever since Davis had taken Éabha's side about the séance.

A murder was a pretty good way of making people put their issues aside.

'Did the girls say anything about what they saw?' Fionn asked.

Davis shook his head. He was sitting on his bed, long legs pulled into his chest, his back against the wall. 'I didn't ask. Éabha was shaking and looked like she was going to pass out, and Raven looked like she was in that place where if you ask the wrong thing, the walls go up and she doesn't talk to you for five years.'

'Ah, I remember that look,' Archer said.

'They definitely saw things I didn't,' Davis said. 'We'll need to do the formal interviews, but I think you should lead them. I was technically there, even if I didn't see everything they did. I could miss something or influence one of their answers without realising it.'

He sounded to Fionn like he was reading a research paper. That was Davis's coping mechanism: science and facts. Someone would need to check in with him, one on one – even if the girls saw more, Davis had still watched a man drown.

Do therapists do group discounts? Fionn wondered. *Because with everything that's happened in the last nine months, we could probably all benefit from it.*

'Before the ... before he ... before, the girls asked me if I could see a man standing by the pool. When I asked if they meant a man sitting on a sun lounger, they said no. Then I realised it was freezing. I went to ask, but before I could ... it happened.'

'I can't imagine what that was like,' Archer said, running a hand through his hair and breathing in deeply. 'What do *you* need right now, Davis?'

'I need to figure out a way to make sure that this doesn't happen to anyone else,' Davis said firmly.

'We'll do that together,' Archer said.

The two looked at each other, nodding, and Fionn knew their Cold War was over for now. Of course, they wouldn't actually talk about it, because apparently no one had learned anything in the last nine months about that either. But this was Davis and Archer, and this was how they'd always been: they butted heads a lot, but they always got past it.

Raven's *rat-a-tat* knock came at the door and Archer leapt up to answer it. He pulled Raven into a hug before she could protest, and for once, she didn't. She hugged him back tightly, and when she pulled back, Fionn could have sworn he saw the beginning of tears in her eyes. She walked into the cabin, kicked off her shoes and climbed onto the bed beside Davis, nudging him with a shoulder. Even sitting, she barely came to his shoulder, and he looked down at her, carefully studying her face before returning her nudge.

We really need to start using our words, thought Fionn.

Éabha walked into the cabin, saw Archer and hesitated. Archer stepped forward, then paused, before opening his arms out. This was the most awkward Fionn had ever seen the two of them around each other, even worse than the morning after Davis had walked in on them kissing in the kitchen for the first time and they'd all had to pile into a car to go and confront The Lady at Hyacinth House.

How did *that* feel like the simple, easy days?

Éabha stepped forward and hugged him, burying her face in his chest and holding him tightly. Fionn looked over at Davis and Raven, who both stared back with awkward 'this is a very confined environment to try and give people space in' looks on their faces. Éabha and Archer broke apart, and sat on Archer's bed side by side, not quite touching, but closer than they had been since the séance.

'Can you talk about it?' Archer asked gently. Beside him, Davis clicked on a voice recorder, a faraway look on his face that made it seem like an automatic rather than a conscious decision.

Raven opened her mouth, and Fionn tensed, anticipating the acerbic onslaught that was likely to come. They all knew it was Raven's defence mechanism, and this had been pretty traumatic.

She had seen someone die in front of her once before – her father, Pádraig – and she had repressed the memories for years before she could face them. This had to be bringing up some of that for her. The others were obviously thinking it too; Davis was watching her with apprehension, while Archer had sounded almost tentative.

'It happened so fast and seemed to last an eternity, which doesn't make sense,' Raven said, shaking her head. A few wisps of hair fell from her plait and she pushed them from her face. 'Éabha and I could see the spirit at the edge of the pool. No one else seemed to, and when Davis arrived, we asked him and he couldn't …'

Davis shook his head in confirmation.

Raven continued. 'The spirit was glaring at the man swimming. Pure hatred. I could feel it coming off him, it was like a hand wrapped around my neck, squeezing.'

'Did it seem personal?' Archer asked.

Raven nodded. 'It was the look you'd give someone you knew well and despised.'

'We should see if there's a link between him and the woman who was locked in the life-jacket container,' Fionn said.

Archer nodded in agreement, writing it in his notebook.

'Then, one minute I'm talking to Davis, the next Éabha screams and when I look back the man is under the water and the spirit … the spirit is kneeling on the side of the pool holding his head down. And his face was partially covered by his cap, but I could see this smile on his face. I saw him let him up to get just a bit of air before he shoved him back under. Like he wanted him to have hope and snatch it away again. It was sadistic. Then Willem jumped in, and he couldn't get him out, and I saw the life ring so I ran to give that to him in case it helped. And I thought, well, if the ghost is corporeal enough to hold the man's head under, surely the rest of him is too? So I tackled him. Or I tried to. I just went right through him. I'm such an idiot.'

Her voice became bitter with self-loathing, and she looked down at her lap, taking a long moment before she raised her head and continued.

'He looked at me with utter fury. And as I looked at him, his face changed – just for a moment and so quickly that part of me wonders if I actually saw it. It was like one of those jump-scares from a horror film. His jaw, it was hanging off, and the top of his head looked … misshapen. Crushed.' Raven looked like she was going to be sick.

'You didn't imagine it,' Éabha said, shuddering. 'It happened at the beginning too, when he first pushed Roy under the water. It's why I screamed.'

Archer shifted a bit closer to her on the bed as she spoke. There was a long silence, and then Raven spoke again. 'I could feel Éabha's energy, trying to push him back psychically rather than physically, so I tried to help her and I think it was working but … it was too late. I should have thought of it sooner.'

'You did everything you could,' Fionn said. Part of him couldn't believe it – that she had told them all that, had even voiced her own feelings. Raven had talked big talk about changing, about not repeating what had happened in the past. But this was the biggest piece of proof so far that she meant it. She was forcing every word, actively making herself not hold back, even though it sounded like they were catching in her throat as she spoke. He could see from the tender expression on Archer's face that he saw it too.

'At least you tried,' Éabha said, her voice even softer than usual. Her gaze was cast down to her lap, her hands twisting in it, fingers interlocking and unlocking in anxious movements. 'I just froze. I screamed, then I stood there, watching. Then, when I finally *did* do something, it wasn't enough. *I* wasn't enough. I didn't have enough energy to push him back on my own. Or at all really. Raven did almost all of it.'

'That's not your fault, Éabha,' Archer said. He gave her hand a gentle squeeze before letting go, as though he didn't want to push it with the tentative peace they seemed to have made.

'Whose is it then?' Éabha asked, a hard edge to her voice. 'I'm a clairvoyant. I have one job, and I couldn't do it because I floated in a pool for half an hour and that used up most of my energy.'

'That's not your fault,' Archer repeated.

'It feels like it,' Éabha muttered.

She kept looking down at her lap, and Fionn wished he knew what to say to make it better. But there wasn't anything that would make this easier for Éabha. He couldn't change what had happened to her, or how it had affected her. The reality was that no one knew when – if – this overwhelming fatigue would go away, not even Lizzie. And Éabha had gone from being powerful but unable to control it, to being in control but with little power.

Then, as though Éabha thought she had said too much, the mask slid into place. Her placid, everything-is-fine expression they had seen so often.

'I don't have much to add to what Raven said. The fury was so vitriolic it made me feel physically ill, almost knocked me off my feet. It was hard to put up walls against it. It definitely seemed personal: the spirit was targeting that man. We need to figure out why.' Éabha frowned, eyebrows furrowed as she thought.

'You've both said more than enough,' Fionn said, trying to think of some form of comfort to offer them.

'He was wearing a uniform with the company crest,' Éabha said suddenly, bolting forward then wincing, like the sudden movement had cost her. 'The boat one. But not like the crew uniform. More like a workman's overalls or something.'

'Great work, Éabha! We should try to find out if Roy has any connections with the company,' Archer said decisively. 'Or Elizabeth Carmichael.'

'And how exactly do we do that?' Davis asked.

'Roy's partner,' Raven offered. 'Though considering she just saw … I don't know how we can speak to her without seeming like trauma-chasing ghouls.'

'I can do that, if someone who was there feels up to coming with me,' Archer said.

'I will,' Raven said.

Archer's eyebrows shot up in surprise, but he smiled gratefully.

'And I can ask Charles what Roy's full name was,' Fionn said. 'I'll do a deep dive online and see what I can come up with. Someone rich enough to be on this boat is probably high-profile enough to have a strong online presence.'

'I'll find Alex. He tried to save Roy, too. He might have seen or experienced something we missed,' Davis said.

'At one point, the ghost pushed him back when he was trying to hold Roy up. See if he mentions anything about that,' Raven said.

'And to com- ... com- ... what's the word again? Prove?'

'Compound?' Raven asked.

Éabha nodded. 'Yes, that. To compound my position as the deadweight of this team, I think I need to rest.' Her eyes were glazed with tiredness and every word sounded heavy on her tongue, like even speaking was almost beyond her.

'It's not weak to need to rest, Éabhs,' Archer said gently.

'Just for an hour or two. You'll wake me up when you've talked to them, right?' Éabha asked.

'Of course,' Davis said.

But Éabha was still looking up at Archer.

'We will. I will. I promise.'

Éabha studied him for a long moment before nodding.

'Come on, I'll help you back to the cabin before we talk to Roy's partner,' Raven said. She gestured down at the oversized hoodie and pyjama bottoms she was wearing. 'Should make myself look respectable too. Meet in me in ten, Little Brother?'

'Aye, aye, Captain,' Archer said, with a weak attempt at a smile.

Éabha slowly shuffled to the edge of the bed, taking a long moment before pushing herself to her feet. She moved like someone four times her age. Raven walked with her to the door, close enough to grab her if she fell, without actually touching her.

'See you later,' Éabha said, her voice slurred with tiredness.

When the door shut behind them the three boys looked at each other.

'I wish I could fix things for her,' Archer said, pain etched onto his face.

'You can't,' Davis said. His tone wasn't harsh, just matter of fact.

'But what you can do is be there for her as she is.'

Archer nodded, then shook himself. 'Right, time to put on a nice shirt and talk to some people.'

Fionn reached over and pulled his laptop towards him.

'Let's see if we can find out who this ghost is.'

'And if there's anyone else he might be targeting,' Davis added grimly.

CHAPTER THIRTY-THREE

IT WAS SURREAL. Davis had seen a man drown a few hours ago, and now he had to put on a suit and make small talk and listen to the other guests discuss Roy's death over dinner like it was the weather.

'I hope they drain the pool and refill it,' he heard one woman say as he made his way to his seat. 'It would be like lounging by the River Styx otherwise.'

A classical allusion didn't stop you from being a self-absorbed vulture, he thought to himself, hoping he'd managed to keep his face neutral.

He let Fionn do most of the talking at dinner, though little was required of them since their tablemates were determined to discuss the 'accident' in excruciating detail. He tuned them out and retreated into his safe space: logic. He couldn't stop mulling over all the facts, trying to make a connection. Cami, Roy and Elizabeth Carmichael had never met, had nothing in common besides being on this ship. Elizabeth had been taken late at night, Roy had been killed during the day. They'd both had champagne, but surely the ghost wasn't targeting based on drinks preference? From the sounds of it, they'd both been obnoxious, but ...

Wait.

Elizabeth had kicked up a fuss about a staff member asking her to leave when she wouldn't put shoes on. Roy had been rude – and racist – to Willem and Alex. And Cami had been pretty creepy to

Charles, knowing he couldn't call her out when he was crew and she was a guest.

Charles had said that when the lights went out, he felt comforted. Safe. Was the ghost targeting people who were rude to the crew? And why? Éabha said he was wearing something with the ship company's logo on it, so maybe that was linked to his death? And now he was … what, protecting the crew? Targeting people for being on the boat? Though the girls had said his face had seemed crushed on one side. How did that happen on a boat? And why would he need to protect the crew from rude guests because of it?

Despite all the questions, Davis couldn't contain the excitement humming in him at the theory. It was just that, an idea, but it was a common thread that linked them all. He forced himself to join in the conversation at the table, steering it away from the death and onto safer terrain as he tried to contain the brimming excitement bubbling up through him. He wished he could just grab the others now and tell them his theory. But no, he needed to make polite chit-chat for another forty minutes at least. He just needed to know if they thought it was likely. It had been driving him mad, trying to find the link between all the victims. He refused to believe it was random. Everyone's actions were driven by some sort of logic, even if it made sense only to them. Even if they were a spirit. And now, after what he'd witnessed this afternoon, Davis needed to find some sort of explanation. Maybe then the wails of Roy's partner, Alicia, as she watched him drown, with no understanding of what was happening or why no one could help him, would stop echoing around his head.

CHAPTER THIRTY-FOUR

FIONN HEARD A FAMILIAR VOICE call his name as he left the dining room after dinner and turned to see Charles walking purposefully towards him.

'Do you have—' Charles glanced around, checking that no guests were nearby, and lowered his voice before continuing, '—any investigation work tonight?'

Fionn thought about the haunted expressions on Raven, Éabha and Davis's faces when they'd got back from the pool, how they were all in varying degrees of shock. The crew had handled Roy's death quickly and discreetly, but the word had spread rapidly and the few guests who had witnessed the drowning had already loudly discussed it. Fionn had sat through an entire meal with the people at his table sipping wine and saying what an utter tragedy it was before immediately starting to worry about whether it would mess with the cruise itinerary and if they personally would feel uncomfortable by the pool now. He'd had to clutch the edge of the linen tablecloth underneath the table not to snap at them when one person had said with a sigh, 'If only it had happened in a less desirable part of the ship.' They all seemed to believe it was a heart attack or something, already glossing over the parts of his drowning that didn't make sense. People did that with traumatic experiences; they rearranged narratives to make them make sense. It was easier to handle than the truth, a lot of the time. Davis had sat beside him, mostly silent, and Fionn genuinely had no idea how his friend had managed not to yell at them.

PSI definitely needed to be careful with this spirit and not rush into anything. And while time was running out – they were halfway through the cruise now – there was nothing riskier than trying to push through when three of them had witnessed something so distressing. They would rest tonight and regroup in the morning.

Though, considering the state of the team right now, it was debatable how all of them would manage to be in the same room together. The temporary truce in the aftermath of Roy's death had been pleasant but, until they resolved everything, there was a good chance it wouldn't last.

'I think it's unlikely,' Fionn said. 'Why?'

'It's a clear night tonight,' Charles said.

Fionn looked at him blankly.

'Sorry, remember how I said I do the stargazing on deck eight for guests? It's scheduled for tomorrow night but, if you wanted, maybe we could look together tonight?'

Fionn felt a little surge of optimism. That was exactly what he needed: a few hours in the fresh night air, away from the stifling tension. He had no idea how Raven and Éabha could stand it when even he, a non-clairvoyant, could feel it. It must be suffocating.

'That would be great, I'd love that.'

Charles beamed at him. 'Meet me on the aft deck in half an hour? I'll have clocked off by then. It's closed to guests, so we won't be disturbed.'

'Absolutely,' Fionn said, grinning. He checked his watch to make sure he knew the right time to meet. 'I should go get changed. I'll see you then!'

Back in his cabin, he shrugged off his suit jacket and unbuttoned his shirt quickly, excited to be up on the top deck under the wide expanse of the night sky. And for some peace and quiet. The woman on Fionn's right during dinner had given him a lot of advice on offshore accounts, which sounded, if not illegal, at least morally questionable. He'd nodded and smiled politely, asking her a question every now and then that set her off on another monologue. It was good in that he hadn't had to contribute much to the conversation, but it had given him a massive headache. He changed into jeans, a T-shirt and a navy jumper, in case it would be chilly out on deck now that the sun had set, and speedily made his way up to the very top of the ship. He took the stairs, enjoying the feeling of the steps underfoot and the way the exertion increased his breathing.

Charles was already on deck eight, on the stargazing platform. He'd laid a chequered picnic blanket on the deck, facing out to sea, while behind him the soft lights of the Corsican coast in the distance were reflected in the lapping water. He'd changed out of his crew uniform into jeans and a grey knitted jumper.

'Hello,' Charles grinned. 'I'm so glad you wanted to do this.'

'I love astronomy,' Fionn said, sitting on the blanket beside him. 'I live on a farm and the sky is pretty clear a lot of the time. Ever since I was a kid I'd sit out and try to spot the constellations.'

Above them, the sky stretched into an infinite expanse of darkness that felt comforting rather than frightening, because it was filled with millions and billions of stars and galaxies, tiny pinpoints of light shimmering overhead. His heart lifted as he tilted his head back, studying them, letting the serenity of the night sky quiet his anxious mind.

'There's the North Star,' he said, pointing. 'Right?'

'Very good,' Charles said. 'And that's Orion, and that's Cassiopeia.'

The next while went quickly. Charles taught him so many tips for finding different constellations that all the worry about the team, the investigation, everything, faded from Fionn's mind.

'And that there, that's …'

Fionn didn't hear what Charles said next. He was suddenly aware that Charles had moved a lot closer to him, leaning on the arm he had placed behind Fionn's back. Fionn looked at him, and Charles's face was inches from his, his wide, brown eyes looking softly at him as his lips curved up in a gentle smile.

Was this … a date?

Was he on a date?

Surely someone needed to *tell* you if you were going on a date?

Panic fizzed through him as he shifted through every interaction with Charles. He had been out as asexual-aromantic for only a few months, but the moment he'd learned the terms they'd felt so right he'd known that was who he'd been all his life. He just hadn't had the language to explain it before. And now that *he* knew it, part of him had just assumed everyone else would too. Not that he thought he wasn't someone a person could be attracted to, but just that … they'd know, somehow. And it wouldn't be something he'd need to navigate.

Foolish.

So foolish, to assume people would somehow just *know* something about him that it had taken him nineteen years of his life to figure out. It wasn't enough to say it out loud once. He'd have to keep saying, keep introducing that part of himself over and over. How had he not realised this before now?

He was not prepared for this conversation. What should he say? What if he wasn't reading this right and it wasn't a date, and he said 'by the way, this can't be a date' and Charles was just like 'arrogant of you to assume that' and never spoke to him again?

What if it *was* a date and he'd said or done something to make Charles think he knew it was, and then he said it wasn't, and Charles hated him and never spoke to him again?

Fionn really liked Charles. He could see them being good friends, and he would be so sad to lose him, or hurt him.

He needed to get out of here. He needed to find someone who could tell him what to do.

'I have to go,' he blurted out, jumping to his feet.

Charles's face fell. 'Are you OK? Did I–'

'Thanks so much it was really fun I just remembered I need to go ... feed ... the EMF meter.'

Fionn was through the deck door leading back below before utter idiocy of his fumbling excuse fully sank in.

He fled down flights of stairs, too anxious to wait for the lift, panic driving him forwards as his brain screamed every mistake he had made at him in rapid succession.

CHAPTER THIRTY-FIVE

ARCHER WAS SITTING IN THE CABIN WITH DAVIS, both going through various files for the case in an awkward silence that felt like a physical weight, when Fionn practically fell through the door. His eyes were wide and panicked, his chest heaving.

'What is it?' Archer asked, leaping to his feet and bounding over to him.

Had Fionn had an encounter? It must have been something terrifying to elicit this kind of reaction. Fionn ran a hand through his hair, making it even more dishevelled than it already was, and opened his mouth, then snapped it shut again, before blurting out, 'I think I accidentally went on a date with Charles, but I didn't know and I have no idea what to do.'

Davis and Archer stared at him in shock.

'H-how do you accidentally go on a date?' Davis asked, perplexed.

'When the other person doesn't tell you it is one,' Fionn wailed.

'But you're aro-ace,' Archer said. The relief that Fionn hadn't, in fact, been targeted by a murderous ghost was overtaken by pure confusion.

'Yes, *I* am aware of that, Archer. But it doesn't always come up in general conversation and I'm not going to start every interaction with "Hi, I'm Fionn and I'm aro-ace just in case that's information you need to know",' Fionn said. He went to his bed and flopped onto it, face down, his next words muffled by his pillow.

'You'll need to stop trying to smother yourself in the bedclothes if you want our assistance,' Davis said.

Archer tried to hold in a laugh, looking at Davis with a tentative grin. For a moment Davis smiled back, then seemed to catch himself and frowned again.

It was a stab to the gut.

Fionn rolled back over, sitting up and pulling his knees into his chest. 'I don't even know if I'm right in thinking that he thought it was a date. Maybe I'm being really full of myself for thinking he's attracted to me. Oh God, am I that guy that assumes every person who's nice to him is flirting with him?'

Archer bit back a smile. 'I can assure you, you're not. And it's not arrogant to think someone could be attracted to you if they're acting like they are. You may not be interested in sex or romance but that doesn't mean other people won't be interested in you.'

'I just assumed people could, like … tell,' Fionn said unhappily, looking down at the sleeve of his jumper as his pulled on it.

Archer raised an eyebrow. 'Fionn, you know there's no one way to express any identity.'

'I do, of course,' Fionn said quickly.

Archer could empathise, he really could. He'd been out as bisexual for a few years, but sometimes he felt like an imposter, and other times he felt that he stood out glaringly. Like when some customers at Forest Fair, the cafe where he worked, looked at his painted nails a little too long. Or, alternatively, when he'd gone to Dublin Pride the summer before and had felt so underdressed in jeans and a T-shirt. The T-shirt had a little cat wearing a witch's hat, all illustrated in the bi-flag colours, but compared to some of the other people there, he'd felt like a sham. He'd got chatting to a really lovely guy at a party, experienced a severe case of bi-panic, and left. So he could definitely understand Fionn fleeing, and even if his sheer panic was pretty entertaining, Archer knew he needed to support him.

'Just go find him tomorrow and talk to him,' Davis said, sitting down on his bed. 'Clear the air and explain the situation. He'll understand.'

'What if he's mad at me? Or thinks I led him on? What if I did?'

Archer climbed onto Fionn's bed and put an arm around him.

'Fionn, unless you turned around to him and said, "Hello, I would like to go on a date with you," you did not say anything untruthful or misleading. He likes you, he wanted to spend time with you, and sure, he'll be a bit disappointed you don't want something similar, but if he's angry at you for that, he's not a good person and not worth having as a friend anyway.'

Davis nodded emphatically. 'Archer's right.'

It was a testimony to how much Davis wanted to console Fionn that he didn't sound in any way bitter saying that, Archer thought, as Davis continued.

'He didn't say it was a date; you didn't agree to one. He was probably hopeful and, if anything, he's probably also freaking out right now too. Put the poor guy out of his misery.'

'I mean, it's the nicest rejection anyone could get. It's not that you don't want him: you don't want anyone,' Archer pointed out.

'Quite literally a case of "it's not you, it's me",' Davis said. 'Not that there is anything wrong with you,' he added quickly and firmly.

'What would you say to Cordelia if she went to hang out with a guy and he thought it was a date and she had to be like "no, I don't like men"?' Archer asked.

Fionn wrinkled his brow. 'But Cordelia's with Raven.'

'If she wasn't,' Archer said, slightly exasperated.

Davis snorted. The familiar sound sent a little spike of warmth through Archer.

'OK, I see your point.' Fionn paused, then looked at them both. 'So I'm not a terrible person? For thinking either he might think it was a date or, if it was a date, not knowing and going without saying anything?'

'Not at all,' Archer said, nudging Fionn affectionately with his shoulder to emphasise his words.

Davis echoed him.

'Thanks,' Fionn said, and exhaled deeply. 'I guess I'll go talk to him. Tomorrow.' He paused, a guilty expression on his face. 'I know I should find him now, but he's probably gone back to the crew quarters since he's not on duty, and I'd have to knock on all the cabins to try and find him and people will wonder why and I just don't think I can handle that right now.'

'Tomorrow's absolutely fine,' Archer said. Poor Charles. He was probably in for a rough night, but he could tell Fionn was one uncomfortable interaction away from completely falling apart and, honestly, the team was hanging on by a thread as it was. *Sorry, Charles.*

'Then after that, all we need to do is find a ghost before they murder anyone else,' Davis said drily. 'Simple.'

CHAPTER THIRTY-SIX

ÉABHA WOKE UP FEELING SOMEWHAT refreshed, despite the nightmares that had plagued her for most of the night. She'd eventually fallen into a dreamless sleep, exhaustion taking over and stopping her tossing and turning as she tried to erase the images of the drowning Roy grasping for the side of pool from her mind. She could tell Raven was awake too, but neither of them spoke. Éabha knew her friend needed to process it by herself first before she even tried to discuss it. Raven was doing better at talking about things, but Éabha knew that she herself couldn't even begin to try to vocalise the awfulness of it, and she assumed Raven wouldn't either.

How did you even begin to deal with it?

They had been right there. And she had been unable to stop the spirit. Unable to do anything other than freeze, then belatedly try to use her energy – her minimal, weak energy – to try and save Roy. And it wasn't enough. She wasn't enough.

She struggled through breakfast, picking at scrambled eggs and making polite chit-chat with the other people at her table. Davis sat with her, politely fielding any questions that asked too specific a question about them. Everyone on the boat thought they were a bunch of rich kids who'd met at boarding school before separating for college. As far as the other guests knew, their trust funds were paying for this extravagant holiday, a chance for them all to catch up and reconnect.

If only she could be that person.

But no, she was the one who saw and felt things other people didn't. Who had watched a man drown and not been able to do a thing to stop it.

She shuddered, her teaspoon rattling against her coffee cup, and she steadied her hand.

Mask on, Éabha.

After a while, Fionn paused by their table to greet them, an anxious look on his face. Charles walked by, his back straighter than usual and his eyes straight ahead, as they talked and Fionn went red, his cheeks almost matching his hair, before scuttling off to find Archer and Raven's table.

'What was that?' Éabha murmured to Davis.

'I'll tell you later,' he said, giving her a wry smile.

It would have been easier to distract herself with small talk and Fionn's odd behaviour than to sit with her thoughts, but she didn't want to push Davis. Instead, she tried to force some more food down as worry gnawed at her stomach. There were so many things to deal with. First of all, they needed to figure out who this ghost was, and how to deal with him, before he struck again. She had no idea where to even begin with that. Then there was how she was going to work with Archer when every time she looked at him another piece of her heart shattered.

She would have to face it eventually, she knew that. And it became all too clear when Raven stopped at their table on her way out, Fionn and Archer going on ahead.

'Meet you in the boys' cabin when you're done?' she said.

Éabha looked down at her half-eaten scrambled eggs and

pushed her plate away. 'I'm done, if you all are,' she said.

Davis agreed, draining the dregs of his coffee before standing up from the table.

'Let's get started,' he said.

Éabha followed suit, getting to her feet and walking after the other two out the door.

Find a ghost.

Stop any more murders.

Be in the same room as Archer without bursting into tears.

She could do this.

CHAPTER THIRTY-SEVEN

'ARE YOU SURE YOU'RE OK to talk about it again?' Raven watched as Archer looked first at her, then Davis and Éabha, as he asked. Éabha was curled up in the corner of Davis's bed, leaning against the wall, while Davis was on the floor his back against it, his long legs stretched out in front of him. Fionn was sitting at the desk, a notebook and pen in front of him.

Raven tried to keep the bite out of her voice as she answered. She could understand why Éabha got so frustrated with him checking on her; it was never enough for him to ask once, or even twice. It was hard not to feel that he didn't trust them to know what they could handle, or to tell him the truth.

In fairness, she had probably contributed to the latter part. Which was why she was going more for 'exasperated older sister' rather than 'snarling wolf' as she answered, for the third time, 'Yes, Archer.'

'You saw a man die.'

'And I want to make sure we don't see another person die, which is what is going to happen if we don't solve this mystery,' Raven countered. She looked at Archer's worried face and softened. 'I promise, Little Brother, honest; if it gets too much, I'll say. Just trust us to make the call.'

Davis and Éabha made noises of agreement. There was a pause, then Archer nodded, leaning back against the cabin wall.

'So, to recap in the most analytical way possible …' Fionn began, checking a sheet he'd written on. '... Raven and Éabha could see the ghost, Davis couldn't. It seemed like he could touch the man in the pool because he was pushing him under, but Raven tried to tackle him and went right through him.'

'Yep, that's pretty much it,' Davis sighed. He reached up and tied his hair back, frowning at the A4 pad in front of him as though willing the answers to magically appear on it.

'OK. That's ... new.'

'Never ones for the simple stuff, this team,' Raven said. She gave a wry grin, but inside her stomach roiled. She couldn't stop picturing Roy's face as he broke through the surface of the pool for brief moments, eyes wide and frantic, mouth gasping for air. Could he see the ghost? Did he know what was happening? Or did it just feel like an invisible, inexplicable force was holding him down? He'd been awful to Willem and Alex, but no one deserved that. Did he have family, besides the woman who'd been at the pool with him? Alicia's screams still echoed in Raven's mind when she closed her eyes.

'... d'you think, Raven? ... Raven?'

It took her a few seconds to realise that Archer was saying her name.

'Sorry, what was that?' she asked.

She met his eyes and nodded to the silent question there. *I'm fine. Please don't ask again.*

She couldn't read minds and, as far as they knew, Archer wasn't clairvoyant, but ever since they were kids sneaking around hotels and houses when they were supposed to be asleep, she and Archer had been able to communicate without words.

'I was saying, do you think limited energy would make him unable to manifest fully? So maybe he had to concentrate on specific things?'

Éabha let out a little 'oh' of excitement, leaning forward to tap Davis on the knee.

'The wood!'

'The ... forest?' Davis asked, giving her a perplexed look.

'No,' Éabha said, with an impatient sigh. She flapped her hands as she spoke, something she had started doing in recent months when she was tired and struggling to articulate things.

'The house, The Lady, when she tried to hit you with the beam. I could see her, you couldn't. Remember?'

Davis's eyes lit up in excitement and he started to write furiously on his pad of paper. 'So we *have* a previous instance of something similar.'

'And she drained the camera and my hearing aids to use her energy to break the timber,' Éabha said.

'There's not a lot of power out by the pool,' Fionn said, biting the end of his pen as he thought.

'I didn't have my hearing aids because we were going swimming,' Éabha said. 'And he wasn't drawing on me or Raven. I was fatigued, but not any more than usual, and Raven–?'

'My energy levels were OK,' Raven said.

'We need to find if there was another power source up there,' Davis said.

'Something that would allow him to be physical with a person without the energy to fully appear,' Fionn mused.

'I wish there was someone besides us who'd had a similar

experience,' Davis sighed. 'We're too close to be objective.'

Éabha slumped back against the wall, like even that bit of excitement had drained her reserves.

The room went silent. Raven wracked her brains, trying to think of something that could help them. At the moment, it felt like the list of questions, not answers, was getting longer, and she hated it.

Someone who had physically interacted with a verified ghost …

There was one person. It was all personal experience, though, because his camera had cut out. And he'd only recalled this part of the experience months later, so there was a chance it was a false memory. She was the only one he'd even told about it so far. And he was hyperbolic at the best of times. But he wasn't a liar, she knew that. Not about this.

'I think there's someone,' she said. Everyone's head snapped to her, like meerkats popping up out of their holes, and she stifled a smile. 'I don't know how enthusiastic you'll be about his reliability though, Davis. But for what it's worth, I think it's genuine. Or at least he definitely believes it is. This is something he's only told me, in private. It's not a clickbait thing.'

'Clickbait,' Davis said, frowning. 'You don't mean …'

'I can arrange a video call with our old pal Jack Gallagher.'

CHAPTER THIRTY-EIGHT

'IS THIS SEAT TAKEN?'

Her voice pulled him from the piece by Ennio Morricone that he was listening to on his earphones. Archer was sitting in the corner of the bar, in one of the deep, squishy leather armchairs that made him feel like he was in a dark academia novel. He had a pile of notes in front of him, from his and Raven's fruitless conversation with Alicia, Roy's partner, and a collection of other testimonies. His heart jolted as he looked up, almost afraid to believe it was that familiar voice, and saw Éabha standing there. The dark circles under her eyes were pushing past the layers of concealer she'd applied, and the smile she gave him was weary, but she was there. She was asking to sit down.

And he was taking an uncomfortable amount of time to answer.

'The seat next to me will always be yours,' he said, pulling his earphones out of his ears.

Just because you feel like you're in a dark academia novel doesn't mean you need to talk like you are, Archer.

Was that relief on Éabha's face? Did she really think he'd turn her away?

She was the one who'd been blocking him out.

'How are the files going?' she asked, nodding at the scattered documents laid out on the table in front of him.

'Honestly? Frustrating. All the crew, previous and present, are accounted for.'

'I still don't think it was a crew uniform,' Éabha said, frowning. She leaned forward and started sifting through the pages in front of him. 'It had the company logo, but it wasn't the pressed white clothes. It was navy and looked like workman's clothes.'

'There's no workmen on the crew, though,' Archer said.

'Now, maybe, but …' Éabha paused and looked over at him, her fingers spread on a sheet of paper. Her nails were chipped, a few broken. In the entire time he had known her, he had never seen her without perfectly shellacked nails. She followed his gaze and curled her fingers under the paper as though she could read his mind.

'I didn't have the energy to go before we left,' she said, a melancholy tone in her voice.

He leaned forwards, covering her hand with his. 'You know you don't need to always be completely put together, right?'

The warmth of her skin under his fingertips sent his heart beating. He'd missed her so much since the séance. His hand always felt empty because it wasn't holding hers. She turned her hand under his to lace her fingers between his, and it took all his self-restraint not to beam with delight. She was opening up to him again.

'I know, but this … this is something I actually like. It's taken me a while to figure out what I was doing because I was trying to be the version of a daughter my parents expected, and what I actually wanted to do myself. And I really like having nice nails. It makes me feel a little more together. And now it's just another thing in the long list of things I can't do.' She frowned, looking down. 'It's a constant reminder that I'm not the person I was before Adrian, and I don't know if I'll ever be her again.'

Archer had never thought himself capable of hatred, but he hated that spirit with a fury that sent acid to the back of his mouth, made every muscle in his body clench. He wished he could burn that painting a thousand times over for what Adrian Fitzgibbon had done to Éabha, was continuing to do.

'You'll get better.'

'I may not,' Éabha said softly. 'It's pretty similar to a condition my GP calls ME. There's no cure.'

'But this is a clairvoyance issue, not a medical one.'

'Physically it's manifesting the same. And Lizzie has reached out to her entire network. No one has ever heard of this happening. And no one knows how to stop it. I think I need to stop waiting for it to magically go away and start figuring out how to live with the reality of where I am now.'

'No, Éabha, you can't give up. You need to stay positive – you need to keep fighting.'

He knew he couldn't fix it all for her, no matter how much he wanted to, but he couldn't watch her give up hope in front of him.

She snapped her head around to look at him, yanking her hand from his.

'Trying to learn how to live my life within the parameters I've been given is not giving up, and you don't know what I need,' she hissed. 'Do you really think I can just positive-think my way out of this? That I'm just not trying hard enough?'

'That's not what I meant–'

'Well, it's what you're saying. First, you undermine me and go behind my back to make decisions based on what you think I can do, not what I tell you I can do. And then when I tell you I have limitations, you tell me I'm just not thinking positively enough about it. Which is it, Archer? Because of all the team, you were the only one *positive* I couldn't do the séance.'

He sat there, reeling. Was that what she thought of him?

'I was trying to protect you because I failed so miserably the last time.'

'You can't protect everyone all the time, Archer. Especially when it's their choice to do something. Either you respect and trust me enough to let me make my own choices, or you don't. Which is it?'

'Éabha, I love you.'

'My parents said that too. That didn't stop them from trying to control me, to make my decisions for me. They would have said they were protecting me, too.'

Archer felt like she'd punched him in the gut.

Éabha stood up, her eyes filling with tears. 'I'll take these sheets back to my cabin and look over them there. I'll see you at the meeting in a few hours.'

He sat there, staring at the empty table in front of him for a long time after she left.

CHAPTER THIRTY-NINE

ÉABHA SLOWLY MADE HER WAY BACK to the cabin, wishing she had the energy to run. She needed to move, to release this writhing coil of tension building inside her. She needed to run from the truth that was screaming at her, because she didn't want to stop and listen.

She knew that when she listened, when she acknowledged it, it would be over.

She and Archer would be over.

And the pain, the feeling of her heart being slowly crushed in a vice whenever she considered a future where Archer was not her boyfriend, made her shy away from the voice whispering *you are not good for each other any more*. The documents she'd taken from Archer were loose in her hands, and she realised how precariously she was carrying them when, at the sound of that whispering voice in her mind, a sheaf of them slipped from her fingers and fell to the floor, scattering everywhere.

'Sugar,' she said, then huffed a laugh to herself. Her parents had forbidden swearing, and even now she still defaulted to the acceptable version. Fionn would always respond 'granulated or icing?' when she said it, an affectionate tone in his voice that made it clear he wasn't mocking her. She crouched down to gather them.

'You're wrecking the gaff, Éabha.'

She looked up to see Davis standing over her, smiling teasingly, before crouching down beside her to help.

'This is just like the first time we were in the office together,' he said, handing her a stack.

'Ah yes, that lovely memory of when you blatantly hated me and I was terrified of you?' Éabha asked.

Davis looked offended. 'I was mistrusting of you. I didn't hate you.'

'Heavily disliked then.'

He laughed. 'OK, maybe, but I saw the light eventually.'

'I'm so grateful,' Éabha said drily. She stood up, and her vision narrowed, spots dancing in front of her eyes. She dropped the sheets again, reaching for the wall to steady herself.

'Éabha? Are you OK?'

She felt Davis's arm support her as she slowly slid to the ground.

'I stood up too fast. That happens now,' she said slowly, her words thick on her tongue. She leaned against the sturdy wall, taking deep breaths and hoping no guests passed by. Davis sat beside her silently, waiting for her to speak.

Eventually, her vision cleared, and she could speak again.

'The doctor calls it POTS, something to do with heart rate and blood flow and a lot of things my brain shut out because concentrating got hard. Lizzie took notes.'

'Sounds pleasant.'

Éabha snorted. Davis had gathered the sheets again and held them in his lap as he looked at her. 'How are you holding up?

'Honestly?'

He nodded.

'Just about. There's just such a difference between what I want to do and what I can do, and every time I think I've figured out my limits, the goalposts change. One day I can do loads, the next nothing. Sometimes a shower wipes me out for an hour or two, other times I'm fine. It doesn't make any sense.' She paused. 'And I feel like I can't pull my weight in the team any more.'

Davis opened his mouth to protest, but she silenced him with a look.

'Don't patronise me.'

'Éabha, when have I ever held back from the truth?' Davis asked.

He had a point.

'I'm listening,' she said. She looked down at her lap, staring at her hands and focusing on the sensation of her fingers intertwining and unlocking, the feel of the skin of her palms under her thumbs as he spoke.

'You can't do things the way you used to. That's a fact. But that just means we need to figure out how to help you do those things within the parameters your body has now. We need to adjust the protocol.'

Wasn't that what she'd said to Archer? That she needed to figure out how to live with these circumstances instead of just hoping it would simply vanish? Davis said it so matter-of-factly, like it was just logical. She didn't know if she wanted to cry or to hug him – either or both would freak him out anyway.

'You really think so?'

'Yes. You haven't lost your gifts – and even if you had, you'd still bring a lot to the team, before you start panicking about that happening.'

How did he know exactly what she was thinking?

'You're just having some trouble accessing them consistently,' he continued. 'So we need a new system. I'll come up with some experiments for us to do when we're no longer on a boat in the middle of the Mediterranean. We can figure out what affects your skills, and prepare a … a pre-investigation protocol for you. Like, don't wash your hair the day you have a survey. And spend a minimum of a full afternoon resting beforehand. No research or prep.'

'Other people will have to pick up my slack, though,' Éabha said, biting her lip.

'Did you see it as me slacking when I had to ask you to do all those survey reports when I was studying for exams and preparing my final presentations?' Davis asked.

She shook her head.

'So think of it as … life prep, equal to my exam prep.'

Had Davis actually … logic-ed her out of being sad? How?

'Thanks, Davis,' she said.

'No need to thank me. I am simply being sensible. Someone on this team has to be.' He got up in one fluid motion, reaching a hand down to her. 'You OK to move or do you need more time?'

'I think I'm OK,' she said, taking his hand.

'Slowly,' he warned as she got up, as if she hadn't just had a very strong reminder of what happened when she moved too fast. She would have rolled her eyes at him if she wasn't worried about triggering the dizziness again. Instead, she just reached out for the papers he was holding for her, which he handed over with a knowing smile, like he could tell she was trying not to retort. They walked back to the cabin in a comfortable silence.

'There's still hope you'll recover, Éabha,' Davis said when they got to her cabin door. He shuffled a little awkwardly, clearing his throat as he spoke. 'But even if you don't, we'll find a way around it. You can be hopeful for the future and realistic about the present at the same time.'

'Is that your scientific conclusion?' she asked.

He grinned. 'Yes. And we all know what an excellent scientist I am.'

Éabha laughed at that, swiping her card to unlock the cabin door.

'See you in a bit,' she said.

'See ya,' he responded, striding purposefully off as the door swung closed.

Éabha felt like a weight had been lifted. Her friends didn't see her as a burden, or a problem to be fixed. Even if she never got better, they'd figure it out. She hadn't realised how badly she'd needed to hear that. Imagine, the logical scientist being the one with the best emotional support. This case was just full of surprises.

CHAPTER FORTY

"SUP, RAVEN? You and Cordelia on a fancy romantic boat trip?" Jack's face filled the screen, a big smile on his face and his curly hair exploding from under his beanie.

'What? No, I'm with PSI investigating a boat. I literally told you that in my message,' Raven said, adjusting the laptop on the desk.

Éabha had to stop herself from laughing.

'Ah, right. Probably for the best. Romance and boats never go well. Caroline's made me watch *Titanic* like five or six times now.' In fairness, with how this trip was going for Éabha and Archer, maybe he had a point. Even if Raven was staring at him with affectionate exasperation.

It still seemed a most unlikely friendship to Éabha, but then she would have said that about her and Raven a few months ago too. Raven and Archer had interviewed Jack for the Hyacinth House investigation. He'd broken into the house just a few weeks before Cordelia hired PSI to investigate it and had a pretty nightmarish experience. He'd originally said he'd blacked out and woken up in the hospital, but he'd confided in Raven that recently his memory was starting to come back. Of the two O'Sullivan siblings, Éabha's money wouldn't have been on Raven being the one to bond with Jack. Jack was a YouTuber, forever trying to convince Raven to do a 'collab' for his channel. He was loud, energetic, excitable and said whatever came into his head at any given point. He was the exact opposite of the kind of person Éabha would have guessed Raven would want as a friend. But something about him had made Raven reach out to him, and she was clearly fond of him.

'You remember Éabha, right?' Raven asked, completely ignoring his *Titanic* story. She'd warned Éabha before the call that Jack could be a bit chaotic, always jumping from one topic to the next, and not to let herself get distracted by him or they'd be there all night and not get the information they needed. She'd told her this affectionately, like she was describing a small quirk and not a character trait Raven would have absolutely found frustrating in anyone else in the world.

'Yeah, of course.' Jack's face grew serious and he looked at her with an earnestness she could almost feel through the screen. 'I'm sorry about what happened to you in the spring. That must have been awful.'

'Thanks,' Éabha said, trying not to let the surprise show on her face.

'Hashtag NotAllMenButEnoughMen, am I right?' Jack said. 'So Raven, you need my wisdom and expertise on something?'

He'd changed the tone so fast that Éabha was momentarily breathless. Raven had described hanging out with Jack as 'like going on one of those funfair rides that whip you all over the place – a lot of fun but you have a bit of a headache after,' and, honestly, she hadn't given Raven enough credit for how accurate that analogy was until now.

'We do. And I swear I wouldn't be asking you this if it wasn't one hundred per cent necessary but … remember how you said bits of your memory had come back? About the night in Hyacinth?'

Éabha could see him visibly shrinking into himself as Raven

spoke. All the bright energy disappeared and he was suddenly pale, looking at them warily.

'Yeah. Only in bits, though. It's not like ... cohesive or anything. And it could be all in my head. Like a false memory. Because trauma. That's what my therapist said.'

'Can you share it with us anyway?' Raven asked gently. 'It won't go further than the team, you have our word.'

Éabha nodded emphatically beside her.

'OK.' Jack said.

Éabha could see his fingers worrying at the ends of the sleeves of his green hoodie, and she felt a surge of guilt. She knew that feeling all too well. But they needed this information, and he was the only person they could ask.

'So, you both know what I recorded online, and what I told Raven and Archer when they interviewed me last autumn. That everything was too hazy to remember, but I guessed I'd tripped, fallen back and impaled my leg on the jagged end of the cracked floorboard. I mean, I'm normally a lot nimbler than that, but I *was* pretty scared so ...'

The bravado, the attempt at a joke, was a flimsy shield against the genuine fear that was threaded through Jack's voice. This was hard – horrifying – for him to talk about. But he was helping them anyway.

Éabha was starting to see why Raven had so much patience for him.

'But yeah, I keep getting these, like, flashes. At first, I thought they were nightmares, but I get them during the day too. And they feel real.' He looked down, away from the screen. 'Not, like, hallucinations or anything,' he added hastily. 'They feel like memories. I'm in Hyacinth, I'm banging on the door and freaking out and then ... Something grabs me by the collar and *pulls*. Hard. I didn't stumble back onto the broken floorboard. I was dragged back.' He looked up at them, eyes almost pleading. 'I'm not imagining that, right? It's possible?'

'From what we've seen on this case, yes, it is,' Raven said grimly.

She and Éabha asked their follow-up questions: what did the pull feel like (a hand, grabbing the collar of his jacket), if he felt any other particular sensations (besides the already established fear and cold, no), if he remembered anything from after that (no, but he'd let them know if more came back).

'Thank you for sharing that,' Éabha said at the end. She kept her voice gentle, wishing she could offer him some kind of comfort.

'Anything for the Ravester,' Jack said, nodding towards Raven.

Raven leaned towards the computer and spoke in a low, firm tone. 'Jack, you just delved into a traumatic memory to help us so I will let you away with it just this once, but you know we've discussed my strong feelings about the name "Ravester".'

Éabha snickered and Raven shot her a look that a few months ago would have made Éabha want to crawl into a corner and cry. Now, she knew Raven well enough to know when she was actually angry or just Raven-angry.

'Sure thing,' Jack said cheerfully, pretending to salute. 'So tell me more about this boat. Besides the spooky stuff, is it nice?'

After warning him multiple times that this was strictly confidential, they told him a bit about the ship and some of the things that had happened, including their séance with Philippa, though they didn't go into detail about the USB stick evidence, just her death. They also didn't tell him about Roy; they didn't know if the family had been notified, and they'd agreed beforehand that it would be wrong to tell anyone before his family knew, even just in a private conversation among friends.

'And no one else has died on cruises or before them?' Jack said, thinking.

'What do you mean "before them"?' Raven asked, wrinkling her nose in confusion.

'You know, like building it. Eight people died building the *Titanic* you know.'

Both girls stared at him, and he shrugged sheepishly. 'After Caroline and I watched the film, I got curious and did a deep dive on the history. It's really interesting. Did you know–'

Jack launched into what Éabha guessed would be a lengthy monologue. At another time she would have been interested, but right now wasn't the time. His words had triggered something in her, a little niggle at the back of her mind, telling her to pull that thread and see what unravelled. She zoned out for a moment before giving herself a mental shake, forcing herself to concentrate on the conversation.

'I better go, but if you need anything else, just text, OK? I have a few videos to shoot, but I'll be about,' Jack was saying. 'And Éabha, if you ever want to do a collab, let me know. It would be fun to have a real clairvoyant and the Rav– Raven refuses. Shockingly.' He rolled his eyes at her with a cheerful grin.

His ability to slip back into 'Jack Gallagher' mode would be uncanny if she couldn't still see the lingering tightness around his eyes. This was his coping mechanism, and Éabha wasn't going to take that away from him.

'Let's double date when you get back, Raven – you, me and the two Cs! Chat soon, Ravester.'

Jack gave her a wink and ended the Zoom, leaving Raven laughing and shaking her head at the same time. Then her face grew serious, and she looked at Éabha.

'Please, whatever you do, do not tell Fionn about the Ravester thing.'

CHAPTER FORTY-ONE

'SO THAT WAS HELPFUL ANYWAY,' Raven said, after making Éabha promise multiple times not to tell anyone Jack's nickname for her. She'd made the mistake of telling Cordelia and her girlfriend had laughed for about five minutes straight and still brought it up. Raven wouldn't survive the boys – especially Fionn – finding out too.

'In more ways than one, I think,' Éabha said, chewing her bottom lip thoughtfully. The two girls were sitting on their beds, Éabha cross-legged, Raven with one knee propped up and the other leg stretched out in front of her.

Éabha leaned towards Raven. 'Did you hear what Jack said? About eight people dying during the construction of the *Titanic*?'

'Yeah, his hyperfixations can surprise me, too,' Raven said.

'No, well yes, but that's not what I mean,' Éabha said. 'The ghost, everyone who's seen him says he's wearing a uniform with the company logo on it. That's what we saw too. But it's not the crew uniform. Right? We both thought it was different.' She grabbed a pile of sheets off the table and started rifling through them until she found the one she needed. 'And here!' She brandished the sheet enthusiastically.

It was the most energetic Raven had seen Éabha in a long time, and she had to suppress a smile.

'The boat had extensive work on it to transform it into the luxury mega yacht it is now. So what if the ghost isn't an ex-crew member? What if he's–'

'—an ex-worker,' Raven said. Anticipation flooded through her, that tingling feeling she got when she knew they were on to something. 'Of course! He's wearing overalls.'

'We need to get more information on the refurbishment,' Éabha said. They looked at each other with excitement.

'We should get the others, too,' Raven said.

With almost comical timing, there was a knock at the door. Raven jumped off the bed to stop Éabha trying to get up to do it and opened it to find Fionn there.

'I'm not interrupting your call, am I?' he asked.

Raven shook her head, opening the door wider to usher him in.

'We have an idea,' Éabha blurted out excitedly as he entered.

Fionn's eyebrows shot up and his eyes scanned Éabha, smiling at her. He could obviously see the enthusiasm bolstering her. They hadn't seen this Éabha in a while.

'We need to find more details about *L'Imperiale*'s renovations,' Raven said. She quickly filled him in on Éabha's idea, Fionn frowning thoughtfully as he listened.

'You genius, Éabha! This is a really good theory.' Fionn paused, opened his mouth then quickly shut it again, a blush starting to rise on his cheeks.

'What is it?' Raven asked.

'It's nothing …'

'Fionn, do we need to remind you that you're in a room with two clairvoyants?' Éabha asked.

She opened a bag of Maltesers and started munching on them, offering the bag to the other two. Raven crunched on a few while Fionn finally started to speak.

'Charles. He mentioned some stuff about the renovation. His dad's construction company worked on it, it's how he heard about the ship. He'd probably know who we could speak to about the records.' Fionn's cheeks were an even deeper pink, and Raven didn't know if she wanted to tease him or hug him. 'But, I don't think I'm his favourite person since …'

'… since you realised you were on a date with him, freaked out and ran away?' Raven asked.

Éabha shot her an admonishing stare and for a moment Raven felt guilty. Damn, that girl was good.

'Pretty much,' Fionn said, shuffling his feet awkwardly.

Éabha patted the space on the bed beside her. 'Come. Sit.'

Fionn did, and she gave him a friendly nudge with her shoulder. 'First of all, if you talk to Charles, I'm sure he'll understand. He probably just feels super-embarrassed right now.'

'I guess,' Fionn said miserably. He groaned. 'I thought one of the perks of being aro-ace was not having to deal with this stuff!'

'Sorry, pal: no one gets to escape the awkwardness of interpersonal relationships,' Raven said. 'Have a comfort snack.'

She threw a Malteser to him and he caught it, putting it in his mouth and chewing sadly.

'You said "first of all": what else is there?' Fionn asked Éabha.

'Secondly,' she pronounced. 'Unfortunately for you, you are the one that Charles knows best, and therefore the one he is most likely to talk to about anything he knows.'

'If he doesn't HATE me,' Fionn grumbled.

'He does not *hate* you, that's impossible,' Raven said. 'I'm the grumpiest person alive and I like you.'

'That is actually quite reassuring,' Fionn said, cocking his head to one side. He gestured at the Maltesers bag and Raven threw another one to him.

'Just go talk to him,' Éabha said gently. 'Be honest. He won't be mad at you for not being attracted to him.'

'You haven't met a lot of guys outside of PSI, have you?' Raven asked.

'No,' Éabha said earnestly. 'Why?'

Fionn and Raven looked at each other and laughed.

'We'll explain toxic masculinity another time,' Fionn said affectionately, patting her on the arm. 'But yeah, Charles seems like a nice guy. Hopefully he won't hold any of this against me.'

'And if he does, I will happily drop-kick him off the side of this boat,' Raven said lightly.

She knew they knew she was serious.

'Are there sharks in the Mediterranean?' Éabha mused, winking at Fionn.

'You're a terrible influence on her,' he said to Raven, shaking his head.

'Look, no pressure, but we do need to figure this out ASAP. So while I know it's awkward and, honestly, I am extremely relieved I am not you, I'm afraid we don't have time to wait. So, choose to go find Charles, please? Before I make you?'

'How are you simultaneously supportive and scary?' Fionn asked.

'It's a gift.'

'It'll be fine,' Éabha said, giving him another encouraging pat. 'And if you need to come freak out afterwards, we are here for you, we promise.'

'Thanks,' Fionn said, and then sighed. 'I really wish Archer had come to check in with you.'

'That would have just delayed the inevitable,' Raven said cheerfully.

Fionn sighed again, even more heavily, and pushed himself to his feet. 'I suppose. Thanks for the slightly intimidating pep talk, pals.'

'Any time,' Raven said.

'Good luck!' Éabha added.

The door swung shut after him and Raven waited until the count of five before she looked at Éabha.

'Odds of that conversation being an absolute disaster?'

'Significant. But I wasn't going to tell Fionn that.'

'He's right. I am a bad influence on you,' Raven said, shaking her head.

Éabha smiled at her, a mischievous little smirk, as she began to sort through more of the sheets of paper in front of her.

'I'm a good influence on you too, though, so it evens out.'

Raven snorted in response.

'Hey, you talk about your feelings, like, once a week now. That's way more than you did before we became friends.'

Raven threw her pillow at her and Éabha squawked as it hit her in the face, before bursting into laughter and throwing it back.

'Throw pillows all you want, we both know it's the truth,' she said with mock-primness.

Raven opened her mouth to retort and then shut it again. Éabha was right: she was a good influence on Raven. And a good friend.

'You're a very good friend to me too,' Éabha said, curving her lips into a gentle smile.

Raven hadn't realised she'd said that last part out loud. But the warm feeling rising up through her made her glad she had. For once, she had blurted out something that made someone happy, not hurt. It was a feeling she could get used to.

CHAPTER FORTY-TWO

FIONN SPENT MOST OF LUNCH HALF-HEARTEDLY picking at a croissant, until Raven asked him if he was creating a new form of confetti, with a pointed look at the flakes of pastry now littering the plate and a good portion of the table. He stilled his hands mid-shred of a new layer, flakes falling from his fingertips even as he paused.

'Sorry,' he said.

'It'll be OK,' Raven said, with more gentleness than she usually had.

'Or it'll be terrible and he hates me,' Fionn said.

'I'm fairly certain it's impossible to hate you,' Archer said from his other side.

Fionn was flanked by the O'Sullivan siblings this meal. Éabha had paused to rest her hand comfortably on his arm and give him a smile, her eyes firmly fixed away from Archer, before disappearing to a table on the other side of the room. Davis had followed her, the momentary truce he and Archer had seemed to make last night already dissolved. Archer had watched them both walk away, his eyes sad and shoulders slumped, before he'd visibly slid on a mask of cheerful support. Fionn had begun to ask him about it, but caught Raven subtly shaking her head as she picked up her coffee cup. So instead Fionn had pretended not to notice and let the two siblings carry on the conversation while he tried not to drown in the pool of dread forming when he thought about the conversation to come. He'd failed to find Charles before lunch, which had just prolonged the apprehension, but the moment he'd spent an acceptable amount of time to be sure he was visible to the other guests at lunch – and long enough to determine Charles wasn't filling in as a server today – he left the others and set off on his search once again.

It took him a while to track Charles down: he wasn't on decks seven or eight, or in the conference room, or stationed in the foyer of any of the levels. Fionn really didn't want to go down to the crew levels and start asking people where to find him. He was turning the corner to head back towards the lift to deck seven, hoping he'd somehow just missed him, when he smacked straight into someone tall, broad and wearing a crew uniform. Fionn stumbled back, hitting the ground hard, and looked up to see Charles standing over him, his face aghast.

'Fionn! I'm sorry!'

'No, I'm sorry. I should corner better. I mean watch corners, I mean … watch where I'm going,' Fionn said, the words tripping over his tongue as he took the hand Charles extended to him and rose to his feet, certain his face was already bright red. He looked down and saw a few sheets of paper scattered on the floor, a few slightly crumpled now, and bent down to pick them up.

'Ah, yes, these are why I was looking for you,' Charles said, his cheeks reddening. 'I found some extra error reports in the server that I thought might be helpful. It's all the times the CCTV has failed in the last few months.'

'Thank you,' Fionn said. Maybe this meant Charles didn't completely hate him?

'It's the least I could do. You know, after ...' Charles trailed off, pulling uncomfortably at the crisp ends of his sleeves. He took a deep breath. 'I'm very sorry if I made you uncomfortable. I thought there was something but ... I am sorry.'

He looked at Fionn, his brown eyes sad, and bit his lip.

'No, *I'm* sorry,' Fionn said. 'I panicked and ran away and that wasn't fair to you. I just ... honestly, I didn't expect to ever be in this position, and I had no idea how to respond.'

He heard footsteps behind them and turned to see a few of the guests walking forwards them. Charles smiled at them, tipping his head as they passed, before turning back to Fionn, his face serious.

'You see–'

More loud voices came around the corner, and they both started.

'Maybe we could talk not in the middle of the corridor?' Fionn said quickly.

Charles nodded, taking a few steps forward and unlocking a door. They darted in just before the voices rounded the corner, and Fionn blinked as Charles snapped on the light in what was a slightly larger-than-average storage closet. It was stocked with cleaning supplies, toiletries and toilet paper, and must be for the cleaning crew to restock the rooms easily.

'A closet? Really?' Fionn asked, before he could stop the words exploding from his mouth.

Charles blinked at him, then started laughing, hard.

'I think only one of us belongs in here,' Charles said.

'Not exactly,' Fionn said.

He took a deep breath. This was the first time he'd told anyone outside PSI about his identity, and now that the moment had arrived, he felt terrified. He'd heard there could be some stigma towards ace people in the LGBTQ+ community, and while Charles seemed lovely, maybe his response wouldn't be what Fionn was hoping for. His palms were sweating, and his heart was beating so loudly he was sure Charles could hear it. Charles raised an eyebrow at his last words, an almost hopeful look entering his eyes.

Oh, he was messing this up again.

'I'm ace. Aro-ace, to be exact. Like aromantic-asexual. So I don't feel sexual attraction, or romantic attraction either. I only figured that out about myself recently, and I guess I forgot that, like ... just because *I* know I am doesn't mean everyone else will? And you're very clever and funny and interesting and I liked your company so much, it just genuinely didn't occur to me that you might like me like that. And if I led you on, or implied that, I'm so sorry. I thought I'd made a new friend, and I was really excited about that.'

He couldn't look at Charles as he spoke, staring down at his laces. There was a long silence.

'You did make a new friend.'

Fionn snapped his head up to look at Charles, who was smiling at him with affection.

'Do you think I would stop being your friend because you're not attracted to me?'

'It's not just you. I mean, objectively, I can see you're really hot–' Fionn began to babble.

Charles threw his head back and laughed. 'This is the most confidence-boosting rejection I have ever received.' He looked closely at Fionn. 'You haven't told many people, have you?'

Fionn shook his head.

'Yes, I can see the nervousness in your eyes that I used to have in mine. "Will they reject me? Will they believe me?"'

Fionn hadn't realised how worried he'd been about that. About not being believed. About claiming that label and having it torn out of his hands, told it wasn't for him.

'Thank you for sharing such a sensitive part of yourself with me,' Charles said. 'I appreciate your trust, and I promise I am not heartbroken. Just mildly disappointed,' he added with a grin.

'Only mildly? Rude,' Fionn joked, before clapping a hand over his mouth. 'Not that I want or expect you to be devastated! I just …'

Charles howled with laughter. When he eventually stopped, he looked at his watch. 'I don't have too long before I need to cover a foyer shift. But I'd like to have coffee with you later, if you don't have PSI duties? We can trade coming-out stories.' He winked.

'I'd love that,' Fionn said. He could feel the weight of the fear lifting off him, as though a thick layer of cement had been peeled off him. 'Actually, there's some PSI stuff I need to talk to you about, if that's OK? About the ship's renovations. Do you have any time now?'

'Of course. Not too long, but I can answer a few.'

'Thank you,' Fionn said, still both relieved and shocked the conversation had gone so well. He flew through his list of questions, Charles answering the best he could, before eventually he looked at his watch. 'I really have to go. Is that enough?' he asked.

'Yes, thank you so much,' Fionn said, nodding fervently. Already his brain was jumping ahead to all the things he and the team would need to check and look into.

'I'll see you later then,' Charles said, putting his hand on the door handle, before pausing. 'Can I give you a hug?' he asked, turning back to Fionn.

Fionn held out his arms and hugged him tightly. 'Thank you,' he said softly.

They both knew he wasn't thanking him for answering his boat questions.

'You're welcome,' Charles said, hugging him a little more tightly for a moment. He opened the door to the closet and stepped out, directly into the path of a very startled Archer. He looked behind Charles to Fionn, taking in where they had just come from.

'A closet? Really?' he asked.

Charles burst out laughing again. 'You two are far too similar. I'll talk to you later, Fionn – and I hope those help too,' he said, nodding to the sheets in his hand.

Fionn had forgotten he was holding them. 'Thanks for these,' he said, waving them at him.

Charles smiled and walked away, while Archer looked at the papers with bright-eyed interest.

'I don't know what I'm more curious about: the conversation or the papers,' he said.

'Cabin in an hour? I need to talk to Neale about these first. I'll fill you in on everything then,' Fionn said.

'It's a plan,' Archer said. 'I'm going to the dining room while it's hopefully empty. I heard someone at lunch saying that there was a chill by their table. Might just be the air con – it's right under a vent – but better to check.'

They split up, and the lightness in Fionn's step as he made his way to Neale's office was almost unbelievable compared to how he'd felt this morning. Now if only the PSI team could sort out their communication as easily as he and Charles had.

CHAPTER FORTY-THREE

DAVIS WAS PRETTY SURE THE CABIN was shrinking the longer they were on this boat. Every time he and Archer were in there together it felt like the walls were closing in. Maybe it was because they were both studiously avoiding eye contact with each other, to the point where they'd both reached for the same piece of paper from the stack on the locker between their beds and recoiled the moment they'd brushed fingers.

Fionn bursting through the door was a welcome distraction from the mounting tension. Davis had hoped Fionn would return to the cabin before Archer did, and judging from the expression on Archer's face when he'd opened the door to find only Davis inside, he'd been hoping that too. Instead, they'd forced out a 'hi' each before sitting quietly in a silence that had immediately thickened and solidified. He was still furious with Archer for what he'd pulled, the trust he'd broken with them all by lying about the séance, but the dark circles under his eyes, the slumped angle of his shoulders, made it impossible to yell at him. So instead they were in this silent emotional stalemate, where Davis was too angry to forgive him, but too concerned to have it out with him.

'I asked Charles about his family's business and the renovations for the yacht. It was a little awkward trying to find a nice way of asking "hey, do you think your dad would cover up workplace accidents?" But he didn't get offended. He said he has a friend he can ask – he kinda hinted that asking his dad before we have proof might cause some issues.' Fionn blurted it all out in one go as he came in, kicked off his shoes and sank onto his bed. 'I also went by Neale's office and checked in with her about a few of the CCTV issues they were looking into. They have no explanation for what caused any of them.'

Davis felt a surge of pride. Conversations like that were hard for Fionn. There was a reason he generally avoided the more people-facing interview aspects.

'You mean the multimillion-euro company that designs luxury yachts for the mega-rich might not be entirely honest?' Davis asked. 'Wild concept.'

Fionn rolled his eyes at him. 'Doesn't stop you enjoying the fancy hot chocolate at breakfast.'

'Technically, the food is part of our fee and I intend to get every penny,' Davis said, folding his arms and pointedly ignoring Fionn's chuckle.

They focused on going through the timeline of CCTV failures, comparing them to the times people had reported incidents, and the next few hours flew by. Fionn shifted uncomfortably every time Davis or Archer directed their observations at him rather than at the room in general, both of them speaking to and through Fionn rather than the three of them being in one conversation, but Davis couldn't bring himself to be the first to soften the hard tension between him and Archer. It was not the pleasantest of environments to be in, and he barely stifled a relieved sigh when there was a knock on the cabin door.

Archer opened it to reveal Charles standing there. He was in his white crew uniform, his tanned skin glowing against it, and he smiled at Archer.

'Is Fionn here?'

'Hi!' Fionn said, bouncing to his feet. 'Do you want to come in?'

Charles shook his head. 'I'm just at the end of break. I have to get back to work: the people need their chilled champagne!' He held out a USB key. 'I just wanted to drop this off – my friend sent over the files on the construction of the ship. I thought they might be helpful.'

'You're amazing, Charles, thank you.' Fionn said gratefully. 'That was so fast.'

'Anything to help PSI,' Charles smiled. His face grew solemn. 'Honestly, morale isn't great. We're all worried the cruise may be shut down if things keep happening, and it's too late in the season for us to find other jobs. Everyone's worried.'

'We'll do our best to make sure it doesn't get that far,' Davis said firmly.

'These are only the things that are easier to access – I asked him to look into any accidents that may have happened, but that could take him a few days to find, so I thought I'd give you this for now.'

'It's a great start,' Davis said.

Charles bade them goodbye, and the door closed heavily behind him. Archer had just sat down and turned his laptop on when another knock came on the door, Raven's *rat-a-tat* this time. She and Éabha stepped into the room as Archer plugged in the USB stick.

'Files from Charles,' he said over his shoulder.

Davis hung back as Archer opened a few files, calling out what they were – some PDFs and a few jpegs – as Raven and Éabha hovered on either side. Davis forced himself to be patient, knowing that the girls had more chance of recognising something to do with the spirit since they were the only people to have seen him. He could go through the files again afterwards. When it didn't involve being so close to Archer.

'What are these images?' Raven asked, pointing at something on the screen.

'Progress updates, mostly,' Archer said, clicking from one to the next, each showing the construction of *L'Imperiale* in increasing detail.

'Wait, go back,' Éabha said suddenly, gripping his arm.

Archer looked at her hand and back up at her, puppy-like hope in his eyes that quickly morphed into hurt as she flushed, letting go of him quickly. The flash of pain that flitted across his face sent a pang of sympathy rushing through Davis. He steeled himself against it; Archer had put himself in this situation.

'Can you zoom in on him?' Éabha tapped the photo, her finger landing on a worker in the background, shovelling something. His face was turned towards the camera, and he appeared to be scowling in anger.

'OK, but it'll blur the more I zoom,' Archer said. He clicked a few times.

'Raven? Do you think …?' There was hesitancy in Éabha's voice.

Raven swore softly. 'It's him. And that's the uniform he was wearing too.'

Davis finally allowed himself to step forward, his curiosity outweighing his animosity. Even with the image blurred from zooming they could see the logo clear on his chest.

'That's our ghost,' Éabha said, tapping the screen with her finger, her voice hollow.

'Now we need to find out how he became one,' Raven said grimly.

'Charles's friend might have something, but we don't exactly have a few days to hang around waiting,' Archer said, frowning.

They needed someone good at digging things up quickly and quietly. Someone who knew how to get people to talk to them.

Davis grinned.

'I think I know someone we can call,' he said.

CHAPTER FORTY-FOUR

'I DID SOME DIGGING,' Audrey Sato said immediately when the Zoom call opened.

'Hello to you too,' Archer said.

'Right, sorry, hi.'

Davis smiled affectionately, a little pang of longing surging through him as he looked at her. Audrey's long, black hair was pulled back, and she was wearing her usual outfit: blazer, T-shirt and necklaces, the multiple piercings in her ears glinting in the light.

He missed her. They'd fought constantly the first few weeks they'd known each other, while he tried to convince her parapsychology was real and she was determined to paint them as frauds, and he'd spent most of his energy trying not to completely lose it with her multiple times a day. But when Éabha had gone missing, Audrey had stepped up.

Their relationship had been brief, her job offer in London arriving just a month or so after they'd got together, and he was already starting to drown in preparation for his final exams anyway. So they'd ended things amicably. Besides, they'd probably have bickered themselves into a break-up within a few months. They would have had fun doing it, though.

Davis snapped his attention back to the conversation at hand. Audrey had a knack for winkling out information from the smallest threads, so he'd sent her the photos, the company name and rough dates, and asked her to work her magic.

She had not disappointed them. By the time they got back from dinner, she'd messaged him that she had something for him, and to call as soon as possible.

Her powers of research had clearly only grown stronger now that she was in London.

'OK, so,' Audrey said, flipping through a notebook to find a page. 'I reached out to a friend who knows someone who is connected to the company.'

'Sounds verifiable,' Davis said.

Audrey glared at him through the screen. 'All vouched for, all sketchy about saying anything until I assured them it wasn't for print and the information would never reach the company.'

'That's interesting,' Raven said.

'I know, right? They were definitely spooked about talking to me.'

'Multimillion-euro businesses seem to bring that out in people,' Davis said.

Audrey snorted. 'Shocking.' She smirked with the air of satisfaction that bordered on but never quite reached smugness that had captivated and infuriated him when they first met. 'But that didn't stop me from wanting to find out why.'

'Of course it didn't,' Davis said.

He knew the affection was in his voice from the little smile Raven couldn't quite conceal; he tried to shut out his friend and focus on Audrey. He was pretty sure nothing could intimidate her. She was pure stubbornness and righteous indignation; it was why they had worked so well together, and clashed so hard, too. Two people who generally believed their convictions were the correct ones and who never wanted to back down from a fight – they had been fireworks, but they just as easily could have been an explosion.

'So, this company took some massive financial hits during Covid,' Audrey began. 'Obviously, the tourism industry suffered hugely, and even when travel resumed cruises, where people were travelling from place to place in close quarters, dropped in popularity. They'd just invested in *L'Imperiale* beforehand, and then all the refurbishments had to be paused for a significant period of time and they were just haemorrhaging money. So, once the restrictions were lifted and the work was allowed to begin again, they were under serious pressure to deliver fast results for the most cost-effective prices.'

'I can see where this is going,' Archer said, frowning.

Audrey nodded. 'They cut corners. Pushed workers to do longer hours, skimped on safety measures, equipment … basically, the place sounds like it was a lawsuit waiting to happen. Except the company was paying the limited staff a decent amount, and they all needed the work, and you don't want to annoy a company like this when it might have a lot of opportunities in the future, or at the very least could absolutely ruin your future chances elsewhere.'

Audrey sighed, sifting through a couple more pages in her notebook. 'So we get to where it gets really grim now.'

'Oh, was that supposed to be the chill part?' Archer asked.

'Yes,' Audrey said, leaning forward. Her face filled the screen, her eyes burning with the intensity Davis still found captivating. 'I only know this last part through a source who it took me a lot of begging to get to talk to me at all, and I promised I wouldn't use their name, even to you. The owner came to visit the shipyard one day and blew up about how long was still left before the ship would be ready. Most of the team just nodded, but their team leader, Henry Talbott, stepped up and said that he needed to protect his team, and he was worried about the safety standards. That they were understaffed, overworked and lacking protocols that were important, and it was only a matter of time before someone got seriously injured.'

'The owner told him that he had "extremely wealthy and actually important" people expecting to board the boat in six months' time, and that he cared far more about their comfort than this "woke leftist nonsense". And if he didn't want to work there, no one was stopping him from leaving. Henry stayed.'

Audrey looked down at her notes and swallowed hard. 'Two days later, there was an accident. He was crushed by falling machinery in the ship's bow.'

Davis swore, and Archer winced. Raven covered her mouth with her hand. 'What an awful way to die,' she said, voice laced with quiet horror.

'The inquiry ruled it was Henry's error, especially because of apparent reports claiming there'd been signs that he'd been drinking on the job. But my informant, they told me Henry was definitely sober and had never given any signs he was intoxicated. He'd had issues with addiction in the past, but he'd worked incredibly hard at his recovery, went to meetings every week. They had no idea who made the claim that he was drinking, but it definitely wasn't anyone on the team, and it wasn't true. My informant said it was an equipment malfunction, most likely an oversight due to the understaffing or the equipment not being maintained well enough, all to save costs.'

'Do you have a photo of Henry?' Davis asked.

Audrey smirked. '"Do I have a photo"? Do you know me at all!' She shared her screen and pulled up a photo.

The team leaned forward as one, crowding close to the screen, to study it carefully. Henry Talbott was smiling in the photo, his arms slung around two crew members, all in identical navy-blue coveralls, but there was no mistaking him: he was the glowering man the girls had pointed out in the construction photo, the man they had seen by the pool.

They had found their ghost.

CHAPTER FORTY-FIVE

RAVEN FELT LIKE THE PIECES WERE slotting into place now. Between Jack, Audrey and Charles, they had the who and the how figured out, and now it was just a case of coming up with a plan on how to handle it. This ghost was angry. If Audrey's sources were true, then he had every reason to be. But it meant they were dealing with a volatile spirit on some kind of revenge mission and, if he was determined to stay, it could be tough to persuade him to cross over.

Éabha and Raven stayed up late after they'd gone back to their cabin, deliberating on the best way to approach it. Raven looked up at the ceiling, remembering the whole two minutes they'd taken to go on the aft deck for some fresh air and the glimpse she'd got of the lights of Livorno dimming in the distance before they'd had to get back to work, briefly allowing herself to imagine a world where she was on holidays with her friends, not trying to figure out how to stop a murderous ghost. Then, the moment of indulgence over, she turned her focus back to Éabha and the reality at hand.

'It feels like he's escalating, like he's getting more and more angry. He's gone from scaring people, to pushing them, to killing them,' Raven said. She tugged on the end of her plait as she thought. 'Why, though?'

'Remember what Lizzie said, back when we were dealing with The Lady?' Éabha said. 'That spirits can get lost in one emotion, be consumed by it. Maybe that's happening to him, and the longer he gets lost in rage, the more it takes over.'

'That makes sense,' Raven said. 'Terrifying concept, but makes sense. Philippa said he was unravelling. It was why she was so scared of him. So we need to get him out of here before he loses it again.'

'Lizzie says the first approach must always be to talk to them and help them over,' Éabha said, chewing on her pen. 'And this time there's no personal connection between us and the spirit, so he may be more open to listening to us?'

Raven cocked her head, considering.

'The Lady already hated us because we'd been there before, and she saw us as a threat to her house. Adrian had taken you.'

Éabha nodded. 'Exactly. So there's a chance this spirit might–'

'–not immediately try to murder us?' Raven said.

Éabha smiled exasperatedly at her. 'We can hope. Look, tomorrow is day six. If we can have a séance tomorrow, hopefully we can get him to cross over, or at least tell us why he's here. That gives us the seventh day to regroup and plan, and the night to try again.'

Raven frowned. 'That's cutting it pretty close.'

'It's actually the least time pressure we've been under for a verified spirit,' Éabha said mildly, turning the pages of a clairvoyance book in front of her.

'I don't know if that's just a sign that we are very bad at managing these situations,' Raven sighed.

Éabha looked at her, then shrugged. 'Only one way to find out, I guess.'

'You're weirdly chill about all of this,' Raven said, leaning back against the cabin wall and studying the other girl.

Éabha looked up and met her eyes steadily. 'I don't have the energy for anxiety right now,' she said.

The weary, final tone in her voice worried Raven far more than panic or upset would have. Éabha sounded broken. Or, if not broken, breaking.

'So I just need to go with what we can do in the way we can do it and hope for the best,' Éabha continued.

Archer had been in a weird mood earlier too, so either something else had happened or it was still the aftershock of their previous argument.

Should she ask? Would it be awkward if she did? Would it be worse if she didn't?

Could she just ... dip out of the cabin, call Cordelia quickly and ask her?

'You don't need to do anything, I'm OK,' Éabha said.

Raven jumped. Her shields were firmly in place, her emotions shouldn't be spilling from her like this.

'I didn't need to read your emotions to know you're panicking,' Éabha said, giving her a small smile. 'I'm OK. But thank you for caring. Honestly, the best thing I can do is just ... focus,' she said, gesturing at the book in her lap.

'I can do that,' Raven said.

The two went back to reading quietly, concentrating on solidifying their séance plan for the next day. As they did, Raven's entire body began to relax, her mind absorbed in the task at hand.

They just needed to get this spirit to cross over; then they could work on mending their fractured team.

It would be fine. It had to be.

CHAPTER FORTY-SIX

ARCHER KNEW HE HAD TO SPEAK TO ÉABHA. He spent the night tossing and turning, thinking about it after the others had turned the lights off. He knew he could have handled the conversation better. All night his mind raced with the many ways he could've explained what he meant. Even when he tried to rest and go to sleep, the look on her face as she walked away from him in the bar hovered at the forefront of his mind. He didn't know what haunted him more – the anger or the hurt on her face. What he did know was that he needed to make things right.

Something had changed between them since Adrian. He would never stop hating the spirit for what he had done to her. And how it had impacted them. He had always known the right thing to say to her, before Adrian. Now everything he said was wrong.

Archer stumbled his way through breakfast, arriving later than the rest of the team, having only fallen asleep in the early hours of the morning and sleeping through the alarm he had set. He joined a table and tried his best to seem normal and friendly, doing a surprisingly decent job. Focusing on asking other people about their lives helped him stop ruminating on the mess that was his own.

Afterwards, Archer searched the boat level by level, combing all the public spaces until he eventually found Éabha on the outside seating section on deck six. She was reading a book – something with a gold cover and what looked like a dragon on it – stretched out on a sun lounger with an umbrella over her, an iced coffee beside her.

'Keeping up appearances,' she said almost sheepishly.

'Very wise,' he said. 'May I join you?'

She nodded and he sat on the lounger beside her, pretending to sun himself. The aft deck was quiet, with just a few people scattered around, none of them sitting close by. The other guests were probably either having late breakfasts or getting ready for that day's port. He didn't even remember what town they were at today.

The warmth of the sun's rays didn't touch him.

The silence stretched on. He took out his phone, pretending to scroll through a few memes on Instagram as he tried to think of how to start the conversation. Why was it so awkward? He'd never had to search for things to say to her before. But now …

He studied Éabha out of the corner of his eye. She was pale and tired, her chipped nails turning the pages of her book slowly.

'You look tired,' he said.

The slow turn of her head made it clear that was precisely what he shouldn't have said.

'Thanks,' she said in a clipped voice.

'No, I just mean …'

'I know what you mean, Archer.'

'I'm sorry, OK,' he said, frustration welling. He slid his phone back into his pocket and turned to face her. He was just trying to take care of her and every attempt was treated like an attack. 'I'm sorry I'm trying to look out for you. I'm sorry I'm trying to stop you from overdoing it or putting yourself or the team in harm's way.'

'You're *not* looking out for me,' Éabha said, putting her book down. 'Or the team, because I've already told you we have a plan to make sure that doesn't happen. You're doing what makes you feel better despite the fact that I've explicitly told you it's not what I want or need. When are you going to listen, Archer?'

'When are *you*?' he snapped back. 'You're not well, Éabha. I can't stand seeing you like this.'

'Then don't look,' Éabha said coldly. 'You keep acting like what happened to me is a personal grievance to you. *You* weren't trapped in a painting, *you* weren't drained of your life force–'

'No. I just fought tooth and nail to get you back only for you to immediately try to endanger yourself again,' Archer said. His voice rose as he spoke, and he noticed a few of the other passengers start to turn and look, obviously keen for a bit of drama. He forced his voice low.

'You don't get to throw yourself into danger and expect us all to watch.'

'Funny. You're the only one who thinks I'm endangering myself,' Éabha said. 'Everyone else trusts me. They respect me enough to let me make my own choices.'

'This isn't about respect,' Archer said, running his hand through his hair in frustration.

'No, it's about you,' Éabha said. 'I'm so sorry my traumatic experience was upsetting for you, but you do not get to decide how I recover or how I deal with it.'

The coldness in her voice swept over him in a frigid wave. It was just such an unfair take on the situation. Was he not allowed to have feelings about what happened to her too? Wasn't he allowed to have nightmares about someone he loved, trapped, while he was powerless to do anything to help her?

He opened his mouth, but Éabha kept talking. 'And if you can't trust me with that, and if I can't trust you to respect the decisions I make ... then we shouldn't be together.'

All the air disappeared from his lungs. He felt like he'd been thrown overboard into the sea.

'You don't mean ...'

'I do.'

Éabha's blue eyes shimmered with tears and resignation, and it was that sight that made him want to crumple into a ball on the deck and never get up.

'You're not acting like the person I fell in love with,' she said, and those words shattered him into a thousand pieces.

He couldn't speak, couldn't weep, not here in front of the rich people pretending not to eavesdrop, not in front of the girl who had just crushed his heart. The person he had always felt safe to cry around before. He got up and walked stiffly to the door back into the interior, then dodged left into the stairwell, pausing at the top to take a few deep breaths to see if he could push back the rising wave of tears threatening to stream from his eyes. He knew immediately he was fighting a losing battle, and began to make his way down the stairs, his pace increasing as his feet moved faster and faster beneath him. He burst from the stairwell on the floor where their cabins were, and as he fled down the corridor into the foyer, Charles appeared in front of him, hazy through the tears blurring his eyes.

'Archer, have you—'

'Not now,' he snarled, the words angry and harsh and not him. Archer had just destroyed the best thing that had ever happened to him, he didn't have time to answer questions. He stumbled past Charles and turned another corner, trying to keep the last pieces of himself together. He was close, so close, to his room, where hopefully Fionn and Davis wouldn't be and he could break down without an audience or an 'I told you so'.

The wall of cold that hit him was the first sign he got that heartbreak was not his only problem today.

CHAPTER FORTY-SEVEN

DAVIS WAITED WITH FIONN for the others to arrive in the cabin to make their plans. Fionn had the updates from Charles, they had Audrey's info and Raven had checked in with Neale about doing a séance tonight. It felt like they were on the verge of getting there, even if they didn't quite know where 'there' was. The girls had even shared their theory about why Henry's behaviour had been escalating, which answered a few questions. It wasn't that he hated Roy more than any of the other victims – he had just unravelled more by the time he got to him. A logical, albeit terrifying, explanation.

Raven's signature knock came at the door and when Fionn opened it she walked in, taking a bite out of a lavishly iced Danish and holding a coffee in her other hand. 'I stopped by the snack bar to show my face as a guest,' she said, shrugging at the boys' looks.

Davis snorted. 'Sure. Definitely nothing to do with the fancy pastries.'

'Fine, I'll keep yours too,' Raven said, dropping the white paper bag that Davis hadn't noticed was tucked under her arm onto the desk.

'I didn't mock your pastries!' Fionn protested.

Raven grinned and handed him a pain au chocolat, then held out a croissant to Davis, dangling it towards him. Davis could smell it from where he sat on his bed, a freshly baked just-out-of-the-oven aroma wafting across the cabin towards him. It was probably still warm. His mouth began to water as he looked at it.

'Who's the best undercover paranormal surveyor?' she teased.

Davis groaned. 'You are,' he said, getting up and taking the croissant.

Raven's delighted cackle almost masked the soft knock at the door. She opened it and Éabha walked in, looking warily around the room before her shoulders relaxed slightly.

'No Archer yet?' she asked, in a casual voice that was in no way casual.

'What's happened *now*?' Davis asked. He probably should have tempered his tone, but the words had left his mouth before he could consider that. Seriously, could Archer go more than five minutes without making a terrible decision?

Éabha flushed, her wan expression becoming slightly livelier as pink spread across her cheeks.

'That obvious?' she asked.

'Subtle as a freight train,' Fionn said.

Éabha sank onto the floor, leaning back against Davis's bed. He couldn't see her face as, in a quiet voice, she said, 'I think we broke up.'

There was only shocked silence, Raven and Fionn looking to Davis as though he would know what to say. He didn't have a clue. His stomach sank as he took in her words. He was cross with Archer for how he'd treated Éabha, but he knew how much his friend loved her. This would destroy him. No wonder he hadn't come back to the cabin yet. Was he crying somewhere, alone? Did Archer think Davis wouldn't be there for him because he was annoyed with him? And what could he say to Éabha? She'd possibly just broken his best friend's heart. But she was his friend, too.

'I'm sorry, Éabha.'

Wow, well done, Davis. Way to emotionally support.

'I suppose you all hate me now,' Éabha said with a shuddering laugh that sounded like the beginnings of a sob.

'Never,' Fionn said earnestly.

Raven shook her head emphatically, and Davis reached forward and squeezed her shoulder, hoping that would say what he couldn't quite manage to find the words for. Maybe her shields were down, and she could feel his sympathy and the pain he felt for both of them. He hoped she could.

'I–' Éabha started to say, but was interrupted by a knock on the door.

'Hey, Charles,' Fionn said after opening it. 'Come in.'

'Is Archer here?' Charles asked, looking around the cabin.

'No, we're not sure where he is,' Fionn answered.

Charles' face fell, and he hesitated.

'What is it?' Raven said, her voice sharp in the way that Davis knew meant she was worried, but made people who didn't know her well think she was going to take a bite out of them.

Charles held out his hand. 'I found this on the floor at the end of the corridor.'

It looked like Archer's phone, and the screen was smashed. Davis got up and took it to check if it definitely was, but the screen was black. Maybe it had broken when it smashed? He'd seen Archer unplug it from his charger just a few hours before. Davis leaned over and connected it to the charging cable, fully expecting nothing to happen. Instead, first the charging symbol appeared and then the screen flared in life. It was definitely Archer's phone: the screensaver was a photo of him and Éabha, a selfie of the two of them lying on the couch at home, her head comfortably on his chest as they both smiled at the camera.

'He had it when he was with me,' Éabha said slowly. 'So …'

'He lost it on the way back to the cabin.' Raven finished.

'This is a dead end though,' Davis said. 'So either he came back to the cabin, changed his mind without coming in and went back or …'

'Something happened between there and here,' Raven supplied. She folded her arms tightly around her as though to stop them shaking.

Charles's voice was sombre when he started to speak. 'I saw him about ten minutes before one of the guests found the phone and brought it to me. He was agitated, brushed me off when I tried to ask him something. He didn't pass back by me in the foyer, where I was on duty. So he definitely went towards your cabin and didn't come back.'

Davis felt a sudden, plummeting drop of déjà vu, of standing in front of a portrait looking at Éabha's face staring out from it. Except this time, they had no idea where Archer was. Did *he* take him?

Considering the ghost's form for what he did to his victims, they might have already run out of time to find out.

CHAPTER FORTY-EIGHT

ARCHER WAS HAVING A NIGHTMARE. He had no idea where he was; his eyes were open, but all he could see was darkness. He could hear a distant hum, like the sound of an engine, but it was faint. He raised his hands in front of him only for them to slam into cold metal almost immediately. He flailed out to the side, the pain of hitting into steel walls reverberating down his knuckles.

He'd never had a nightmare so vivid before. He could feel his lungs taking shallow breaths that filled the air around him with the noise of short, panicked gasps. The cold of the metal slab underneath his back was creeping through the thin material of his shorts and T-shirt, almost burning into the bare skin of his forearms and calves. He tried to shimmy down, but his feet hit a solid wall almost immediately. He took a breath through his nose, trying to place the strange chemical smell that seemed both familiar and unplaceable at the same time.

He'd never smelt something in a dream before.

Focus, Archer.

He was trapped in a metal container barely bigger than he was. Blood pounded in his ears, his heart thumping so hard he thought it would burst through his ribs. He wanted to wake up now. He *needed* to wake up, to be in his cabin with Fionn's snores and the sound of Davis tossing and turning in his sleep. To be in a familiar, comforting darkness, not this oppressive, threatening inkiness that was swallowing him whole. There had to be a way to wake himself up.

When had he gone to bed? His head hurt, and he tried to retrace his steps, as though establishing the timeline would help him return to waking, to claw his way out of the dream that was currently consuming him.

He'd had a fight with Éabha. She'd ended things. He remembered that with a painful pang that, for a fleeting moment, drove away the panic threatening to consume him. He furrowed his brow, thinking hard. He'd stormed off. Charles had tried to ask him something, and he'd brushed him off. He'd been pretty rude: he'd have to find Charles and apologise. He just hadn't been confident he could speak without bursting into tears.

He'd turned the corner and … it had been cold. Like walking into the freezer section of the supermarket. His heart started to pound again, his mind almost protesting as he pulled on that thread of memory. Screaming at him that he wouldn't like what he found when he got to the end of it.

The lights had flickered. There had been a man. A figure that got closer each time the lights came back on, with a face twisted in rage and a grip so cold it burned. And everything had gone dark. Archer couldn't stop the whimper that escaped from his lips.

This was no nightmare.

This was real.

Panic overtook him and he began to scream, banging over and over again at the metal surrounding him, praying to a god he didn't believe in that someone would hear him, find him.

But no one came.

And suddenly the memory hit him of where he'd smelt this chemical scent before. And he wished he hadn't remembered.

A morgue.

He was in the ship's morgue: probably locked in one of the refrigerated drawers. The hysterical thought bubbled through him that at least they wouldn't need to move his body if they didn't find him in time.

The darkness seemed to close even tighter around him, and his mind raced, trying to figure out if the air felt thinner than it had just moments before.

Only the urgent thought that he needed to preserve what little air he had left stopped him from starting to scream again.

CHAPTER FORTY-NINE

ÉABHA COULD FEEL THE PANIC RISING as she raced around the ship looking for Archer. The team had split up to cover more ground quickly, with her taking deck five, and every time she had to slow to pass a guest, pretending to simply be making her way to one of the amenities, a wave of frustration rose in her. She had her senses out, hoping to pick up a trace of him, but so far, she'd felt nothing. All she had was a driving sense of urgency and a voice in her head shrieking *quickly, quickly, quickly*. She poked her head through the door of the gym, scanning the treadmills and weights section hoping Archer would be sweating out his feelings. But no, there was one lone person, a man seemingly more intent on taking photos of his muscles in the mirror than exercising. She kept going, every room she didn't find his smiling face in and hear a bemused 'Éabhs, I'm fine, I was just …' making her heart clench more. The adrenaline had kicked in enough that she didn't feel the heaviness in her legs, the fog in her brain lifting for once. All she could think of was Archer.

That couldn't be the last conversation she ever had with him.

She loved him, she really did. She was angry with him, sure. And though she knew deep down they weren't right for each other, that didn't stop her from loving him. She needed him in her life, somehow.

She couldn't exist in a world that didn't have Archer in it. As she thought that, the lights flickered above her, momentarily plunging the corridor into darkness before the brightness returned. Was the ghost nearby, watching her panic and laughing to himself? Something was draining the lights.

What had he done that required this much energy to replenish his own?

Éabha shoved that thought away, focusing on the task at hand. She ploughed on, forcing a smile as she passed Cecily in a robe, clearly on her way to the spa, before speeding up again once the other woman had passed her by.

Was this how he had felt, when he got to the Merrion Hub and she was gone? When he found her in the portrait and realised who – what – had taken her?

It was a living nightmare.

They reconvened an hour later, all with pale faces and grim expressions, in the boys' cabin.

'Nothing?' Raven asked, her voice tight.

'Nothing,' Davis confirmed grimly.

'What the *fuck* is the point of being psychic if I can't find my own brother on a bloody boat,' Raven said. Her face twisted in frustration, and she turned and punched the wall. 'He could be–' She drew her fist back again and Davis stepped over, grabbing her arm.

'Breaking your hand is not going to help things,' he said calmly.

Raven gave him a long look, then shook her arm out of his grasp, turning away for a few moments, shoulders tense and head bowed. When she turned back, her face was calm, though anger still flashed in her eyes.

Raven was right. What was the point of having clairvoyant powers if they couldn't help someone they loved when they were in danger? Éabha was the stronger at picking up on the energies of the living, and a nagging voice told her that if she was at full strength, she would be able to sense Archer.

Unless he isn't alive ...

She shoved that thought away the moment it surfaced, her stomach clenching, acid rising in the back of her throat.

'I'm not strong enough to find him,' she said, as tears pricked her eyes. 'I'm sorry, I should be able to throw my energy out and find his, but I can't ...'

She couldn't look at the others, couldn't witness what was probably written all over their faces: agreement. Resentment.

'You need a boost,' Raven said.

Éabha snapped her head up. Raven's eyes were bright with hope. 'Like in the portrait, remember? You boosted me and I got away.'

'Lizzie said that's too dangerous,' Éabha said. 'I had to draw on the entire team and I could have drained them completely. I don't know how to control it. We just got lucky that time.'

'That's why we don't use the entire team,' Raven said. 'Just me.'

Davis and Fionn immediately started to protest, but Raven raised a hand, her palm flat out in a 'stop' motion. They both silenced instantly. She folded her arms, a determined scowl on her face. 'What's the one thing I am best at?'

'Blocking off your energy,' Éabha said, a glimmer of excitement fluttering in her stomach.

'Exactly. We don't risk Davis and Fionn: that could cause more problems than it solves. But we can do this, Éabha, you and I, together. I trust you. You won't take too much.'

Éabha opened her mouth to profess her doubts at that.

'Besides, you know I can cut you off the moment I need to,' Raven added.

That was true. And comforting.

'Éabha,' Raven said, walking over and taking the other girl's hands in hers. Her eyes bored in to Éabha's, determination and fear shining through them in equal measure. 'We. Are. Running. Out. Of. Time.'

Éabha nodded, just once, bracing herself. 'Let's do this.'

They settled cross-legged on the floor across from each other. Éabha glanced around the room, taking in the expressions – of hope on Fionn and Davis's faces, conviction on Raven's – before taking Raven's hands and shutting her eyes.

Éabha breathed in: long, slow breaths. Everything in her was shrieking at her to hurry, to rush, and she firmly told that voice to pipe down. If she rushed things, she wouldn't do it right and this needed to be done correctly.

There was too much at stake.

Éabha murmured the usual breathing exercises, the familiar routine Lizzie had them do at the beginning of every class, and the pounding adrenaline of anxiety and fear and hurry-we're-almost-out-of-time began to ebb.

'Bring the wall down, brick by brick,' Éabha said. Hers dropped instantly – keeping it in place was always more of a challenge for her than letting it down – and she let her energy move out in a slow wave to brush against Raven's. She could feel the other girl's wall dropping, slowly, achingly slowly, and she kept breathing steadily. There could be no rush. There could be no threat.

She felt Raven's energy brush with hers, start to merge, Raven's purple with Éabha's blue.

'Think of Archer,' Éabha said. 'See him in your mind, how it feels to be around him.' She sent their energy out in her mind's eye, a rushing wave darting down stairwells and along corridors in the ship, searching for him.

Level by level, they moved through the ship in their mind's eye, waiting for the familiar pull, the call that said he was close. There was so much activity, so many little balls of light of different people's energies. Some of them felt vaguely familiar, others completely alien. They had never thrown their energy out like this before, never tried anything like this in such a busy place, or even at all. Every time Éabha felt her energy start to falter, Raven's was there, boosting her, sweeping her along in its strong pull.

Éabha's energy cried out for more, craving that boost, that power. For a moment she opened up, pulling on it, lost in its heady power.

They were on the second-lowest deck and Éabha tried to stop despair creeping in. They needed calm, stasis.

Then.

The faintest pull.

She could feel the surge of excitement from Raven, rising then falling as though she had squashed it down. They picked up speed, their energy racing towards that faint, familiar pull of Archer.

It grew and grew until …

'Where are you?' Éabha asked. She wasn't sure if she was speaking the words out loud or just in her mind. She could feel rather than hear Raven echo the question.

Where are you where are you where are you?

Then, hitting her with the force of a steel truck: panic. Fear.

A dark, enclosed space. Hard metal under her.

And cold. So cold she knew that if she opened her eyes, she'd see her breath in clouds in front of her.

Then their energy was rushing back into them, separating, and Éabha was back in her body. She snapped her eyes open just as Raven did the same, and they stared at each other.

'He's alive,' Éabha said, adrenaline and relief coursing through her. Then she registered the fear shining in Raven's eyes, and the rush was replaced by sinking dread.

'Could you hear him?' Raven asked.

Éabha shook her head.

'His breathing, it's so shallow. He's either panicking or running out of air. Or both.'

'Where is he?' Davis asked urgently.

Éabha shook her head again. 'We didn't get a room. It's a few levels down. I could feel cold, freezing cold. He's lying on metal, maybe on some kind of steel panel? And it's completely dark.

'It's narrow,' Raven added. 'You can't hear any people or footsteps. Just the hum of the engines and Archer's breath.'

'It's not enough,' Éabha said, tears of frustration pricking at her eyes.

'We need to think,' Fionn said, pacing. He stopped, then strode to the desk and rifled through some of the documents until he pulled out the ship's schematics.

'We know he locks them somewhere small, right? Claustrophobic, probably to echo how he died. What you sensed backs up that he's done the same to Archer.'

Éabha shuddered at the thought. Of what had happened to Roy, and what she had felt happening to Archer right now.

'And it's cold,' Davis added. 'It's not the kitchens, because we checked there. So he's not in one of the industrial fridges.'

'Is there anywhere we haven't checked?' Raven asked, crossing to stand beside Fionn. 'There has to be somewhere ...' She scanned the blueprints, her brow furrowed. 'What's this?' She asked suddenly, her finger setting on a section. The paper shook slightly under her touch and she frowned angrily at it, like it was betraying a secret.

'I ... I'm not sure,' Fionn said.

'I didn't see an entrance in that part of the ship,' Davis said. 'I'm sure we covered it in our search.'

'Could it be hidden?' Éabha asked.

'Why would anyone hide a door on a ship?' Fionn asked.

'If it's something they don't want the guests to see?' Davis asked out loud.

'What, like access to the plumbing or something?' Fionn asked. 'Rich people don't want to be reminded they poop.'

'Yes, poop and mortality, the rich's deepest fears,' Raven said sarcastically. She gasped.

'Mortality. If someone dies on a cruise, where do they put the body? Like, if what happened to Roy had happened while we were at sea or if weather was too bad to get to port, they'd need somewhere to keep him, right?'

'That is a grim thought I hadn't considered before,' Davis said.

'There's an M on this room,' Fionn said, leaning close.

'Morgue,' Éabha said.

The team looked at each other, then bolted from the room. They got a few curious looks from other passengers, but Éabha couldn't bring herself to care. Nothing was more important than Archer. They collided with Neale one level down, and frantically asked her about their theory.

'Yes, it's the freezer and there's a facility for a body too, like a miniature morgue. The door is always locked, but it's covered in the wallpaper we use on the corridors, to stop any guests getting curious, just in case someone forgets to lock it.'

Raven grabbed Neale's arm and started hauling her down the stairs before she even finished speaking. It probably wasn't how they were supposed to treat their employer, but if Raven hadn't done it Éabha would have. Probably by her hair, if Neale had hesitated.

'You have a key, right? We need to unlock it, now.'

'I walked down that corridor,' Davis said, aghast. 'How did I not hear him?'

'He may not be conscious,' Neale said. 'And that room has very thick soundproofing, because of the noise of the refrigeration.

He was conscious a few minutes ago. And he was terrified.

Religion had always been her parents' thing, not Éabha's, but she still found herself praying to *something* as Neale went to unlock the door. The captain's hand was shaking so much she couldn't get the key in the lock, and Raven yanked it from her hand to open it herself. Éabha was too anxious to worry about being polite right now, and silently thanked Raven for being the same. They burst in the door, and she paused just a moment to take it in, scanning frantically.

Icy cold hit her, her panting breath forming clouds in front of her. The room was narrow, with just enough space for her and Davis to stand side by side, but no more.

There. In front of them, the only thing in the icy room. A long metal door. Behind them, the door to the room swung shut, almost completely silencing the hum of the engines.

Allowing them to hear a faint noise, a weak thud.

Coming from behind the metal door. The others realised it at the same time she did, and Davis bolted to it, wrenching it open.

She caught a brief glimpse of metal shelves, before his body blocked her view, stooping to pull out a long metal shelf. Pale hands appeared around his neck as he lifted someone up and off the metal tray that had emerged from the depths of the fridge. Archer threw his arms around Davis's neck, burying his face in his shoulder, and even Éabha could hear his sobs of relief. Raven flung herself at the two of them, holding him tightly.

'I thought I'd lost you,' she said, her words thick with emotion. Tears flooded down Éabha's cheeks as she watched them, relief and fear and heartbreak all merging as one.

He was alive.

Her words were not the last thing he'd hear. Davis released Archer just long enough for Fionn to hug him.

'You scared us,' he said.

'I was pretty scared myself,' Archer said shakily. His legs seemed to give out underneath him and Fionn lowered him gently to the floor, supporting him as he leaned back against the wall. 'But I knew you'd find me. I knew it.'

He looked over Fionn's shoulder at Éabha, and his pale,

tear-streaked face made her heart break all over again.

'Arch–' was all she managed to get out before she burst into proper tears, deep wrenching sobs. She didn't know how she ended up on the floor with her arms around him, but she did, inhaling his familiar smell and clutching him to her. He was cold, freezing really, and trembling violently, but he was alive.

'I didn't ... I couldn't ... I couldn't stand the idea that something would happen to you while you thought that was how I really felt about you. I couldn't, I love you so much,' she said. She wasn't even sure if he could understand her with all the sobbing, but he clutched her tighter, his breath warm against her neck, his tears falling on her shoulder.

'I love you too, Éabha. I'm sorry, I'm so sorry, for everything,' he said.

'We both said and did things that weren't fair,' she said.

'I'm sorry to interrupt,' Neale's voice made the whole team whirl. They'd all completely forgotten she was there. 'But I really need to insist that Archer see the medic.'

'I'm fine,' Archer said.

Neale gave him a firm look. 'That was not a request, Mr O'Sullivan.'

'You should be checked out, Arch. You were in there a while,' Raven said softly. She reached for his hand, wincing at the icy touch of his skin as she helped him to his feet. 'I'll come with you.'

The look of joy he gave Raven made Éabha's heart swell even more. She studied him as he stood, still trying to reassure herself that he was alive, he was safe, that she hadn't failed him. His hand was at eye level with her as she got to her knees to stand up herself, and she suppressed a shudder at the deep purple of his fingers.

It had been close.

'We'll meet you at the cabin afterwards,' Davis said.

'It won't take long,' Neale said. She led Archer, walking slowly and shakily, Raven's arm wrapped around his waist, from the room.

Davis pulled out an EMF meter, scanning the room.

'Nothing abnormal now,' he said.

'How did you even remember to do that?' Fionn asked. He was still so pale he looked like he might pass out at any moment.

'Logic makes my brain stop screaming,' Davis said simply.

Éabha could feel the adrenaline ebbing from her, and with it the urgent realisation that she was just a minute or two from collapsing back onto the floor. But Davis was right, they needed to do the checks. She pulled the tourmaline bracelet off her, and took the earrings from her ears, before silently holding them out to Davis.

'I might need you to catch me,' she said to Fionn, who nodded seriously, taking a step closer to her.

They were with her. She was safe. She could do this: for Archer.

And neither of them questioned whether she could or not.

Éabha closed her eyes, taking a deep breath and letting her wall come down. Sending her energy out, probing. Then, taking a deep breath, she placed a hand on the shelf Archer had been lying on.

She had never regretted psychometry being her strongest skill until now.

She doubled over, her hand still firmly on the container. Fear, unimaginable fear coursed through her. Her heart raced, her breath quickened. She was going to have a panic attack.

No. Not her. Archer.

Dig deeper.

There: a tendril of energy that didn't feel like Archer. That was rage, pure rage, like nothing she'd felt before, yet somehow familiar.

It was what she'd felt as the ghost held Roy under the water.

She pushed the shelf back in and closed the door, holding the handle firmly to see if she could pick up anything else. It was more of the same.

'It was definitely him,' Éabha said, turning to the others. 'I can't pick up on anything else, like why he chose Archer. Maybe he mistook him for a guest? But the ghost only picks rude ones. I know Charles said Archer was a bit abrupt with him, but surely he wasn't rude enough to warrant … this.'

'I don't think anyone could be rude enough to deserve this,' Davis said, staring at the metal door like he was going to be sick. 'Maybe Archer will have some answers.'

Éabha had to struggle to focus on his words. Using her gifts had drained the very last of her energy, and everything was getting fuzzy. She swayed slightly and felt Fionn's arm wrap around her waist. She sank against his comforting solidity gratefully.

'Maybe we should discuss this back at the cabin?' Fionn suggested.

His voice sounded far away, like it was underwater or when her hearing aids died or when she had a cold.

They led her to the cabin together, Fionn's arm around her waist, one of her arms tucked into Davis's elbow. Even with their support, her feet barely lifted off the floor, but being carried was a last resort: it would draw too much attention, spark too many awkward questions if they were seen. She almost stumbled through the door when they unlocked it, Fionn's support the only thing stopping her from face-planting onto the floor.

'I'll just rest until the others get back,' she said. Her words were slurred, even though her mouth was working hard to articulate each one. She didn't even know whose bed she landed on, sleep claiming her the moment her head hit the pillow.

CHAPTER FIFTY

RAVEN SAT IN SILENCE AS ARCHER was checked out by the medic.

'You're in mild shock,' she said after she'd done a bunch of reaction tests Raven didn't understand the purpose of but just needed to trust were important. 'But otherwise you're in good health, considering. Far better than the last person I saw,' she said grimly.

She was the one who had ruled Roy deceased, Raven remembered. She had a feeling the ship would be looking for a new medic soon.

Archer thanked her politely and the two of them left. Raven couldn't stop watching him out of the corner of her eye, as though if she took her gaze off him for one moment, the ghost would seize him again. He was pale, and his eyes looked haunted. She knew they'd need to ask him what happened as soon as possible, while it was all still fresh, but she just wanted to shut him in his cabin and keep him there until they got to shore, and she could get him as far from this cursed vessel as humanly possible.

And then she would find a way to become the first person to murder a ghost.

The sympathy she'd had for what happened to Henry Talbott had evaporated the moment he took her little brother. Had locked him in that place. If they had taken any longer to find him ... she shuddered.

Better to focus on the seething, protective rage burning through her than to think about the alternative. Because if she did, she would start to scream and never stop. Even now, the memory of another room, another ghost, another family member dropping to the floor in front of her while she was helpless to save him was trying to barge its way into her mind.

And if she gave it space, she would never get it out.

So she would focus on this task, on the ghost that had just made this case extremely personal and the brother she would do anything to protect. She'd let him down enough in the last few years – she never would again.

As they opened the door to the cabin, Davis and Fionn leapt to their feet. Éabha was asleep on Fionn's bed but woke up immediately. She sat up slowly, her bleary eyes fixed on Archer. The boys both hugged Archer again, as though checking he was still real, while Davis fired a list of questions about the tests the doctor had done. Apparently, he'd spent the time they were gone Googling what the medic should check, to make sure she'd covered everything. Raven sat on the end of Fionn's bed, giving Éabha what she hoped was a reassuring smile, but she suspected might have looked more like a grimace.

'You know a science degree doesn't make you a doctor, right?' Archer asked, trying to smirk as he sat at the desk. 'You didn't even do biology.'

'Humour me,' Davis said.

Archer rattled off the answers, while Davis nodded approvingly. This was how he coped: logic and questions and not looking an emotion in the eye in case it pounced on him.

'Do you need to rest?' Raven cut in when Archer finished his medical report.

'No. I need to figure out how we stop this from happening again.'

'Arch, you've been through a lot,' Éabha said gently. 'Do you think you need time to process?'

Archer shook his head. 'I should tell you all now, when it's fresh. Before my mind can start playing tricks.'

'OK,' Davis said. 'You know what you can handle best.' There was no pointedness in his tone, no intent, so Raven knew he wasn't saying it to prove a point, but she felt a surge of protectiveness towards Archer at his words.

A flicker of understanding flashed across Archer's face, his head jerking to look at Éabha, who was staring up at something apparently very interesting in the corner of the ceiling.

'I've got a recorder ready,' Fionn said, placing it on the desk beside Archer. 'Ready?'

Archer nodded and drew a breath. 'This is Archer O'Sullivan. We are on day six of the *L'Imperiale* survey and I am reporting a personal experience of a paranormal encounter,' he said clearly.

Raven could feel the panic that had engulfed her start to ebb. This was all familiar. This was what they did. These were the systems and the language they used. It could almost make her forget.

Almost.

'I left the deck around eleven a.m. Éabha and I had had an argument …'

Raven glanced over to see Éabha look down at her feet, her hands twisting in her lap. Archer continued.

'I just needed to be alone. I bumped into Charles and he tried to ask me something and I snapped "not now", at him and kept walking.' A blush rose on Archer's cheeks and he looked miserable. 'I can't believe I spoke to him like that. I was just so frustrated and about two seconds from bursting into tears and I know that's not an excuse, but ...'

'It's OK, Arch,' Raven said gently. 'Trust me, I'm the queen of snapping at people unfairly. Just explain to Charles and say sorry. It was one out-of-character moment.'

'I turned a corner and felt this wall of icy cold. I knew, just knew I was in trouble the moment I felt it. It wasn't like "the air con is a bit too high" cold. Then the whole corridor flickered. The light came back on and there was a figure at the end of it. I recognised him immediately: the uniform, the expression of utter anger on his face. And it was completely focused on me.' Archer shuddered. 'The lights flickered again and when they came back, he was right in front of me, so close I jumped back. I turned to run, but I felt a hand close over my mouth and then just ... nothing. Darkness. I came to in the ... in the ...' Archer swallowed hard. 'In the morgue cabinet.' He shuddered, his eyes haunted.

Raven would do anything to never see that expression on her little brother's face again.

'I don't know how long I was awake for,' Archer said. 'It felt like days, but I was only in there a few hours. So I can't accurately say how long I was out for, or how he knocked me out either. One minute I was standing there, fully conscious, the next I was in the morgue.'

There was a long silence, as the reality of what had happened to Archer, how close they had come to losing him, sank in.

'How is he transporting people?' Davis said, breaking the silence.

He was staring into space, but his eyes were focused, like he was looking at something the others couldn't see. 'Someone would notice an unconscious Archer being dragged around the ship, and the amount of energy it would take to ... how is he even doing it? Can ghosts teleport? Is that even possible?'

'Henry is powerful,' Raven said quietly.

'Maybe even more than The Lady,' Éabha said. 'Or Adrian. And *he* ...'

They didn't need a reminder of what Adrian had done.

'That's it,' Fionn said, snapping his fingers. 'Éabha: Adrian pulled you into the portrait.'

Everyone turned to look at him.

'I know. I was there,' Éabha said, with a dryness that took Raven by surprise.

'Yes, but your body. Raven went in as a spirit, astral-projecting during the séance, but you were *physically* taken in. What if Henry Talbott can do that?'

'Pull someone into the spirit realm and then back out in another physical place?' Davis asked.

His eyes were starting to light up, the way they did when he had a theory or was about to start a very long-winded debate. The boys turned to Raven and Éabha, both still sitting on Fionn's bed.

Éabha bit her lip. 'It's possible, I guess. I mean ...'

'We haven't exactly covered it in Clairvoyancy 101 yet,' Raven said, shrugging.

Her heart was pounding, though. It was scary enough that she and Éabha could be under threat, but a ghost that could grab anyone, even a non-clairvoyant, and haul them into the spirit realm? That was terrifying. What if next time he didn't return them to the physical world?

'Adrian needed my energy to keep me there,' Éabha said, like she was answering the question Raven hadn't spoken out loud. 'So it probably takes a lot to do it, even briefly. He'll need to recharge.'

'So now would be a good time to go after him,' Archer said.

'Except for the fact that we just pulled you out of a metal box, like, two hours ago,' Raven said.

'And every hour that passes is an hour that he can replenish his energy and do that to someone else. Someone we may not find in time,' Archer pointed out.

'Tomorrow night is the last night of the cruise too,' Davis said gravely, looking around the room. 'He might know he's running out of time if there's anyone specific he wants to target. They'll be out of his reach by the day after tomorrow. So if he has anything else he wants to do, he's going to do it the moment he's recharged. Can we really take that risk?'

Raven felt her heart sink into her stomach.

Archer was right. They were out of time.

CHAPTER FIFTY-ONE

'WE NEED A PLAN. I don't think this ghost is just going to toddle off into the afterlife because we ask him nicely,' Archer said.

The realisation that they needed to do something urgently had left a stunned silence in the room, quickly replaced by a resolve that spurred them all into action. Éabha felt a bit better after her nap, but she could feel the sucking fatigue that made every movement like wading through heavy mud that meant another crash was on the way.

There wasn't time for her to sleep for fourteen hours, though, so several energy drinks and letting Raven take the lead on the energy work was the right call. It was the only call. Even if Éabha hated to admit it: she would be no use to the team if she tried to do too much and ended up being possessed again.

The fact that Éabha had to think *again* made her wonder if she should stop and take a long, hard look at her life.

'You'd think after two other ghostly showdowns, we'd have an effective strategy,' Fionn sighed.

'I wish either of those had involved a safe way of getting the ghost to move on that didn't involve destruction of the place they haunted. But The Lady burned the house down and Raven shoved her foot through the portrait of Adrian,' Davis said.

'Then I set it on fire,' Raven added helpfully.

'We can't just burn things on every investigation.'

'I mean …' Fionn and Raven said in unison, looking sideways at each other. Davis groaned.

'It's worked two out of two times,' Fionn pointed out.

'The ghost is haunting a boat. *That we are currently on*,' Davis said. He huffed loudly, an exasperated look on his face.

'Besides, lads, no one is going to hire us if the reviews are like "Pros: they found the ghost. Cons: they burned my property down",' Archer said reasonably.

'We barely escaped the enquiry for Hyacinth House,' Davis said in a considerably more irritated tone, folding his arms.

Raven laughed. 'Relax, we were only like …' She looked at Fionn.

'Sixty per cent?' he suggested.

'Sixty per cent serious.'

'THAT'S TOO HIGH A PERCENTAGE!' Davis shouted.

Raven and Fionn broke into peals of laughter, Éabha echoing them almost immediately. After a moment, Archer half-reluctantly joined in, looking at the three of them with affection.

Davis threw up his hands. 'Well, I'm glad committing actual felonies as a business plan is so entertaining to all of you.'

That only made them laugh harder, and eventually a begrudging smile spread across his face. 'Yes, you're all hilarious. Can we plan now, please?'

All the mirth drained from Éabha as she thought about the situation they were in. What was at stake.

'Why do we never have time to plan properly? We always start off slowly then it's like "bam, if we don't do this right now, there will be terrible consequences",' Raven sighed.

'She's right, we always get pushed into a drastic move, either through time or threat,' Archer said.

Éabha nodded fervently, wishing that for once they could do things at their own pace.

'Pushed ...' Davis said slowly.

'What do you have in mind, O Science One?' Fionn asked.

Davis thought, his brows furrowing. Then he looked around, his eyes lighting up.

'Go ask Charles for a whiteboard. I need to outline.'

CHAPTER FIFTY-TWO

AFTER ARGUING WITH ARCHER FOR fifteen minutes, Raven was beginning to have sympathy for everyone who had to deal with her. Davis had outlined his plan on a hastily procured whiteboard – they'd use Raven's ability to turn her energy into a weapon to literally push the ghost into crossing over – and then they'd worked through the practicalities of whether that was possible. She'd turned her focus to trying to convince Archer to sit this one out, since he was already a target for the ghost and he'd, you know, almost died earlier that day. But he flat-out refused, his arms folded and mouth set in the stubborn line that said he meant business.

'I need to be there, Raven,' he insisted. 'I'm not hiding. You didn't; Éabha didn't. Why do you expect me to?'

'That's not the same,' Raven said.

'How? You don't get to risk yourself constantly and then complain when other people do the same. And need I remind you that only one of us has offered to trade themselves to a ghost?'

'That was also not the same,' Raven snapped.

'Because it was you, not me?'

'Because I'd already been dragged out of a burning building, knowing you were trapped inside! And then today I had to face the fact that we might not find you in time. Surely I get a break for not wanting you to risk yourself immediately? I was scared, Arch.'

Raven's voice cracked a little and she saw Archer soften. He pulled her into a hug and she wrapped her arms around him tightly, her eyes closed because that made it easier for her to talk about her feelings.

'I don't want to lose you,' she said, her voice muffled.

'Good thing you'll be able to keep a very close eye on me then, isn't it?' Archer said.

She huffed a reluctant laugh.

'I'm not going to win, am I?' she asked, pulling back out of the hug.

'Nope,' he said cheerfully.

Raven sighed. 'Fine. Just make sure I don't end up in a position to say I told you so.'

'Wouldn't dream of it,' he said cheerfully.

Her phone buzzing in her pocket stole her attention. She pulled it out to see a string of messages from Cordelia.

I'm so glad Archer is OK.

Please be careful.

Don't do anything foolish.

Raven smiled and tapped out a message – *When have I ever been foolish?* – adding a little angel emoji.

Cordelia: *Do I really need to bring it up yet again?*

Raven: *Believe it or not, you are not the first person to mention that today. And I promise, it's very much not on my to-do list.*

Cordelia: *Good. Because if you even think about pulling that again, I will fly over there and drag you off that boat myself.*

Raven snorted.

I mean it.

The second message came through as though Cordelia could see Raven's reactions in real time.

Being known so intimately was slightly terrifying.

'You're smiling at your phone again,' Davis said in a sing-song voice.

Raven rolled her eyes at him, the warmth in her chest alleviating any need to respond snarkily.

I know you do, she texted back to Cordelia. *Don't worry, I'm coming home to you.*

In some ways, typing those words was scarier even than the prospect of the murderous ghost they were about to face. Because longing was rising in her in a way that was utterly unfamiliar to her. It was a homesickness for a person, not a place.

Cordelia.

CHAPTER FIFTY-THREE

'FIONN.'

Charles was standing on the other side of the door when Fionn opened it. Behind him was a stream of other guests, all holding day bags and chatting about plans. The itinerary meant that they were due to spend the afternoon and evening on shore – thankfully, this stop was such a highlight that no guest had opted out. PSI would have the ship to themselves for what they needed to do.

'They say you're going for the ghost,' Charles said, taking Fionn's arm and leaning in close, his voice low. Fionn looked around, making sure no guests were in earshot.

'We are,' he said.

'Is it ... Do you know if ...?'

'If the ghost is from the work your dad's company did?' Fionn asked gently.

Charles nodded.

'We're pretty sure it's Henry Talbott,' Fionn said. 'We won't know one hundred per cent until we try to talk to him but ... we're pretty sure.'

'I spoke to my father,' Charles said. 'The renovations happened when he was off sick for a period. His partner was in charge at the time. He had made some risky investments pre-Covid, and everything depended on getting *L'Imperiale* ready as soon as possible.'

'So he was probably desperate enough to cover up an accident?' Fionn asked.

Charles nodded, frowning.

'My father said he'd make some calls and get back to me as soon as possible. But I'm guessing ...' Charles trailed off again, looking into the cabin over Fionn's shoulder at the rest of PSI, who were efficiently gathering equipment and packing things into backpacks.

'We don't have time,' Fionn finished.

'I heard about Archer,' Charles said, sympathy on his face.

'We got lucky,' Fionn said quickly. He couldn't think too much about it, how close they'd come to losing Archer forever, or he'd fall apart and never piece himself back together again.

'If you hadn't brought his phone to us ... we might not have found him in time. We all owe you massively.'

'It was nothing,' Charles said, with a wave of his hand. He spoke quietly, but Archer's head snapped up at the sound of his voice.

'Charles, I was hoping to see you' he said, coming over. 'I'm so sorry, that was really rude of me earlier.'

Charles shrugged. 'You were upset. I was just worried I'd intruded. It definitely didn't call for ...' he trailed off as Archer forced a smile onto his face.

'If only the ghost had agreed with you on that,' he said.

The sudden sound of the speaker system interrupted them. 'All passengers, the gangways are now ready for you to disembark,' Neale's voice said.

'I should assist with that,' Charles said. 'If you need anything, just let me know.' He gripped Fionn's shoulder for a moment before turning and walking briskly down the corridor. Fionn shut the door and turned to look at the others.

'So the cover-up theory is getting more official looking,' he said.

Davis looked at the whiteboard. 'If we had more time, maybe we could explore it further …'

'At this point, the why doesn't matter,' Raven said fiercely. 'He needs to go.'

Éabha bit her lip. 'We're supposed to always try to talk them into crossing over first,' she said softly. 'Do you think going straight on the offence could backfire?'

'He went on the offence when he took one of us,' Raven said. She zipped up the bag she was packing with a yank.

Éabha looked at Archer, her face set with determination, and nodded. She was still pale, the dark circles under her eyes even more pronounced. Fionn had practically had to carry her back to the cabin after they'd found Archer, and the way she had sunk all of her weight onto him, like she didn't have it in her to even hold herself up, had broken his heart.

As though she'd heard his thoughts, Éabha turned to look at him.

'Raven's doing the heavy lifting for this one,' she said. 'I'm the back-up.'

'Éabha's the negotiator while I'm the muscle,' Raven said lightly, nudging Éabha with her shoulder. The other girl smiled at her.

'Both valuable roles, though one currently more necessary than the other,' Davis said.

The tightness in Éabha's eyes ebbed at their words. Fionn never quite knew what the right thing was to say in these circumstances. He tried just to listen, ask what Éabha needed and do that, but

Davis and, surprisingly, Raven, seemed to know instinctively what Fionn had to grasp for cues about.

He'd managed to do a bit better than Archer anyway.

There seemed to be an unspoken truce between Archer and Éabha. Fionn had seen how terrified Éabha was when Archer was taken, and the reality of what they were facing seemed to make them put every personal issue to the side. Maybe once they'd finished this investigation, they'd figure things out.

Once nothing went horribly wrong during this one, and they all walked off the boat together. A year ago, that wouldn't have been a worry. But now … they'd had too many near misses to be confident.

Sometimes Fionn yearned for the foxes and electrical faults. Not so much the electrical faults that were, in fact, ghosts trying to burn them alive, though. He shuddered, blotting out the memory of smoke and screams.

That wouldn't happen this time.

'Third time lucky,' he muttered to himself, shouldering a backpack and picking up a tripod.

'Let's do this,' Archer said grimly.

CHAPTER FIFTY-FOUR

EVERY STEP ÉABHA TOOK FELT as though a heavy weight, a shackle, was clasped around her ankle, slowing her down. She'd let the others carry the equipment, focusing instead on downing the energy drink Raven had silently handed her as they left the cabin. A few weeks ago she would have insisted on trying to help, desperate to prove that she could be an equal member of the team. But Davis's words kept echoing in her head now; that needing help didn't make her less important or valuable. And that every time she said 'actually, I need help with this,' or 'I should let someone else do that, so I have the best energy for this' she was emphasising that she knew her own limits and how to manage them.

She hated it, but this was her life now, at least for the moment. She'd never give up hope that things would get better, but she couldn't put her life on hold waiting for it. She had to adapt. And, annoyingly, sometimes that meant letting other people do the things she wished she could do herself.

Besides, even as she felt the caffeine and taurine and whatever other things were in the drink swirl through her, she knew she needed it.

She hated Adrian Fitzgibbon so much it made her stomach cramp. Then she hated him even more for turning her into someone who could hate so fiercely. Whenever the surge of anger rose through her, the hot wave that made everything in her tense, her jaw tighten and her fingers curl into fists, she felt like he'd taken another part of her.

'Maybe he unlocked it,' Raven had said to her last night, when she'd finally confessed how she felt over late-night snacks and how mixed up it made her feel. Raven, she knew, would understand. Éabha had seen her constantly battle the part of her that got angry, that made her lash out.

'What?' Éabha had asked, so startled she asked with her mouth still full.

Her mother would have admonished her deeply for that.

'Not all anger is unhealthy, Éabha,' Raven said. 'In fact, sometimes a healthy dose of rage is exactly what someone needs.' She'd given her a frank, knowing look. 'I'm aware that this is coming from the poster girl for unhealthy coping mechanisms. But anger, it makes us stand up for ourselves, advocate for ourselves – and others. You spent your entire life being controlled and lied to and shamed by other people. And you swallowed it all down, pushed it aside to be the good, nice person everyone said you had to be. Maybe Adrian was the final straw? And that's not necessarily a bad thing, once you direct it at the right places. Like taking down murderous ghosts, yes. Good time for anger. Yelling at Archer because he's – understandably – wound you up? Maybe that needs to be more of a ... warning snap than an outright bite back.'

Éabha had gaped at her, open-mouthed. She knew Raven was far more sensitive than she ever let on, perceptive too, but it was like the other girl had seen into her soul. Raven's words were like pebbles hitting the surface of a lake, a *plink plink plink* of recognition.

'Have you always been this wise?' Éabha had asked eventually.

Raven had smirked, even as sadness crept into her eyes. 'I tend to hide it by making the worst possible decisions.'

'Not recently,' Éabha said. 'If anything, you're the most emotionally stable of all of us.'

'Now that is a terrifying thought,' Raven laughed.

They'd finished their snacks without any more deep chats, but her words had stuck with Éabha. She didn't think even Raven knew how strongly they had resonated with her. She'd tell her, but the other girl would probably sprint out of the room. Telling Raven something nice about herself and getting her to acknowledge it was a pretty intense challenge.

Éabha looked at the other girl's plait swinging as the team marched purposefully down the corridor to the dining room. The last few guests had disembarked, so they had a couple of hours. They had arrived in Cannes, France, and this stop allowed the guests to visit Monaco. Monaco was the ultimate place of prestige, filled with expensive yachts and oozing wealth and decadence. That, alongside the famous casino at Monte Carlo, meant that almost all the passengers were keen to spend the full day on shore, or at least long enough to take a few boasting selfies and try to track down a Formula One driver. That would keep them out of the way for at least a while. They technically had the whole day as a stop, but there were always a few who, once they'd taken a few shots for their social media, decided they just wanted to lie by the pool and have cocktails brought to them. Anyone who came back to the ship would be told that deck four was closed for maintenance – the handy thing about Henry's consistent draining of the lights was that enough passengers had commented on it to not raise suspicions. Deck four held only the dining room and a single outdoor lounge and sun deck, so guests were unlikely to be unhappy about being kept away for a few hours – there was no real reason for them to be there until dinner.

Four hours is enough to exorcise a ghost, right?

'We'll make it be enough.'

Éabha hadn't realised she'd asked the question aloud until Raven answered her.

Davis hung back to walk beside her.

'You feeling good?' he asked. His steady pace, brisk but not rushing, and calm expression steadied her. Ahead, Archer and Fionn laughed at something – humour forever their coping mechanism – while Raven stomped along in her usual manner, effortlessly texting with one hand and holding a large bag with the other.

'Sufficient,' Éabha said with a smile. Davis nodded.

They reached the doors to the dining room, the others having disappeared through them already, and he held one of the heavy doors open for her.

'After you,' he said. 'It's showtime.'

Éabha swallowed, hard.

What if she'd overestimated herself? What if she couldn't do it, and let everyone down? What if she messed up and someone got hurt, again?

'Éabha,' Davis said, reaching out a hand and stopping her. 'You're not alone. You can do this, and we're all here if you need help.'

'Thanks, Davis,' she said, automatically slipping her mask back into place, her composed facade of togetherness. For a moment, she thought Davis shook his head, as though disappointed, but she dismissed that suspicion quickly.

In the centre of the dining room the others were already efficiently setting up candles and cameras. The long, thick curtains, which usually framed the windows for decoration had been pulled, blocking all natural light from the room. Raven had started to form a large circle of salt and crystals. She turned to look at Davis and Éabha, her hands on her hips.

'OK: less staring, more sprinkling,' she said, the affection in her voice taking the sting out of her words.

Éabha huffed a laugh and stepped forwards, taking a container of salt and completing the circle.

They were already quite practised at setting up, and within twenty minutes they had everything ready. Needing to use real candles made Éabha anxious, and she knew even before taking off her bracelet and earrings, she wasn't the only one. Davis's gaze flicked to the flames regularly, while Fionn looked everywhere but at the candles. His avoidance was as loud as Davis's stare.

'OK,' Éabha said, clapping her hands together. 'PSI's first exorcism. Let's go.'

CHAPTER FIFTY-FIVE

THERE WAS A SIXTY PER CENT CHANCE that Archer was going to throw up. He took a long sip of water, taking a few deep breaths to try and settle himself. Éabha was about to take off her jewellery and Raven would bring down her mental shields that blocked out her clairvoyance, and he didn't want them to know how utterly terrified he was. He needed them focused, and odds were that Éabha would worry and Raven would ... well, probably get mad. And while, most of the time, he appreciated having a protective older sister, especially after he'd spent years thinking she didn't care about him at all, right now she needed the clear mind of an unrattled clairvoyant.

They were all sitting cross-legged in the large circle of salt and crystals the girls had created, candles lit and flickering on the nearby tables they had moved to make room for the circle. Raven was at the top, Éabha to her left and Archer to her right, while Davis was to Éabha's left – Archer felt a pang as he realised that's where he would have been – and Fionn to Archer's right. Raven had placed a printed-out photo of Henry Talbott in the centre of the circle, beside the burning cedar and other herbs Archer had still forgotten to ask the identity of, and Éabha's tourmaline jewellery as well as Raven's own tourmaline stone. She rarely even took it out of her bag, her problem being opening to energy, not cutting it off, and Archer had been surprised to see it make an appearance, but Raven told him they'd brought it as an extra just in case. The tourmalines weren't close enough to touch the girls or affect them, but in easy enough reach that if one of them needed to shut themselves off, they could grab them easily. They really had planned everything thoroughly to make sure it was as safe as possible.

Raven led them through the familiar breathing exercises, in the same calm, assured way she had led the previous one. The one Éabha should have led. Guilt surged through him and his eyes blinked open to see Éabha frown from across the circle. She'd sensed it. He clamped down on his emotions, focusing on his sister's voice, the smell of the herbs, the feel of his body sitting on the floor: anything to take his mind off the cresting wave of fear rising through his body.

'We ask the spirit of Henry Talbott to join us in our circle. We invite you to join us in this circle, if you mean us no harm,' Raven said. 'We wish only to help and come in good faith.'

Well, they had every intention of sending him on, willing or not, but the manner depended on him, so technically it was true.

There was a long silence as they waited, and Archer's heart began to beat faster. He focused on taking long, deep breaths, as Raven patiently repeated the words.

Archer felt the cold first. A creeping, chilling cold that for a moment made him feel he was back in a dark, cold box, running out of air, his throat hoarse from screaming. Raven clasped his hand even more firmly and he catapulted back into the present.

'Join us,' she said again.

The chill intensified, and Archer opened his eyes to see the candles extinguish one by one, in tandem with the moving, creeping cold's progress around the circle.

He was here.

As the final candle guttered out, the room falling into a darkness punctuated only by the dim light from the corridor outlining the doors and the herbs burning in the centre, a figure gradually appeared.

It was him.

CHAPTER FIFTY-SIX

RAVEN WAS DOING HER BEST TO STAY CALM. First, there was the pressure of leading the séance, and then there was the fact that part of her wanted to fling herself at the figure in front of her and beat him to a bloody pulp.

Henry Talbott had hurt her brother. He had almost killed him.

She had watched him kill someone else, someone she hadn't been able to help in time.

She wanted him to pay.

Éabha's hand tightened on hers, and she felt a rush of calming blue energy flow through her, damping the fire that roared inside her, steadying her.

'What do you want?' Henry's voice echoed all around them, a discordant tone underpinning it making her ears shriek. From the winces around the circle – she really hoped Éabha's hearing aids had already been drained – everyone felt it.

'It's time for you to move on,' Raven said in a firm, composed voice. The man – Henry – was exactly like his photo: white skin, deep brown eyes, a tuft of sandy hair emerging from under his cap. He met her gaze, simmering fury shining from his eyes.

'And why should I care what *you* think?' Every word he spoke made her nerves scream, a primal instinct yelling *go, run, get away now*.

'Because we can make you cross over whether you want to or not,' Raven said, shoving that sensation aside. 'This way you can pretend it's your decision.'

Fury spread across his face and, as it did, he – glitched. That was the only word her brain could offer to describe it. His face morphed, his jaw gaping, hanging by a single ligament, skin torn, blood down his face, the top portion of his skull crushed in so all she could see were shards of white bone and glimpses of something greyish-pink and squishy that made her stomach churn as she registered what it was. Henry turned, slowly studying the other members of PSI, his face shifting between his regular face and how he must have looked after being crushed to death. Éabha's face was neutral, giving nothing away. Davis's jaw was set in determination. Fionn met Henry's eyes, held his stare, even though every muscle in his body was tensed like he was about to run away. And finally, slowly, Henry turned to study Archer. Her brother didn't flinch, didn't move, his face resolute, and pride surged through her.

'You escaped,' Henry said.

'I was rescued,' Archer replied. 'Was snapping at someone because I was upset really grounds for … for that?'

Henry's expression hardened, a coldness radiating from him that still sent icy chills through Raven, even with his face returned to how he'd appeared in life. 'You're all the same: willing to trample over the people beneath you to get what you feel you're entitled to.'

'I said "not now" to someone,' Archer said.

Henry frowned. 'No, it was more than that … I knew I needed to protect them from you …' Confusion battled with consternation on his face and he grabbed at his head, shaking it, fingers clutching his hair.

He truly didn't remember. Not everything. He was unravelling. What had Éabha said that Lizzie had told her about The Lady?

That, with time, spirits could become consumed by one emotion? Had Henry started off as someone trying to find justice and then slowly become more and more consumed by anger?

A twinge of doubt started to rise in Raven.

Were they doing the right thing? Did he need their help as much as the passengers?

She cast a glance at Éabha, who was looking at her, lips slightly parted in a small 'o', the same realisation dawning in her eyes. Raven nodded.

'Why do you do this?' Éabha asked gently. 'What are you trying to achieve?'

'I want to protect them,' Henry said. 'The way I wasn't. I want people to see the truth.'

'And what's that?' Éabha asked. The softness in her voice, the soothing energy flowing from her in waves towards him, it all seemed to be working. Calming him, his eyes becoming more lucid again.

'That they LIED,' Henry bellowed, his face shifting, his voice a hollow roar that somehow still emerged from him even as his jaw hung gaping, tongue wet and loose and glistening.

Rage pulsed from him, shoving back Éabha's blue, and Raven knew with a sinking heart that they had lost him.

'They didn't follow the safety protocols and then, when I died, they lied and said I relapsed, that I was drunk on the job. So my wife, my son, they didn't get the insurance money. And they think … they think …'

The rage was momentarily replaced by grief, and Raven thought she might drown in it. *This man, he has been wronged so badly.*

Henry looked like his pre-accident self again, eyes wide with pain and grief and he hunched over into himself, arms wrapped around his torso like he was holding himself together.

How would she react in his place? Hopefully not by murdering people. But still.

'And killing people who've got nothing to do with it is the right way to deal with that?' Raven asked carefully.

'They … they're complicit. They'd do the same …' Henry shook his head. 'I didn't mean to kill them, just scare them. Teach them not to treat the crew like they're nothing.'

'You held a man's head under the water until he drowned,' Raven said, a harsh tone creeping into her voice as the memory flooded her brain. The fear. The helplessness. The sound of screaming. Éabha shot her a warning look.

'I didn't …' he said vehemently, shaking his head. 'I wouldn't.'

He was being consumed by rage, enough that it was messing with his memory, and taking over.

'I just … I was so …' he continued. 'You have no idea what it's like. Trapped in the place that killed you, not knowing how your family is, no one able to see you or hear you and watching all the people who could be next to end up like you. I wanted to help.'

'They don't need your help,' Éabha said. 'Not like this.'

'They brought us here to help them,' Raven said.

The moment the words left her mouth she knew she'd said the wrong thing.

'You're working for THEM.'

Fury blasted out from Henry, a red wave that almost choked her. Instinctively, Raven pulled on Éabha's energy, channelling it through her to throw out a wall of energy, blue and purple melded together just in time to shield the others. It slowed but didn't fully stop the wave of red. Despite the team's efforts, they were still thrown backwards, narrowly avoiding breaking the circle of salt. Henry lunged towards Raven.

Raven threw her hands out, ropes of purple energy shooting from them, wrapping around Henry, holding him in place. She could feel herself draining by the moment, hear Éabha's laboured breath as threads of blue, not as thick as her purple ropes, but solid and steady, joined them. She chanced a quick glance to her right, where Éabha was kneeling, pale and determined, a sheen of sweat already glistening on her forehead.

They needed to finish this quickly, before it took too much from her.

From both of them, she realised.

Digging deep, Raven pushed harder as Henry howled with fury, writhing against his bonds, glitching faster and faster between his two forms.

'Let. Me. Go.' He roared with a ferocity that made her want to duck, made her expect things to shatter, lights to explode, the windows of the boat to blow out from behind their curtains. Miraculously that didn't happen, but an instinct told her that the moment she slipped, stopped being able to restrain him, that would change.

He was strong. Stronger than Adrian, filled with a single-minded rage that was currently fixated on her. She couldn't think, couldn't form a thought or a plan, because everything was concentrated on holding him back.

Raven felt something brush against her mind and she recoiled, the walls halfway in place before she realised the familiarity of it.

Éabha.

We need a plan.

Are we reading each other's minds right now?

We can figure that out later. Focus.

Right, the ghost. The angry ghost that looked like he wanted to wrap his hands around her throat.

She'd already had one ghost try to strangle her. That was enough for a lifetime.

Exorcism?

Exorcism, Éabha confirmed. She could feel the other girl's regret as she said it, but her determination too. It was the only choice.

Taking a deep breath, Raven opened her mouth to begin.

They had no idea what would happen. If it would work. If opening a hole to the spirit world to send him through would have unexpected consequences.

But they were out of options. Out of ideas.

'We–' they began.

Until.

'Um, Mr Talbott?' A voice came from behind them, by the doors to the dining room. 'I think I can be of some assistance.'

CHAPTER FIFTY-SEVEN

FOR A MOMENT, FIONN THOUGHT he was hallucinating. He'd hit his head pretty hard when the ghost had thrown them all back. But no, here was Charles, in his neatly pressed crew uniform, holding a sheaf of papers and walking slowly but surely towards the circle of chaos that was probably moments away from turning into an all-out shitshow.

'Charles, it's not safe,' Fionn said urgently.

'He wouldn't hurt crew, would you, sir?' Charles said.

Henry looked at him, affronted. The energy around him began to ease, the pressure alleviating. Out of the corner of his eye, Fionn could see Éabha and Raven exchanging a look even as he stayed focused on his friend, who was approaching Henry as though he were a guest with an enquiry.

'Of course not,' Henry scoffed.

'I believe I can be of some assistance to you,' Charles repeated.

As Henry focused on Charles, Éabha and Raven crawled closer together. Éabha was pale and covered in a sheen of sweat, while Raven looked weary but determined.

Something told Fionn they had used a lot more energy than he had been able to see.

'You were wronged,' Charles said.

Henry's face darkened, and he stood upright, a faint crackling coming from all the equipment around them.

'Charles,' Davis said warningly, his eyes on his EMF meter.

'I can help you get justice,' Charles continued.

The beeping and crackling paused.

'Impossible.' Henry looked at Charles, as hope spread across his face. 'How?'

'There was a cover-up. A faked autopsy, with altered records. I have access to the real one. And, as we speak, the other partner in the business is consulting with lawyers about how to go about this.'

'How does a deckhand know this?'

'Because my father owns half the company.'

It took a split-second for them all to realise he'd said the wrong thing. A bellow of fury erupted from Henry, his eyes flashing with anger as his body shifted and Charles let out a horrified scream. Henry rose up in the air, static crackling around him as the EMF meters began to beep in a cacophony of shrill sounds. Éabha and Raven were both on their feet, hands out, feet set on the floor like they were pushing back against something the rest of them, without their clairvoyant sight, couldn't see. Éabha's head was down, every muscle in her body trembling, while Raven's expression was all gritted teeth and fierce determination.

'He didn't know,' Charles cried.

'That's what they all say,' Henry said.

One moment, everything was steady. The next, a chair flew through the air, narrowly missing Charles. Fionn had just struggled to his feet when he saw the table closest to him start to shiver. He reached Charles a second before it did, jumping over the salt line so it didn't break, pushing him the ground as the table legs whisked a hair's breadth over them.

'Enough,' a voice bellowed.

Fionn turned his head back to the circle to see Éabha, the locks of her pixie cut blowing back in an invisible wind, her blue eyes glowing with a light that he had seen once before. She was holding Raven's hand, and both stretched out their free hands out towards the ghost. For a moment, Fionn thought he could see faint shimmering tendrils of purple and blue flowing from the girls to the spirit. As Henry struggled against something invisible, the furniture all thumped back to the floor.

'Listen. You have been lost in anger for long enough,' Éabha said. Her voice was different: deeper, more authoritative.

She turned to look at Charles, who was staring at her and Raven with an expression that said, of all things, he hadn't expected this.

Fionn could relate.

'My father,' Charles began, rallying impressively quickly. 'He was sick during the renovations. His partner ran it all. We, myself and the PSI team, that is, did some digging. We found the proof that the accident wasn't your fault. That it was covered up. The coroner crumbled the moment he was challenged about the autopsy results. Your family will get the money. They will know the truth. And the people responsible, they'll go to prison.'

Or buy their way out of it, Fionn thought.

Raven shot him a warning glare and for a moment he wondered if he had said it out loud. Her eyes widened slightly as her concentration returned to the figure in front of her.

'Why should I trust you?' Henry asked.

'Because you protected me,' Charles said. 'If you don't trust me, why would you do that?'

The figure was becoming less solid, less easy to make out. From what the girls had said, the amount of energy he would use to manifest so clearly, let alone start throwing tables around the place, couldn't be sustained for very long.

'You don't need to stay,' Éabha said gently. The light was dimming from her eyes now, returning them to their usual colour. Raven's hand was lowering inch by inch, her wary gaze still firmly on Henry.

'Aren't you tired?' she asked. 'You've protected the crew. Everyone knows the truth. You can move on.'

An expression of longing spread across his face.

'I would like to move on, since I can't go back,' Henry said. He looked at each of them in turn, an expression of almost-guilt on his face when he met Archer's eyes.

'I wanted to protect them,' he said, a pleading look on his face.

'You did,' Archer said.

'Even when you didn't need to,' Fionn added. Maybe he was being petty by saying it, turning the knife in the distressed spirit's back.

But part of him wished it would turn into an Adrian-style showdown, and they'd get to see Raven pummel the energetic crap out of him. Henry had almost killed Archer. He'd killed Roy. But now, as Henry looked around the team with more clarity, the rage ebbing from his face, Fionn realised the others were right. Henry had been trapped in the one emotion. It had skewed his logic beyond reason.

Fionn could almost have sympathy for him.

Almost.

The best he could do was watch quietly as Henry moved on to the afterlife. Not curse him as he crossed over.

'That's enough,' Raven said, looking at him with an understanding smile.

She didn't realise he hadn't said that out loud, did she?

He wasn't sure what he expected. A light? A portal to open? Instead, the man slowly faded in front of them, like a pencil drawing being erased, getting fainter and fainter until he disappeared completely.

'Is he …?' Davis asked eventually, a frown on his face.

Éabha and Raven nodded in unison.

'He's gone. We felt it,' Raven said.

Davis opened his mouth to ask what was sure to be the first of many questions. Éabha saved them all from his flood of enquiry by fainting.

CHAPTER FIFTY-EIGHT

RAVEN SPENT A SIGNIFICANT AMOUNT of the time she sat by Éabha's bedside trying to sort through the endless questions that were welling up inside her. She'd practically thrown Davis out of the cabin once they'd carried Éabha back through the thankfully still-empty corridors. She'd seen the questions building up in him too and knew she needed to dam them before they began to flow. In fairness, he'd waited until Éabha was safely in bed before opening his mouth, but Raven wasn't ready to attempt answering his questions.

The truth was she had no answers.

She needed to talk to Éabha to make sense of it. There were too many things she didn't understand, was already second guessing.

Éabha's eyes had glowed. Raven had felt it, connected by their hands. Éabha had plunged into depths they hadn't experienced before. It sounded like the others' accounts of what had happened to her in the Merrion Hub, except she had drawn on them to access it. Éabha's energy had been merged with hers, but she hadn't drawn too deeply, hadn't taken too much from Raven.

But it was still ... unexpected.

Hopefully, Éabha would have answers.

Raven sat on Éabha's bed, her back against the wall and a book in her hand, alternating between keeping an eye on Éabha and not wanting to just watch her sleep. That felt creepy. She texted Cordelia the moment the others left, to let her know that everyone was safe and nothing was on fire, and promising to call her ASAP. Then she'd put her phone down and stared at book pages she couldn't fully see. Her mind kept crowding the words out with all her questions, and she couldn't stop scrolling through the events, trying to process them.

First of all, Lizzie's repeated declaration that talking it out with the spirit should always be the first port of call had finally been proven correct. A small tendril of guilt snaked through her. Of *course* the one time they wanted to go in all guns blazing, the spirit could actually be reasoned with.

Henry had murdered someone and nearly killed Archer, so really it was on him. But still. What would have happened if Charles hadn't shown up when he had? Raven was glad they wouldn't have to find out.

They could leave it as the last of the growing list of questions. Éabha had glowed and Raven ... Raven had a few things to figure out on her own.

Mainly why people had looked confused when she'd responded to what they'd said or asked.

She'd noticed it with Éabha a few times recently, but had tucked it away under 'stuff to figure out when no longer on *L'Imperiale*.' She assumed it was a clairvoyance-link thing, since they spent so much time using their energies together anyway.

But today ... Fionn had given her a look that made her wonder had he, in fact, not spoken aloud. And that raised a whole other line of questioning.

Being inside her own head was hard enough. She didn't need to be in other people's, too. If that was what was happening here, she would respectfully decline.

Then not-so-respectfully decline if she needed to.

She'd sent the others to talk first to Charles, then to Neale. The first guests would be arriving back soon, expecting a fully set dining room in its usual immaculate condition. She felt like they might owe the crew an apology for the tables that had been sent flying by a furious ghost.

At least they hadn't burnt the boat down.

Though, to the average person, that was probably an incredibly low bar.

Raven sighed audibly, hugging a knee into her chest and propping her chin on it.

Every time she thought something was starting to make sense, something else cropped up to perplex her. It was frustrating, confusing, and she was pretty sick of it at this point.

That was an understatement.

She glanced at the sleeping Éabha, who was curled on her side, a lock of hair over her forehead and a frown on her face. It could be hours more before she woke up, Raven knew that. And she knew she should let her rest and recover for as long as it took.

The need she had for Éabha took her by surprise. She wasn't used to this, to relying on others. But she and Éabha, they were a team. They were in this together. And Raven desperately wanted her to wake up.

'You don't have to yell,' Éabha's sleepy voice mumbled.

Raven started.

'Go back to sleep, Éabha. You need your rest,' Raven said in a soft voice, hoping the other girl would drift back off.

'Hard to do that when you're screaming in my dreams.'

Éabha yawned, struggling upright. Her eyes were bright with

concern that made Raven simultaneously feel secure and like she wanted to run from the room.

'I didn't mean to,' Raven said awkwardly.

'I know,' Éabha said. She reached for the glass of water on her bedside table and downed it.

'Looks like we have another thing to figure out, don't we?' she asked.

'Just another quiet investigation with PSI,' Raven said.

The two of them looked at each other for a long moment, before they burst out laughing simultaneously.

'Davis is going to have a field day with this,' Éabha said, shaking her head.

'As if he didn't badger us enough,' Raven said plaintively.

'Should we talk it over ourselves before we let them know I'm awake?' Éabha asked.

Raven played with the end of her plait as she thought. 'I feel like we'll get a lecture on how we might influence each other by discussing things together,' she said reluctantly. 'And the others might be offended that we left them out.'

'Like a little clairvoyance clique,' Éabha said, nodding thoughtfully. She sighed. 'You're right. We should get the others. I've given too many lectures on trusting me to be open about things to hide stuff now.'

'And I still owe them for all the stuff I already hid,' Raven added. She tossed her plait back over her shoulder. 'I guess it's time for us to figure out what the hell is going on. Again.'

CHAPTER FIFTY-NINE

'SO, SECOND TIME ALMOST DYING,' Éabha said, perching on a deck chair beside Archer's sun lounger. He'd been lying out in the late-afternoon sun, catching the last bit of warmth in the day. They'd spent the morning debriefing Neale and reassuring the crew that the ghost had passed on. They'd also told her that Charles needed a raise. Yesterday might have gone a lot differently if he hadn't arrived.

Archer took a deep breath of sea air. He didn't want to admit it, but he needed to be in wide, open spaces and fresh air. Even the cabin, which was spacious for a boat, felt too cramped, too confined. Neither Davis nor Fionn had said anything when he'd left the light on beside his bed all last night. He was grateful for that. He just couldn't deal with being in darkness – his brain started to tell him he was back in the morgue container, and this time no one was going to find him.

He turned his head to smile at Éabha, pushing those thoughts from his mind. She was pale, but her eyes were bright. The sixteen hours she'd slept since the showdown must have helped.

'Would not recommend. One-star experience,' Archer said. He hoped his voice sounded as light as he intended it to.

'We did it,' she said. 'He'll never hurt anyone again.' Her gaze drifted past Archer. He turned to look over his shoulder, to where Alicia was walking slowly along the deck, her shoulders slumped. 'I wish we had managed a bit sooner,' she said.

Archer sat up, leaning forward to take her hand and then stopped, his hand extended in mid-air. He didn't know where they were, *what* they were. Her panic and fear when he was gone, her relief when he was found, he knew that was real. They loved each other – his mistakes hadn't changed that, at least – but something had shifted. He didn't know how to interact with her now.

He knew they needed to talk, but part of him wanted to put it off as long as possible. He suspected, unhappily, that he knew what the outcome would be.

'It's not our fault,' Archer said finally. 'We did our best. Sometimes … sometimes that just isn't enough.'

Éabha looked at him sadly. 'A running theme on this investigation, isn't it?'

She was so beautiful sitting there with her tousled hair, her wide, blue eyes, the sun's rays bathing her with golden light. Archer thought his heart would break just looking at her.

'I'm sorry I hurt you,' he said. He was still so ashamed about some of the choices he had made that it was hard to look at her, but he forced himself to, determined that she see how earnestly he meant it.

'I know,' she said.

'I need you to know, it's not that I ever doubted you. I believed – believe – in you, Éabha. I should have trusted you, and I never should have lied to you.' The wave of pain surged in him. He knew he had destroyed what they'd had. They couldn't go back, not after that. He wished she could feel how sincerely he meant it.

His eyes fell on the chunky black bracelet on her wrist.

'May I?' he asked, pointing at it.

She frowned for a moment, confused, before understanding spread across her face and she slid the bracelet off her wrist and handed it to him. Archer placed it beside him on the sun lounger, then leaned forward and took her hand, pressing it against his chest, directly over his heart. He shut his eyes and let it all rise up: how much he loved her. How sorry he was. How deeply he cared for her. And the sadness, the heartbreak he felt at finally understanding what she clearly knew too: that they could not give each other what they needed in a relationship.

He stayed there, the heat of her hand on his chest warmer than the sun, his hand on hers, savouring this moment. Eventually she slid her hand out from under his and he opened his eyes. Tears were streaming silently down her cheeks, and she raised her hand to cup his cheek. He leaned into her touch, the gentleness of it making tears form in his own eyes.

'Thank you,' she said softly. 'I wish there was a way I could let you feel what I feel too.'

'You can tell me,' he said. 'All of it. The good and the bad.'

'I love you so much,' she said, her voice trembling. 'You were my first friend in a long time. You brought me into PSI, you gave me a home when I was kicked out, you've been by my side the whole time. I love our in-jokes, the shows we watch together, the way I can take one look at you and know what you're thinking. You're my best friend. When the ghost took you, I finally understood how it felt for you when I was taken. I felt so helpless, so powerless, so terrified something would happen to you before I could get to you. I will never forget that fear. And I understand now why it's been so hard for you,' She took a deep, shaky breath.

'But I don't think we're right for each other, romantically. Your instinct is to take care of everyone and I ... I need to stand on my own two feet. I know your intentions on the night of the séance were good, but you took my autonomy, you doubted me. And you made me doubt myself. I was so hurt, so angry, so broken by it. You were the one person I trusted above anyone else. And you broke that trust.'

He would never stop feeling guilty for that night, never stop regretting it.

She gave him an understanding look, and he realised she had felt his regret rolling from him in waves.

'I know where it was coming from, and I forgive you for it. But I think ... I think I need to stop relying on everyone else. I know it's OK to need others, to ask for help, but I let everyone else tell me who I am and what I should do. I let people step in even when I could handle things myself. I lean on you too much, I know that. And you ... you need to stop putting so much on yourself. I know you're the leader of this team. I know you have a responsibility to us. But there is always going to be a degree of risk in this job, and you need to learn to trust that we understand that, that we make our decisions knowing that. There is a cut-off point for what is your responsibility and, as long as we're in a relationship, I think that's always going to stay blurry. You deserve to be taken care of, too. I don't think we can do that while we're together.'

'I do trust you, I really do. I was just ... so scared of losing you,' Archer said. 'And I felt so helpless not being able to do something make you get better. I let that fear and helplessness take over. It's not an excuse and it doesn't make what I did OK. I just need you to know that.'

'I understand,' Éabha said gently.

'I know that won't change anything,' Archer said. 'And, for what it's worth, you've always taken care of me, too.'

He meant it. Éabha had been the person who got him to stop trying to pretend everything was always OK, stop constantly peacemaking at his own expense.

'That means a lot,' Éabha began. She stopped, her voice trembling. 'I don't want to lose you as my friend, or my teammate. But I understand if you don't want that, if you need time or space. I can go, I can leave PSI …'

Archer's head snapped up as his stomach dropped. Éabha thought he would ask her to leave PSI? They were her family now, too.

'I would never ask you to do that,' he said. He let out a snort. 'Besides, the others would murder me if I did.'

Éabha smiled faintly at that, a slight air of surprise on her face. She still didn't fully get how much the whole team cared about her, did she? Even after Davis had sided with her. He paused, thinking about the reality that yawned in front of them, about being there beside Éabha and not being able to kiss her, or hold her. Knowing their relationship had changed forever.

'It'll take time, for it to feel normal again. For it to stop hurting. But I love you, Éabha. And I would rather have you as my friend and teammate than not in my life at all.'

He could see the relief visibly settle on her, her shoulders relaxing, her eyes widening. She lunged forward, hugging him tightly.

'I love you, too. You'll always be my best friend,' she said. Then she stiffened and pulled back. 'Is it OK if I hug you? Can we still do that?'

Archer couldn't help laughing at the panicked expression on her face. 'Yes, we can hug.'

He pulled her back in, holding her tightly. How could he simultaneously feel relieved and heartbroken at the same time? He knew in his gut that this was right for them but … it hurt, more than he thought he could bear.

'I feel the same,' Éabha said softly, squeezing him tightly.

Having a clairvoyant ex-girlfriend would either be very helpful or very annoying. Or both.

'So, what do we tell the others?' Éabha asked.

'The truth,' Archer said. 'That we chose this together. And we're sad, and it's going to be weird for a while, but it won't change our friendship or the team dynamic.'

'That sounded very official and grown-up,' Éabha laughed.

He handed Éabha her bracelet and she put it on.

'Well, I *am* the leader,' Archer said.

He stood up, extending a hand to help her up. She stood up and let go of his hand. Her fingers slipping from his made his heart feel like it was being crushed.

He would never walk down the road holding her hand again. Never curl up with her legs over his or his head in her lap and her fingers in his hair as they watched a film. Never sneak kisses when the others weren't looking, never …

Focus, Archer.

This would hurt. But they would get through it. And, one day, he would meet someone who was right for him. And he would cheer Éabha on when she met someone right for her. He hoped. One day.

Hopefully not too soon a day.

But first he needed a good cry. Or two. Or three. However many it took for the ache inside to start to ebb.

But, as he and Éabha began to walk back to the door that led below deck, even as it felt like a part of his heart had been ripped out, the faintest glimmer of hope began to shine, joining the sunbeams dancing across the deck courtesy of the setting sun.

CHAPTER SIXTY

IT FELT STRANGE NOT HOLDING ARCHER'S HAND as they walked along the corridor. Even stranger to realise she might never hold it again. Part of Éabha wanted to go curl up in her cabin and sob, to weep for the future she'd thought they had together.

What if she'd made a mistake?

Deep in her gut, she knew they hadn't. Knew it from the faint sense of peace that crept over her when they'd finally admitted it out loud.

The doubts still crept in, though. It was hard not to crawl back towards what was familiar, to when it felt like nothing could go wrong when he was holding her. She missed that already and they hadn't even made it back to the cabin. It hurt with a deep ache, like a part of her had been cut from her.

It would probably hurt for a while.

She just needed to make it through one more night on this boat, a flight home and then she could be back in Lizzie's house: home. Drink tea with her aunt and share everything that had happened. See if Lizzie had any insights, both for whatever was happening with her and Raven, and to help ease this ache in her chest about Archer.

The debrief the night before had left more questions than answers, the boys staring incredulously at them as they described everything they had been able to see and feel. Davis had scribbled copious notes the entire time, while Fionn had immediately hypothesised about which equipment to check to see if it had registered any of this. Archer had just listened, until the two of them stopped talking.

'So that's it,' Raven had said awkwardly, shrugging.

'You read people's minds?' Archer had said, his voice stunned.

'Possibly?' Raven had said, sounding like she sincerely hoped that wasn't the answer.

Archer had started laughing. 'Of all the people. You can barely stand being in your own head,' he said, shaking his head.

'That's exactly what I thought!' Raven had said. After a moment she'd started laughing too, a laugh that was almost disbelieving. 'What is my life?' she had asked, her tone half-mocking, half-despairing.

'I've asked myself that a lot lately,' Fionn had said.

'I think we all have,' Éabha had added. She'd looked over at Raven, who had started to chew on her bottom lip, and leaned over to take her hand, giving it a reassuring squeeze. 'But we'll figure it out, together.'

The memories of that warmed Éabha's chest as Archer opened the door to the boys' cabin. Everything was changing and it would take a while to adjust to it all, but they still had each other. None of them would ever give up on a member of PSI. They'd figure this out, the way they always had: together.

ACKNOWLEDGEMENTS

THE PSI INVESTIGATIONS are books about horror, but they are also books about hope, acceptance and love, and the global climate over the last few years has made me even more determined to write stories where people are their authentic selves and are loved and accepted for that. For anyone who sees themselves in these pages, I hope they remind you that you are not alone. It feels surreal to be writing the acknowledgments for the third PSI novel when three years ago I was quietly (i.e. to anyone who would listen) panicking about publishing the first. And yet, here I am, filled with many feelings but a limited word count, and with so many people to thank it makes my heart feel very full.

I'm only able to keep writing these books because people want to read them, and I'm incredibly grateful to every bookseller, librarian, schoolteacher, book reviewer and reader who has been so enthusiastic about and supportive of PSI, talked about them, posted about them online or recommended them to others. It makes such a difference to writers and truly means so much.

To everyone at The O'Brien Press, thank you for giving PSI a home and letting me tell their stories. So many people work incredibly hard across every department, from editorial to production to sales to marketing to rights, and I appreciate every single one of you. A special thank-you to my wonderful editor Paula, who grounds my chaos and is the reason anyone in this book knows what day it is. Thank you also to Helen for the proofread and Emma for the gloriously chilling cover.

Thank you, Gabbie, for your insight and encouragement. Thank you, Courtney, you are not just extremely wise but also incredibly kind. Thank you, Clarey, for being such a supportive and enthusiastic friend. Rebekah, I can't thank you enough for the plot chats, the friendship bracelets, the listening to endless meltdowns and the constant hyping of PSI. I promised you a boat book, so I hope this will do.

Thank you to Stacy, my Style Boy for life, and to my Chronic Coven, Jess and Lucy.

Thank you to Carol for your friendship, your book recommendations and for caring about the PSI books so much – I promise *WTSH* is longer than *WWTP*, and all the extra words are for you. Carrie, thank you for being my friend, for understanding that sending reels is a form of conversation, and always being down for a ridiculous movie marathon.

Brian, *sono incredibilmente fortunata ad averti nella mia vita. Ti amo.*

Mum and Dad, there's so much to thank you for and not enough pages but I hope this encompasses it all: thank you for everything.

Emma (Sib), you're always there for me, through both the inchidents and the wins. Thank you for being the best sister anyone could ask for; here's to always laughing at our own jokes.

My four-legged helpers, Bailey and Coco Swift (and guest supurrvisor Milo), thank you for having zero interest in what I am doing: it keeps me humble.

And finally, thank *you*, dear reader. There are so many books in the world and you chose this one – I hope you found what you were looking for in its pages.

Also by Amy Clarkin
from The O'Brien Press

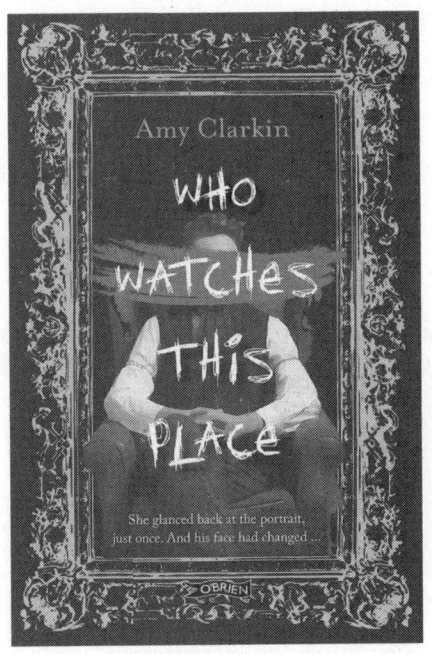